Praise for Chuck Palahniuk and

DOOMED

"A wickedly grim satire on current American life—its obsession with celebrity and religion and meaningless pursuit—and a rather upstanding morality tale."
—*The Guardian* (London)

"[Palahniuk] has a singular knack for coming up with inventive new ways to shock and degrade."
—*The New York Post*

"Funny, always on the edge of reality and bloodied by the profound horror of narcissism." —*Playboy*

"Place this bet in your time capsule: Chuck Palahniuk's novels will be required reading in American literature classes one hundred years from now."
—*The News-Press* (Fort Myers)

"Chuck Palahniuk is one of the most intriguing writers of our time." —*Tucson Citizen*

CHUCK PALAHNIUK

DOOMED

Chuck Palahniuk's twelve bestselling novels—
Damned, Tell-All, Pygmy, Snuff, Rant, Haunted, Lullaby, Fight Club, Diary, Survivor, Invisible Monsters,
and *Choke*—have sold more than five million
copies in the United States. He is also the author
of *Fugitives and Refugees,* published as part of the
Crown Journey Series, and the nonfiction collection *Stranger Than Fiction.* He lives in the Pacific
Northwest.

www.chuckpalahniuk.net

Also by Chuck Palahniuk

Fight Club

Survivor

Invisible Monsters

Choke

Lullaby

Fugitives and Refugees

Diary

Stranger Than Fiction

Haunted

Rant

Snuff

Pygmy

Tell-All

Damned

DOOMED

. .

CHUCK

PALAHNIUK

DOOMED

..

Anchor Books
A Division of Random House LLC
New York

FIRST ANCHOR BOOKS EDITION, JULY 2014

The Library of Congress has cataloged the Doubleday edition as follows:
Palahniuk, Chuck.
Doomed / Chuck Palahniuk. — 1st ed.
p. cm.
1. Ghosts—Fiction 2. Future life—Fiction 3. Dead—Fiction.
4. Microblogs—Fiction I. Title.
PZ7.P1754Do 2013
[Fic]—dc23 201204095

Anchor Books Trade Paperback ISBN: 978-0-307-47654-8
eBook ISBN: 978-0-385-53315-7

Book design by Michael Collica

www.anchorbooks.com

Printed in the United States of America
14   16   18   19   17   15   13

DOOMED

. .

Life Begins at Preconception: A Prelude

Posted by Hadesbrainiacleonard@aftrlife.hell

ood and evil have always existed. They always will. It's only our stories about them that ever change.

In the sixth century B.C. the Greek lawmaker Solon journeyed to the Egyptian city of Sais and brought back the following account of the end of the world. According to the priests at the temple of Neith, a cataclysm will sweep the Earth with flames and poisonous smoke. In a single day and night an entire continent will founder and sink into the sea, and a false messiah will lead all of humanity to its doom.

The Egyptian seers predicted that the Apocalypse will begin on a quiet night, on a lofty hilltop perched high above the kingdom of Los Angeles. There, the ancient oracles sing, a lock will snap open. Among the great walled houses of Beverly Crest, a stout bolt will slide aside. As recorded by Solon, a hinged pair of security gates will swing wide apart. Below these, the realms of Westwood and Brentwood and Santa Monica await, sleeping, laid out in a spider's web of streetlights. And as the last clock tick of midnight echoes away, within those wide-open gates will dwell only darkness and silence until an engine can be heard rumbling to life, and two lights will seem to lead that noise forward. And from out of that gateway will issue a Lincoln Town

Car which slouches forth to begin its slow descent down the hairpin curves of upper Hollywood Boulevard.

That night, as depicted in ancient prophecy, is tranquil, without a breath of wind; nevertheless, with the Lincoln's slow progress a tempest begins to mount in its wake.

As it descends from Beverly Crest to the Hollywood Hills, the Lincoln stretches as long and black as the tongue of someone strangled by a noose. With pink smears of streetlights sliding down the burnished black shell of it, the Town Car shines like a scarab escaping a tomb. And at North Kings Road the lights of Beverly Hills and Hancock Park blink and go dark, not house by house but blocks and blocks of the grid are blotted out in their entirety. And at North Crescent Heights Boulevard, the neighborhood of Laurel Canyon is obliterated; not merely the lights but the noise and late-night music are vanquished. Any shimmering proof of the city is erased as the car flows downhill, from North Fairfax to Ogden Drive to North Gardner Street. And thus does darkness wash over the city, following in the shadow of the sleek car.

And so, too, does a brutal wind follow. As foretold by the priests of ages past, this gale makes thrashing mops of the towering palm trees along Hollywood Boulevard, and these sweep the sky. Their clashing fronds cast down horrible, soft shapes that land with screams against the pavement. With beady caviar eyes and scaly serpent tails, these fierce, soft shapes hammer the passing Town Car. They drop squealing. Their frenzied claws scratch at the air. Their slamming impacts do not break the windshield, because the glass is bulletproof. And the rolling tires of the Lincoln rumble over them, pulping their fallen flesh.

And these plummeting, shrieking, clutching shapes are rats. Cast to their deaths, these are the flailing bodies of opossums. The tires of the Lincoln burst this red carpet of crushed fur. The windshield wipers clear the driver's view of the still-warm blood, and the crushed bones do not puncture the tires, because the rubber, too, is bulletproof.

And so relentless is the wind that it rakes the street, pushing along this burden of crippled vermin, trundling this tide of suffering always in the wake of the Town Car as it reaches Spaulding Square. Fissures of lightning fracture the sky, and rain is pushed into great curtains that strafe the tiled roofs. Thunder blasts a fanfare as the rain plunders the city's garbage cans, loosing plastic bags and Styrofoam cups.

And hard by the looming tower of the Roosevelt Hotel the boulevard is otherwise deserted and the army of trash advances on the city unimpeded by traffic lights or other automobiles. Every street, every intersection is deserted. The sidewalks are empty, as the ancient soothsayers have promised, and every window is dark.

The boiling sky is without the roving lights of aircraft, and the choked storm drains leave the streets awash in rain and fur. These streets slippery with offal. And by Grauman's Chinese Theatre is all of Los Angeles reduced to such butchery and chaos.

Yet not far ahead of the car, in the 6700 block—there the neon lights still shine. In that single block of Hollywood Boulevard the night is warm and still. No rain wets the pavement, and the green awnings of Musso and Frank Grill hang motionless. The clouds above that city block are open like a tunnel to reveal the moon, and the trees along the sidewalks are motionless. So coated in red are the headlights of the Lincoln that they cast a scarlet path for the car to follow. These glaring red beams reveal a young maiden on the sidewalk, and she stands across the street from the Hollywood Wax Museum. And there in the eye of this awful storm she gazes down on a star shape cast in pink concrete, sunk flush in the sidewalk. In her earlobes she wears dime-size, dazzle-cut cubic zirconia. And her feet are shod in counterfeit Manolo Blahniks. The soft folds of her straight-line skirt and cashmere sweater are dry. Masses of curled, red hair cascade about her shoulders.

The name cast in the pink star is "Camille Spencer," but this maiden is not Camille Spencer.

A pink gob of dried chewing gum, several gobs, pink and gray and green, deface the sidewalk like scabs. Printed with the marks of human teeth, the gum is also printed with the zigzag tread of passing feet. The young maiden pries at these with the pointed toe of her faux-Manolo until she can kick the scabrous gum away. Until the star is, if not clean, cleaner.

In this bubble of still, placid night the maiden grips the hem of her skirt and brings it close to her mouth. She spits on the fabric and kneels to polish the star, buffing bright the name cast there in brass, embedded in the pink concrete. When the Town Car pulls to the curb beside her, the girl stands and steps around the star with the same respect with which one would step around a grave. In one hand she carries a pillowcase. Her fingers, their chipped white nails clenched in a fist, hold this sack of white cloth sagging heavy with Tootsie Rolls, Charleston Chews, and licorice whips. In her opposite hand she holds a half-eaten Baby Ruth.

Her porcelain-veneered teeth chew idly. A margin of melted chocolate outlines her pouting, bee-stung lips. The prophets of Sais warn that the beauty of this young woman is such that anyone seeing her will forget any pleasure beyond eating and sex. So physically appealing is her earthly form that her viewer is reduced to nothing more than stomach and skin. And the oracles sing that neither is she alive nor dead. Neither mortal nor spirit.

And parked, idling at the curb, the Lincoln is dripping red. The curbside rear window hums down a crack, and a voice announces itself from the plush interior. In the eye of that hurricane, a male voice asks, "Trick or treat?"

A stone's throw in any direction, the night remains churning behind an invisible wall.

The maiden's lips, glossed with a *red*-red lipstick—a color called "Man Hunt"—her full lips curl into a smile. Here, the air hangs so calm that one can detect the scent of her perfume, like flowers left in a tomb, pressed flat and dried for a thousand years. She leans close to the open window and says, "You're too late. It's already tomorrow. . . ." She pauses for a long, lustful wink blanketed in turquoise eye shadow, and asks, "What time is it?"

And it's obvious the man is drinking champagne, because in that quiet moment even the bubbles of his champagne sound loud. And the ticking of the man's wristwatch sounds loud. And his voice within the car says, "It's time for all bad girls to go to bed."

Wistful now, the young woman sighs. She licks her lips,

and her smile falters. Half-coy, half-resigned, she says, "I guess I violated my curfew."

"Being violated," says the man, "can feel wonderful." In turn, the Lincoln's rear door swings open to admit her, and without hesitation the maiden steps inside. And that door constitutes a gate, the prophets sing. And that car is, itself, a mouth gobbling candy. And the Town Car shuts her within its stomach: an interior as thickly upholstered with velvet as a casket. The tinted window hums closed. The car idles, its hood steaming, its polished body streaming, edged now with a red fringe, a growing beard of coagulated blood. Crimson tire tracks lead up whence it came to where it now sits parked. Behind it, the storm lashes, but here the only sounds are the muffled ejaculations of a man crying out. The ancients describe the sound as a mewing, like rats and mice being crushed to death.

Silence follows, and after that the rear window once more slides open. The chipped white fingernails reach out. Dangling from them is a latex skin, a smaller version of the girl's white pillowcase, a miniature sack hanging heavy. Its contents: something murky white. This latex sheath is smeared with the *red*-red lipstick. It's smeared with cara-mel and milk chocolate. Instead of dropping this into the gutter, still seated in the car's backseat, the girl brings her face to the open window. She places the latex sack against her lips and breathes it full of air. She inflates it and deftly knots the open end. The way a midwife would secure the umbilical cord of an infant. The way a carnival clown would knot a balloon. She ties the inflated skin, sealing the milky contents within, and her fingers twist it. She bends and twists the tube of it until the shape becomes that of a human being with two arms, two legs, a head. A voodoo doll. It's the size of a newborn babe. This foul creation, still candy-coated from her lips, murky with the man's mysterious soupy contents, she flings into the center of the waiting pink star.

According to the prophecies writ down by Solon, that small effigy is a sacrifice of blood and seed and sugar, laid there on that sacred pentagram shape, an offering made beside Hollywood Boulevard.

On that night, with that ritual begins the countdown to Doomsday.

And once again the automobile's mirrored window fills its frame. And at this instant, the storm, the rain and darkness, these swallow the car. As the Lincoln departs the curb, bearing the young maiden away, the winds herd her castoff thing-baby. That knotted bladder. That graven image. The wind and rains shepherd their bountiful harvest of slaughtered vermin and plastic trash and dried chewing gum, tumbling and driving it all in the direction of gravity.

entle Tweeter,

It's worth noting up front that I have always conceived of my mind as a digestive organ. A stomach for processing knowledge, if you will. As a looping, wrinkled mass, a human brain unmistakably *looks* like gray intestines, and it's within these thinking bowels that my experiences are broken down, consumed to become my life story. My thoughts occur as flavorful burps or acrid barf. The indigestible gristle and bone of my memories are expelled as these words.

Writing an honest blog is how you unlive your life. It's like uneating an entire peanut butter cheesecake, and just as messy.

The convoluted, creased, and folded gray entrails of my mind exist as a kind of tummy of the intellect. Tragedies ulcerate. Comedies nourish. In the end, rest assured, your memories will long outlast your flesh—witness me. My name is Madison Desert Flower Rosa Parks Coyote Trickster Spencer, and I'm a ghost. Meaning: Boo! I'm thirteen years old, and I'm somewhat overweight. Meaning: I'm dead *and* fat. Meaning: I'm a piggy-pig-pig, oink-oink, real porker.

Just ask my mom.

I'm thirteen and fat—and I will stay this way forever.

And, yes, I know the word *ulcerate*. I'm dead, not illiterate. You've heard the term *midlife crisis*? Simply put, I'm currently suffering a "mid-death crisis." After some eight months lodged in the fiery underworld of Hell I now find myself stranded as a spirit in the living-alive physical world, a condition more commonly known as Purgatory. This feels exactly like flying at Mach 1 aboard my dad's Saab Draken from Brasilia to Riyadh, only to be trapped circling the airport in a holding pattern, waiting for permission to land. Plainly and simply put, Purgatory is where you unwrite the book of your life story.

Regarding Hell, you mustn't feel sorry for me. We all keep secrets from God, and it's exhausting. If anyone deserves to burn in the unquenchable lake of eternal flames, it's me. I am pure evil. No punishment is too severe.

For me, my flesh is my curriculum vitae. My fat is my memory bank. The moments of my past life are archived and carried in every obese cell of my ghost blubber, and to lose weight would be for Madison Spencer to disappear. Bad memories are better than none. And rest assured, whether it's your fat or your bank account or your beloved family, someday you'll struggle with this reluctance to abandon the living-alive world.

When you die, trust me, the most difficult person to leave behind is yourself. Yes, Gentle Tweeter, I'm thirteen and a girl and I know the term *curriculum vitae*. What's more, I know that not even the dead want to fully disappear.

DECEMBER 21, 6:05 A.M. CET

How I Came to Be Cast out of Already Being Cast out of God's Good Graces

Posted by Madisonspencer@aftrlife.hell

entle Tweeter,

I would not be stuck here on the stony Galápagos that is Earth, drinking the warm tortoise urine that is human companionship, were it not for the Halloween caper cutting of a certain three Miss Slutty O'Slutnicks. On the Halloween in question I'd been strangled to death with my blood flushed out for only eight months, tops. I'd been damned, yes, for committing a horrible murder that will be revealed here soon enough. One of the chief torments of Hell is that we all know, secretly, why we deserve to be there. How I came to escape is, as per custom, on All Hallow's Eve the entire population of Hades returns to Earth to forage for salted nut clusters and Raisinettes from dusk until midnight. I was thus gainfully occupied, scavenging suburban neighborhoods for Twixes and Almond Joys to enrich the treasury of Hell, when a breeze carried my name out of the nighttime distance. A chorus of girlish voices, these wheedling, piping tweenaged voices were chanting my name: ". . . Madison Spencer . . . Maddy Spencer, come to us. We command you to come do our bidding."

To you predead people, like it or not, postalive people are not your bitches. The dead have better things to do than respond to your dumb-ass Ouija board queries concerning

10

lottery numbers and who's going to marry you. You and your séance games, your table-tipping, ghost-baiting she-nanigans. I had, at best, four hours of darkness to gather Kit Kat bars, and here I was getting summoned by a giggling cadre of Miss Coozey Coozenheimers. They sat on my former bed, in the room of my former boarding school in Locarno, Switzerland, and bade in unison, "Appear to us, Madison Spencer. Let's see if your big ass looks any skinnier dead." And they laughed into their slender hands.

Shushing each other, the crew of Whorey Vander-whores chanted, "Show us your secret ghost diet." This playground taunt reduced them to giggles, toppling them sideways, their shoulders bumping one another. They were sitting cross-legged, soiling my bed linens with their shoes, an occasional foot kicking my former headboard, eating popcorn around some candles burning on a plate. "We've got potato chips," they taunted, and shook a bag of the same. Barbecue flavored. "We've got onion dip." One voice intoned, "Here, Madison . . . Here, piggy, piggy, piggy . . ." All the voices combined to sing, "Soooooeeeee . . . !" Loudly were they hog calling into the frigid Halloween night. "Here, piggy, pig, pig, pig, pig . . ."

They snorted. They grunted. They called out, "Oink, oink, oink." Chewing noisily, their mouths crammed with high-calorie snacks, they shrieked with laughter.

No, Gentle Tweeter, I did not slaughter them in my rage. At this writing, they continue to be very much alive, albeit humbled. Suffice to say I arrived in a black Lincoln Town Car and answered their hillbilly yodeling. On the Hallow-een in question I prompted the infamous enemy trio of Miss Skeezy Skeezenheimers to void the meager contents

11

of their anorexic bowels. So shame, shame on me. In my favor, I was a mite anxious and distracted by my impending curfew.

To linger even one clock tick past midnight meant my banishment to tedious Earth, so I remained hypervigilant as the big hand of my wristwatch ascended minute by minute toward the twelve. Once the three Miss Sleazy O'Sleazenicks were well laminated in pelts of their own fragrant upchuck and gummy doo-doo, I hightailed it for my waiting Town Car.

My trusty getaway vehicle remained where I had left it: parked at the frosty curb beside the snowy lawns of the school residence hall. The keys dangled from the ignition. The dashboard clock read eleven thirty-five, a reasonable allowance of time for my return trip to Hell. I climbed behind the steering wheel and fastened my seat belt. *Ah, Earth,* I thought somewhat indulgently, even nostalgically as I glanced at the old edifice where once I'd crept, nibbling on Fig Newtons and reading *The Parasites.* Tonight, every window blazed with light, and many were thrown wide-open to the wintery Swiss clime, their drapes flapping in the frigid wind which blew down from the glacial slopes of the tedious Alps. Of those wide-flung windows all now framed the heads of wealthy schoolgirls who leaned out and puked long banners of foody yuck down the building's redbrick facade. The sight was vastly too pleasing to abandon, but now the dashboard clock gave the time as eleven forty-five.

Bidding it all a fond adieu, I twisted the key in the car's ignition.

I twisted the key again.

I stepped my sensible Bass Weejun on the gas pedal, giving it a little stomp. The dashboard clock said eleven fifty. I double-checked that the tranny shift lever was set firmly in Park, and tried the key a third time.

Ye gods! And nothing happened. No car-ish sounds reverberated from beneath the vehicle's hood. To those of you blogosphere busybodies who think you know everything—especially concerning cars—no, I had not neglected to turn out the headlights and thus exhausted the battery. And, double no, the car was not short on dinosaur juice. Desperate, I tried the ignition repeatedly while watching the clock creep steadily to eleven fifty-five. At eleven fifty-six the car phone began to ring—issuing one old-school *bah-ring* after *bah-ring*—which I ignored in my frantic efforts to open the glove box, locate the driver's manual, and troubleshoot my mechanical crisis. The phone was still ringing four minutes later when, almost in tears, I grabbed the receiver from its cradle and answered it with a curt *"Alors!"*

Through the line a voice said, " '. . . Madison was almost weeping in frustration.' " A wheedling male voice said, " 'Her sweet triumph over her bullying schoolmates had turned to bitter panic as she found her getaway vehicle would not start. . . .' "

It was Satan, the Prince of Darkness, no doubt reading from his dreck manuscript, *The Madison Spencer Story*—a supposed story of my life which he claims he'd penned even before my conception. In those pages, every moment of my past and future is allegedly dictated by him.

" '. . . little Madison,' " Satan continued reading, " 'recoiled in shock at the sound of her supreme master's voice over the Town Car's telephone—' "

Interrupting, I asked, "Did you monkey with this car?"

" '. . . she knew,' " the telephone voice said, " 'that her Great Evil Destiny awaited her on Earth. . . .' "

I shouted, "No fair!"

" '. . . Maddy soon would have no choice but to venture forth and trigger the end of days. . . .' "

I shouted, "I'm not triggering anything!" I shouted, "I'm not your Jane Eyre!"

The dashboard clock now read midnight. A bell in the steeple of *eine* far-off alpine *kirche* commenced to toll. Before even the sixth knell, the receiver in my hands began to evaporate. The entire Town Car was disappearing around me, but the voice of Satan continued to drone. " '. . . Madison Spencer heard the distant church bell, and she realized that she didn't exist. She'd never existed save as a puppet created to serve the supremely sexy, insanely handsome Devil. . . .' "

As the driver's seat dissolved, my tubby, chubby-girl bottom was slowly settling to the pavement. The last stroke of midnight echoed into the canyons and ravines of tedious Switzerland. The windows of the school residence hall were closing. The lights winking out. Their curtains drawn. The safety belt, which only a moment earlier had squished my generous tummy, now became as insubstantial as a shred of mist. Nearby, as if dropped in the street, sat the fake Coach purse that a friend, Babette, had left in the car's backseat.

With the stroke of midnight the Lincoln had dwindled to nothing more than a nebulous fog bank, a small gray cloud in the shape of a Town Car. I was abandoned, sitting in the gutter with Babette's soiled, faux-leather handbag, alone in the blustery Swiss night.

In place of church bells, the wind carried only a tinny synthesized dance tune. It was the song "Barbie Girl" by the Europop band Aqua. A ring tone. It was a PDA I found buried among the condoms and candy bars in the purse. Listed on the screen was a Missoula, Montana, area code. A text message said, "URGENT: Stow away aboard Darwin Airlines flight #2903 from Lugano to Zurich; then catch Swissair flight #6792 to Heathrow and American Airlines flight #139 to JFK. Get your butt to the Rhinelander hotel. Go now!" The text, it was from a certain postalive, blue-haired punk rocker currently serving hard time in Hell, my friend and mentor Archer.

My Homecoming

Posted by Madisonspencer@aftrlife.hell

entle Tweeter,

If you asked my mom she'd tell you: "Religions exist because people would rather have a wrong answer than no answer at all." Meaning: My parents didn't believe in God. Meaning: My family didn't celebrate Christmas.

If my parents ever imagined God it was as a towering, mountain-size Harvey Milk healing the ozone hole with winged dolphins in place of cherubim. And rainbows, lots of rainbows.

Instead of Christmas, we celebrated Earth Day. Sitting zazen, we celebrated Swami Nikhilananda's birthday. Maybe we'd Morris dance, naked, around the base of an old-growth California redwood, its branches lavishly festooned with the soiled hammocks and poop buckets of crunchy-granola tree sitters mentoring spotted owls in passive-resistance protest techniques. You get the picture. In place of Santa Claus, my mom and dad said Maya Angelou kept tabs on whether little children were naughty or nice. Dr. Angelou, they warned me, did her accounting on a long hemp scroll of names, and if I failed to turn my compost I'd be sent to bed with no algae. Me, I just wanted to know that someone wise and carbon neutral—Dr. Maya or Shirley Chisholm or Sean Penn—was paying attention. But none of that was really Christmas. And none of that Earth

First! baloney helps out once you're dead and you discover that the snake-handling, strychnine-guzzling Bible thumpers were right.

Like it or not, the road to Hell is paved with sustainable bamboo flooring.

Trust me, Gentle Tweeter, I know whereof I speak. While my living-alive mom and dad have burned soy-based candles and prayed to John Reed for the better part of a year, I've been dead and learning the real truth about everything.

Alone at My Own Welcome-Home Party

Posted by Madisonspencer@aftrlife.hell

entle Tweeter,

While hardly the fragile homesick type, in light of my current circumstances I do seek out an old family haunt. For as long as I can recall my parents have kept a penthouse at the Rhinelander hotel. There, sixty-five stories above Lexington Avenue, across from Bloomingdale's, my first impulse would be to hide in my old bedroom among my stuffed animals and Jane Austen novels and watch on-demand streaming episodes of *Upstairs, Downstairs* on television until next Halloween. Possibly, I'd reread *The Forsyte Saga*. The coast should be clear, because, according to Page Six in the *Post*, my parents are at sea aboard their three-hundred-foot yacht, the *Pangaea Crusader*. At present they're in the Bering Straits attempting to foil the wholesale factory ship slaughter of killer whales or some other fancy-pants endangered bluefin sushi fish. All this fuss is being shot as B-roll footage for my mom's new feature, *Sperm Whales in the Mist*, where she plays a courageous Dian Fossey–type marine biologist who gets harpooned in her sleep by ruthless Japanese fisherfolk. Principal photography wraps next week, and Page Six says the project has got Academy Award written all over it.

Trust me, for my mom that's not really acting; she's been harpooned in bed more times than you can count.

And, yes, in response to the lecherous comment posted just now by HadesBrainiacLeonard, the story line includes three scenes—yet another tip-off from Page Six—wherein my mom's world-renowned breasts are fully exposed as she swims, naked and blissful, encased in a slippery pod of friendly sperm whales.

The way you, the future dead, experience a motion picture, as a flat-ish visual reality with sounds but sans smells or flavors or tactile sensations, that's how the living world appears to us ghosts. I can move among living people as their noise and action swirl around me, but alive people don't see me any more than actors in a film see the audience. At the risk of seeming too self-deprecating, as a blimpy seventh-grader wearing glasses and a school uniform, I'm more than accustomed to feeling invisible in the world. What takes more patience is accepting the fact that I'm no longer limited by physical barriers; I can stroll through closed lobby doors and hotel doormen as easily as you might saunter through smoke or fog, experiencing little more than a tickle in my ghost throat or an overall shuddering chill.

On the downside, not only do strangers look right through me; they also *walk* right through me. They don't merely stumble into physical contact, or grope you. You're actually penetrated. You commingle. You're violated by the roving physiology of these shopping, eating, fornicating slabs of animated meat. You feel smeared and confused and vertiginous, as does the idiot predead person who's just barged through you.

And, yes, I fully intend to use words like *vertiginous,* so get used to it. I might be a dead heifer, but I'm not going to play dumb just because you feel Ctrl+Alt+Insecure about your puerile vocabulary. And, no, nope, I definitely am *not* going to use slangy Internet lingo. Jane Austen made a deliberate choice not to enliven her wry narratives with emoticons, so I shan't either.

To repeat, becoming a ghost does take some getting used to. Hotel elevators, for example. Stupid living-alive people just keep cramming themselves into the elevator car. At the Rhinelander, I rode up to the penthouse floor standing half inside some gross collagen-stuffed tax exile and half inside her twitchy overbred Chihuahua. Physically, the sensation is like nothing so much as swimming or diving in silicone-polluted Evian. I can taste the saltiness of her Botox. The sour beta-blockers in her bloodstream make me light-headed, and being immersed in the warm bath of chemicals that make up a Chihuahua—ye gods. After riding sixty-five floors steeped in Mexican dog biology, I cannot wait to take a shower and shampoo my ghost hair.

I dissolve through the hallway door, number PH—no neighbors, no pets, no smoking—where I emerge in the penthouse foyer. For the first moment since I arrived in tedious New York, I step into absolute unalloyed silence. No horns honk. No obnoxious predead people gibber loudly on their mobile phones in gobbledygook United Nations languages. Furniture fills the PH's main living room, every chair and table and bookcase shrouded in white muslin dustcovers. Even the hovering chandeliers are wrapped in white cheesecloth, the fabric gathered at the bottom of each and trailing like filmy tails of ectoplasm. The overall impression is of a silent party attended by numerous ghosts, but comic-book ghosts wearing bedsheets and ready to wail, "Woooooo." This roomful of specters feels like a weirdly themed welcome-home party staged to ridicule me. A convention of large and small spooks. To be frank, I feel more than slightly Ctrl+Alt+Offended by this not-sensitive reception.

Out of long habit, following my mom's official house rules enforced from Tokyo to Managua, I slip off my shoes and leave them inside the foyer door.

Beyond the aforementioned soiree of faux ghosts, the PH's high, wide windows look down on the architecture of Manhattan. The rows of tightly packed buildings, those grim skyscrapers suggest nothing so much as a field of gray tombstones. These crowded towers look like broken columns and spires and obelisks, a collection of the monuments with which humans mark their burial sites. Beyond the windows lies this cemetery on a stupendous scale. The Big Apple. A burgeoning boneyard of the future dead.

Please understand, Gentle Tweeter, it's not my intention to be a wet blanket. A deceased party pooper. But I suspect that I'm suffering from a form of postmortem depression. Once the novelty of being newly dead wears off, a sense of malaise does tend to settle in its stead.

To answer the emotionally sensitive post from Mohawk-Archer666, yes, a ghost can get lonesome. If you want to know more, I feel a smidgen sad and discarded, forgotten by the entire world. My heart would swell like a water balloon filled with hot tears, swell and explode if I saw my folks, saw them and had them *not* see me. Isolated, alone with only my thoughts and feelings, as a ghost with no means to communicate, I've become the ultimate outsider.

Not merely godforsaken, I feel forsaken by everyone.

Down a PH passageway, padding in my ghost stocking feet past my mom's yoga studio and my dad's cigar room, I find the door to my bedroom is locked. Of course the door's locked, and no doubt the air conditioning is still cranked to meat-locker cold, and the drapes are drawn shut to protect my clothes and toys from sun fade. To preserve my room as a little shrine to a dead beloved daughter. For an idiotic moment I try to guess my mom's password to the security system. My first choice is: *CamilleSpenceristhegreatestlivingactorunder40*. As my second guess, my mom's security password is: *NoIdidnotkillmychildstinysweetkitten!* My next choice is: *IwouldvelovedMadisonatonmoreifshedweighedafewpoundsless*. Any of these is most likely correct, but then I realize that I can simply walk through.

Stepping through a door or wall feels only slightly less unpleasant than sharing molecules with a Chihuahua. I notice the flurry of sawdust, the oily sensation of too many coats of pale blue latex paint.

My bedroom presents a tableau similar to the PH living room: It's filled by a bed, a slipper chair, a bureau, each piece of furniture masked by a white dustcover . . . but stretched the length of my bed, hidden beneath the white muslin sheeting, is the prone shape of a person. At the foot of the bed, the shape peaks to suggest pointed toes, then thin legs. It spreads to suggest hips, a waist, a chest; then the muslin dips at a seeming neck and rises to cover a face, tented across the tip of a nose. In this Goldilocks moment, someone occupies my bed. On the muslin-draped bedside table a discarded wig of blond hair coils to form a nest. Settled in the center of that blond nest, like eggs, are a set of dentures, a hearing aide like a pink plastic jumbo prawn, a pack of Gauloises, and a gold cigarette lighter. Displayed beside these artifacts is a framed cover from *Cat Fancy* magazine, a two-shot of my mother and me hugging a bright-eyed orange-striped kitty. In contrast to my mom's Botox-steeped features, my smile is a frozen moment of genuine blissful laughter. The headline reads: "Film Star Gives Cinderella Kitten a Happy Ending."

To PattersonNumber54, yes, even a ghost can feel sadness and terror.

Death isn't the end of peril. There are deaths beyond death. Like it or not, death isn't the end of anything.

Nobody wants to wander into a lonely, way-quiet hotel room and find a dead body, especially not one lying in her very own childhood bed. It's the corpse of an inconsiderate stranger abandoned here, no doubt some Honduran hotel maid who elected to commit suicide in my nice bed, surrounded by my imported Steiff bears and limited-edition Gund giraffes, probably with a belly full of my mother's Xanax, decomposing her nasty Honduran bodily fluids into my hand-stitched Hästens mattress, ruining my sixteen-hundred-thread-count Porthault sheets.

As my mounting rage surpasses my fear, I step forward. I grip the top edge of the muslin dustcover and begin to draw it down, revealing the body: an ancient mummy. A hag. Her gums pucker and frill without teeth to support them. Sunk in a pillow, sparse gray hairs wreath her head. I pull back the white fabric in a single yank, throwing it to the bedroom floor. The old woman lies, legs together and hands crossed over her chest, every bony finger sparkling with flashy cocktail rings. Her dress I recognize, a haze of aquamarine velvet heavily trimmed with sequins, rhinestones, and seed pearls. A slit cut in the skirt reveals a skeletal leg from wasted thigh to the blue-veined foot encased in a Prada sling-back sandal. The shoes are so new the price tag pasted to the sole of one is still legible. The blond wig, the gown, they all look vaguely familiar. I know them. I recognize them from a funeral held about a hundred thousand years ago. Miracle of miracles, I can smell the old lady's cigarette smoke. No, I swear, ghosts can't smell or taste anything in the alive world, but I can smell the cigarette stench that wafts from her. And without thinking, without conscious intent, I say, "Nana Minnie?"

The old woman's eyelashes flutter. The outside end of one spidery false eyelash is peeling off, making her look a touch demented. The old lady blinks, lifting herself to her elbows and squinting her milky eyes in my direction. A smile splits the wrinkled width of her face, and her pink lisping gums say, "Pumpkinseed?"

To CanuckAIDSemily, this blows. Even after you're dead it hurts just as bad when your heart swells up, stretched bigger and bigger like an aneurysm of tears getting ready to boom.

My nana's gaze bounces from me to the skirt of her dress, from me to the sequins and velvet that fall away to reveal her aged legs, and the woman says, "For crying out loud . . . would you just *look* at the whore's costume your mama buried me in?" With one shaky, bejeweled hand she reaches to the bedside table and plucks at the pack of Gauloises. Saying, "Come on and give your Nana Minnie a light," she brings the butt of a cigarette to her mouth, and her slack, wrinkled lips collapse into a kiss shape around the filter tip.

entle Tweeter,

Sprawled on the satin coverlet of my bed, Nana crosses her spindly legs at the ankle, affording me an unwelcome glimpse up her slit skirt. Cringing, I ask, "Did we bury you . . . not wearing underpants?"

"Your stupid mama," she says by way of an answer. Her gown is sleeveless, and she stares down at a thorny tribal tattoo that encircles her wrist and marches up her arm to her elbow, continuing to her shoulder. The inky black forms barbed letters, like briars, that spell out, "I [heart shape] Camille Spencer . . . I [heart shape] Camille Spencer . . ." with a tattooed rose blooming between each iteration. Nana spits on her thumb and rubs at the words on her wrist, saying, "What's this happy horseshit?" She can't see it, but the words run from her shoulder to circle her neck like a choker, terminating in a large tattooed rose that covers most of her right cheek. These repetitive declarations were needled into her aged, sunbaked hide postmortem, at my mother's insistence.

Her head propped on the bed's pillow, Nana Minnie glances down at the full breasts swelling within the bodice of her dress. "For the love of Pete . . . What did your mama do to me?" With the gnarled talon of an elderly index finger, she pokes tentatively at one firm breast, obviously another postmortem renovation.

She's smoking a ghost cigarette, blowing secondhand smoke everywhere, and with her free hand she pats the bed for me to come sit beside her. Of course I sit. I'm bitter and resentful and angry, not impolite. I merely sit, not talking, certainly not hugging and kissing her. My borrowed fake Coach bag rests on the bed beside my hip, and I dip a hand into it and dig among the turquoise Avon eye shadows, Almond Joys, and condoms. I fish out a strange PDA and start keyboarding my evil thoughts into words . . . sentences . . . bitchy blog entries.

If I'm honest here, you'll decide that I'm simply the most hard-hearted thirteen-year-old ghost ever to walk the face of the Earth, but I am already wishing my beloved long-dead Nana Minnie would get lung cancer and die a second time.

Between drags on her coffin nail my nana asks, "You ain't seen a spiritualist skulking around, have you? Terrible skin? A big, tall drink a water with his long hair braided down his back like a Chinaman?" She cocks a wrinkled eye at me.

To reassure you, HellHottieBabette, I am taking good care of your handbag.

My Nana Minnie was my mom's mother, and in her palmier days she was probably a madcap jazz baby bobbing her hair and rouging her knees, dancing the jitterbug on cocaine-dusted speakeasy tables with Charles Lindbergh and roaring through the West Egg night in Stutz Bearcats, wrapped in raccoon coats and gorging on live goldfish, but by the time I knew her, my nana was fairly worn down to dust. Probably raising my mom didn't help her stay young any.

By the time I was born Nana Minnie was already collecting buttons and nursing her sciatica. And chain-smoking. I remember that when I'd go visit her upstate, she'd brew tea by sticking an old pickle jar full of water in a sunny window. All that Norman Rockwell–ness aside, my nana's house smelled like vacationing with dirty cavemen, as if she cooked every meal by combining raw ingredients she wrenched from some plot of dirt, and then heated to create food *right inside her house* and never just texted Spago or the Ivy or the Grill Room at the Four Seasons and had them deliver *moules marinières tout de suite.*

After you used my nana's bathroom, no Somali maids slipped in quietly to sanitize everything and distribute new *pamplemousse*-scented shampoos. It's no mystery why my mother opted to run away as a teenager, become a world-famous Hollywood star, and marry my billionaire father. There's only so long you can pretend to be Laura Ingalls Wilder before that barefoot-hillbilly game wears thin. While I was banished to the Elba of tedious upstate, my mother would be off with a UNESCO film crew teaching safer-sex condom techniques to the bushmen of the Kalahari. My father would be orchestrating the hostile takeover of Sony Pictures or cornering the international market on weapons-grade plutonium, and I'd be stuck feigning interest in the rustic mating calls of wild birds.

I'm not a snob. You can't call me a snob, because I'd long ago forgiven my nana for living on a farm upstate. I'd forgiven her for buying domestic Havarti and for not knowing the difference between sorbet and gelato. To her credit, it was my Nana Minnie who introduced me to the novels of Elinor Glyn and Daphne du Maurier. To score a point in my favor, I tolerated her obsession with growing her own heirloom tomatoes when Dean & Deluca could've FedExed us infinitely better Cherokee Purples. I loved her *that* much. But no matter how judgmental this sounds, I still have not forgiven her for dying.

Picking a fleck of tobacco off her tongue, using the chopstick-long fingernails my mom had her retrofitted with for her funeral, my nana says, "Your ma hired some fella to ghost-hunt you, so stay on your toes." She adds, "I can tell you this much: He's like a private dick who finds dead folks, and he's here in this very hotel!"

Sitting here in my old hotel bedroom, surrounded by my Steiff monkeys and Gund zebras, all I can see is that lit cigarette. That legalized form of suicide. And, yes, in response to the comment posted by HadesBrainiacLeonard, this is distinctly ungenerous of me. Allow me to be frank. I'm not entirely without empathy, but to my mind she left me behind. My nana abandoned me because cigarettes were more important. I loved her, but she loved tar and nicotine more. And today, finding her in my bedroom I resolve not to make the mistake of ever loving her again.

My mom never forgave her for not being Peggy Guggenheim. I never forgave her for smoking and cooking and gardening and dying.

"So," my Nana Minnie says, "Pumpkinseed, where you been keeping yourself?"

Oh, I tell her, around. I don't tell her anything about how I died. Nor do I offer a word about being condemned to Hell. My fingers keep typing away on my PDA; my fingertips are screaming everything I can't bear to say aloud.

"I've been there. To Heaven," says Nana Minnie. She jabs

her cigarette toward the ceiling. "We was both of us saved, me and your Papadaddy Ben. The problem is Heaven adopted one of them strict no-smoking rules." Henceforth, she says, in the same way office workers must brave the weather and huddle outdoors in order to puff their cancer sticks, my dead nana must descend as a ghost to indulge her vile addiction.

Mostly I just listen and search her face for signs of myself. Child and crone, we create a kind of before-and-after effect; her hooked parrot's nose is my cute button nose, except irradiated by the ultraviolet rays of a hundred thousand upstate summer days. Her cascade of variously sized chins duplicates my dainty girlish chin, only in triplicate. I steer the conversation to the weather. Sitting on the edge of the hotel bed, where she lies inhaling a cigarette, I ask whether Papadaddy Ben is also skulking around the Rhinelander hotel.

"Sweet pea," she says, "stop fussing with that pocket calculator and be sociable." Nana Minnie rolls her ghost head from side to side on the pillow. She blows a jet of smoke at the ceiling and says, "No, your papadaddy ain't hereabouts. He wanted to be in Heaven to welcome Paris Hilton when she come."

Please, Dr. Maya, give me the strength to not use an emoticon.

Paris Hilton is going to Heaven?

This I can't Ctrl+Alt+Fathom.

Sitting here, looking at my nana's face, it strikes me that I can't see her thoughts. Thoughts ... thinking ... the very proof which René Descartes cites for our existence is as equally invisible as ghosts. As our souls. It seems that if science is going to dismiss the possibility of a soul for lack of physical proof, scientists should also deny that thinking occurs. With this observation I glance at my sturdy, functional wristwatch and observe that only a minute has passed.

My nana catches me with my elbow cocked, my wristwatch twisted for me to look at the time, and she says, "Did you miss your old grandma, kitty-kins?" She exhales another plume of smoke toward the ceiling.

"Yes," I lie, "I did. I missed you," but I keep keyboarding to the contrary.

It doesn't escape me that this is the central conflict of my life: I love and adore all of my family, except when I'm with them. No sooner do I enjoy a reunion with my long-dead Nana Minnie than I yearn to have my chain-smoking, half-blind beloved granny euthanized.

The unhappy reality is that medical euthanasia is at best a onetime solution.

Then it happens: a sound.

From the PH foyer it comes: a laugh.

I ask, "Is that your long-haired paranormal private detective?"

Nana Minnie points her cigarette in the direction of the ruckus, a man's laugh, and she says, "That's how come you ought not be here, duckling." She taps the ghost ash off her ghost cigarette and brings the butt back to her mouth. "Myself, I'm conducting a little covert investigation," she says, taking another puff. "You think I enjoys laying here surrounded by your lousy kiddy toys? Maddy, honey," she says, "you done walked into a stakeout."

A Tryst Revealed!

Posted by Madisonspencer@aftrlife.hell

entle Tweeter,
From elsewhere in the hotel suite comes the sound of a door, the dead bolt snapping open with a heavy clunk. No knock heralds it. No polite announcement of "Housekeeping!" or "Room service!" It's the door which opens from the hotel hallway into the living room. The latch clicks. The hinges give a little sigh, and muffled footsteps sound against the marble tile of the suite's foyer.

Sad to say, the dead can still suffer excruciating bouts of self-consciousness. Like you, the predecomposed, the postalive can feel utterly mortified by their own sordid confessions.

Take, for example, the following admission: I spent the fondest hours of my childhood with my ear pressed to the outside of my parents' bedroom door. On the not-infrequent occasion when sleep eluded me in Athens or Abu Dhabi or Akron, I took great pleasure in eavesdropping on my parents' carnal panting. Their coital groaning acted upon me as the sweetest lullaby. To my childhood ear those grunts and snorts were assurance of continued familial bliss. My parents' bestial ejaculations guaranteed that my home wouldn't crack up as had all those of my wealthy playmates. Not that I had playmates.

Rapping. Tapping. The culture of spiritualists is rife with

ghosts knocking loudly. For souls stranded in a physical world it's only common courtesy. Plainly put, no one wants to enter a room and witness a predead person pooing or vigorously engaged in performing the Hot Nasty.

Thus, ghosts always knock before they enter a room. Including me. Especially me. In the PH of the Rhinelander hotel, as I follow the sound of my father's laugh, the unmistakable Thoroughbred stallion *clip-clop* of his shoes, accompanied by the time bomb *tick-tock* of Manolo Blahnik high heels, my pursuit leads to the closed door of my parents' New York bedroom. The instant before I step through the enameled wood, a voice from within says, "Hurry, my love; we're desperately behind schedule. We should've been screwing hours ago. . . ."

The voice, my father's voice, arrests my entry. What's there to say concerning the renowned Antonio Spencer? The shape of his head is like that of a very handsome boulder. A landmark. Usually he speaks with a phony NPR intonation, but today his voice sounds naked and hairy.

In lieu of dissolving through the door and possibly witnessing a primal scene, I pace the foyer, enervated with guilt.

In the PH foyer, an electrical outlet catches my eye. We'll revisit this practice in greater detail soon, but for the present please accept the fact that I pour my ghost ectoplasm into the tiny holes of a three-pronged outlet and worm along the copper wires buried within the hotel walls. Picture Charles Darwin navigating the steamy Amazonian river system. Arriving at a junction box, I guess the next wire and follow it to a new outlet. Soon I encounter the prongs of an extension cord. Shimmying along copper, I jump the gap of an open switch. Tunneling upward, I reach a dead end, lodged within a lightbulb. Not a roomy Thomas Edison incandescent bulb, mind you; this is a convoluted compact fluorescent lightbulb installed in a bedside lamp. Surrounding me, a vellum shade screens my view of the hotel room. I'm twisted inside a dark bulb, exactly the energy-efficient, eco-friendly option that my parents would choose, and the mercury tastes Ctrl+Alt+Foul. Surrounded by the lamp shade, I can only gaze down onto the wood-grain surface of a bedside table. There, like the elements of some torrid modern still life, my cramped view includes a PDA, a room key attached to a brass fob, an alarm clock, and the torn packaging leftover from a not-present condom.

Hark, the comforting slurp-some din of my parents frantically taxing their aged pleasure centers.

Please note, you future dead persons, whenever you shut off a fluorescent bulb or a cathode ray tube and see a residual photon-green glow, that glow is trapped human ectoplasm. Ghosts are forever being snared in lightbulbs.

Even now, coiled within a dark bulb, I indulge my ghost self by covert eavesdropping. Screened as I am, I can't see them, but I can detect my father's hoarse endearments. "Oh," he says, "slow down." My dad says, "I love what you're doing, baby, but wait." He says, "You're going to send me right over the edge. . . ."

At that, a hand snakes under the bottom edge of the lampshade. It's a bony spider of a hand. Plaited with smooth muscle, it's a serpent of an arm, its skin as smooth as a lizard's scales. The fingernails are painted with chipped white polish, and pink stripes run from the base of the palm down the inside of the forearm, like a few furrows plowed in a fallow upstate field. These parallel pink lines run almost to the elbow. Ragged, they suggest the scant few inches of sodbusting accomplished by some old dirt farmer before he dropped dead of a lonely heart attack.

These scars, so rudely cut and freshly healed, they brand the bearer as a would-be suicide. Gentle Tweeters, I recognize these scars. I know this arm.

I know the desolate visuals of a hardscrabble upstate lifestyle.

A thin crescent of brown shows under each nail. It's chocolate, the brown. To an expert eater, it's clearly milk chocolate smudged from the outer layer of a Baby Ruth. Her touch is slippery with sweat and sticky with caramel. Her fingers fumble against the glass sides of the bulb, effectively fondling my face, soiling my hair. Caressing and molesting the ghost me contained here. These fingers smell like my father's undershorts fermenting in the bottom of an overly heated Tunis laundry hamper. They smell the way my mother smelled when she'd giggle and stay belted in her bathrobe all morning. Those mornings, my mother would serenely pour organic wheatgrass juice, her cheeks ruddy and raw from my father's morning stubble.

Not wearing my mother's canary yellow engagement ring, this groping hand is not my mother's hand.

Attached to the spidery fingers is the snake arm, a skinny shoulder, a slender neck. A face cranes from the bed, and two eyes peer under the lower edge of the lamp shade, looking directly at me as the fingers locate the switch and twist it. A face no older than that of a pretty high-schooler, in the new sixty-watt glare, it's not my mother's face.

Lipstick is smudged around this stranger's mouth. Her

cheeks are livid from whiskers which ought to be abrading my mother's face. She's looking up the bottom of the lamp shade as if she's peering up a skirt. This strange lecher smiles into the glow of my hiding place, and she whispers, "What time is it?"

A Shout-out for Backup

Posted by Madisonspencer@aftrlife.hell

entle Tweeter,

In death as in life I am betrayed by my peers. This girl we find canoodling so freely with my very married father, until recently she professed to be my devoted friend and mentor in Hell. It's likely that she's also violated her Halloween curfew, but how she can manifest a physical body and carnally interact with the predead is a mystery.

To my remaining friends still lodged in the fiery underworld, I make a special request. Unbeknownst to you—smarty-pants Leonard, athletic Patterson, misanthropic Archer, and dear little Emily—during the normal course of events in Hades I inadvertently made contact with my living-alive parents. It was by telephone, an accident, and they were understandably upset about speaking to the daughter they had just buried. To quell their weeping I offered my mom and dad some advice on how to conduct their lives. This advice, most likely, will land them in the Pit.

Please, my underworld friends, if my parents die during my yearlong absence, please protect them. Make them feel at home.

The Tryst, Continued
Posted by Madisonspencer@aftrlife.hell

entle Tweeter,

Seeking forensic proof of my parents' lust for each other, as a predead child I would pillage the dirty laundry. The pong and sogginess of damp bed linens served as the physical evidence that my mom and dad were still in love, and these lustful stains documented their romance better than would any florid handwritten poetry. Their carnal discharges proved that all was stable. The squeak of bedsprings, the slap of skin against bare skin, these spoke a biological promise more lasting than wedding vows.

In those revolting smears of bodily fluids was writ proof of our mutual happy ending. That, it would seem, is no longer the case.

"For the love of Madison," gasps my father's voice, "are you trying to fuck me to death, Babette?"

Those familiar eyes framed in turquoise eye shadow, edged in mascaraed eyelashes, they're the flesh-eating flowers of a Venus flytrap. Her earlobes strain with the weight of dime-size dazzle-cut cubic zirconia. Making her voice a bedroom purr, continuing to gaze upon me in my lightbulb, the young woman, Babette, asks, "Do you miss her?"

My father responds with silence. His hesitation stretches to a cold eternity. At last he asks, "You mean my wife?"

"I mean, do you miss your daughter, Madison?" prompts Babette.

Gruff, indignant. "You're asking if I *hit her*? Did I ever *beat* her?"

"No," Babette says. "Do you *miss her*?"

After a long beat, his voice wry with chagrin, my father says, "I was stunned to find out that Heaven even existed. . . ."

"Madison wouldn't lie," says Babette, baiting me. "Would she?"

"This is going to sound terrible," my dad's voice begins. "But I was even more surprised to hear that Madison got past the gates." A chuckle. "Frankly, I was dumbfounded."

My own father thinks I ought to be in Hell.

Stranger yet, I suspect that Babette can see me. I'm certain she can.

Quickly, dryly, my dad adds, "I could imagine Madison getting into Harvard . . . but Heaven?"

"But she's there now," says Babette, even as she sees me here, trapped on Earth, hovering within an arm's length of their adulterous postcoital dialogue. "Madison spoke to you from Heaven, didn't she?"

"Don't misunderstand me," my dad says. "I loved Maddy as much as any parent ever loved a child." His silent pause here is long and infuriating. "The truth is that my baby girl had her shortcomings."

As if making a token effort to resolve the topic, Babette says, "This must be painful for you to admit."

"The truth is," says my dad, "my Maddy was a little coward."

Babette gasps in theatrical shock. "Don't say that!"

"But Madison was," insists my dad, his voice exhausted, resigned. "Everyone saw it. She was a spineless, gutless, weak little coward."

Babette smirks up at me, saying, "Not Maddy! Not spineless!"

"Those were the empirical findings of our entire team of behavioral experts," my dad's voice affirms dismally. Downhearted. "She hid behind a defensive mask of false superiority."

The statement roils in the cramping bowels of my brain. My ears gag on the words *team* and *findings*.

"Those eyes of hers watched everything and they judged everything," my father declares, "especially her mother and me. Madison decried every dream, but she never had the courage or strength of convictions to pursue any vision of her own." As if laying down his sad trump card he adds, "Nothing led us to believe poor Maddy ever had a single friend. . . ."

That, Gentle Tweeter, is an untruth. Babette was my friend. Not that she's such a great endorsement of friendship.

Too quickly, too gently, Babette says, "We don't have to discuss this, Tony."

And too fervently, my dad responds, "But I do." His voice simultaneously righteous and defeated, he says, "Leonard warned us. Decades ago. Long before she was born, Leonard said Maddy would be very difficult to love."

Narrowing her eyes, grinning up at me, Babette prompts, "Leonard? The telemarketer?"

With an almost audible shaking of his head, my father says, "Okay, he was a telemarketer, but he made us rich.

He warned us that Madison would pretend to have friends." My dad laughs quietly. He sighs. "Over one winter break Madison spent the school holiday entirely alone. . . ."

Oh, for the love of Susan Sarandon, I can't be hearing this! My ghost brains bloat and ache, stretching, painfully, the swollen belly of my memory.

"She told her mother and me that she was spending the holidays with friends in Crete," he continues. "And for the next three weeks, she did nothing but eat ice cream and read trashy novels."

Gentle Tweeter, fie! Ye gods! *Forever Amber* is *not* a trashy novel. Neither am I weak and a coward.

Babette's voice sounds syrupy as she coos, "A pretty girl like Madison . . . That's impossible." Her urine-hued eyes, however, guffaw heartily at my expense.

"It's true," says my dad. "We watched her over the entire holiday via the school's security cameras. The poor, lonely, fat little thing."

entle Tweeter,

Such a nature boy is my father that his copious grunting regales us. Volcanic blasts erupt, not muffled by modesty or any intervening closed and locked door. Having left the bed and padded across the room barefoot, he's installed himself astride the commode in the en suite bathroom, from whence the tiled surfaces amplify a host of wet sounds.

In his absence Babette once more cranes her head to peer up into the lamp shade where I take refuge. "Madison, don't be angry," she whispers. "Believe it or not, I'm trying to help you."

My father's voice calls out, "Babs, you say something?"

Ignoring him, Babette whispers, "Don't delude yourself. Do you think it was an accident when the autodialer connected you with your parents?" Whisper-yelling, she says, "Nothing that's happened to you is an accident! Not *The Voyage of the Beagle.* Not EPCOT." Exasperated, she says, "And the people you think are your dead friends . . . they're not your friends. The nerd and the jock and the punk, they're in Hell for very good reasons!"

If Babette is to be believed, you, HadesBrainiacLeonard, PattersonNumber54, and MohawkArcher666, you're all miscreants. She claims you're bent on subverting creation and imposing your own eternal plans. You befriended me in Hell. You put me to work on the phones. She says this is all part of a grand scheme that goes back for centuries.

"They call themselves 'emancipated entities,'" Babette insists. "They refuse to take sides with either Satan or God."

In the background a toilet flushes.

"Don't let them fool you, Maddy." Wagging a chocolate-smeared finger at me, she says, "Girlfriend, you wouldn't believe the kinky shit your so-called friends planned for you. . . ."

She hisses, "I'm still your best friend. That's why I'm warning you." As footsteps approach from the bathroom, she whispers, "You just watch, Maddy. Satan is going to win this thing! Satan is going to get all the marbles, and you need to get on his side while you still can."

The Tryst, Part Three

Posted by Madisonspencer@aftrlife.hell

entle Tweeter,

Tinny music fills the hotel bedroom. It's the Beastie Boys singing "Brass Monkey." It's the PDA on the bedside table announcing a new text message.

Restored to the bed, my dad explains, "We asked a panel of doctors to study the security videos." His hairy hand reaches into view, patting the tabletop in search of the ringing phone.

Words Ctrl+Alt+Fail me. Not even emoticons can convey the horror I feel upon hearing this. Like the subject of some patronizing panocular coming-of-age saga in the dirt-eating hinterlands of New Guinea, my not-clothed childhood antics have been observed! My formerly faithful, formerly devoted father is blatantly cheating on my mother, yet he deems me flawed and not likable! Yes, Gentle Tweeter, I might be emotionally withheld and lacking in superfluous, superficial social bonds, but I am not unproud of the fact that I failed to self-stimulate my virginal hoo-hoo for the Peeping Tom anthropological kicks of some voyeuristic child psych consultants. It's monstrous, the idea that strangers watched me. Even my parents. *Especially my parents.*

Babette asks, "Antonio?"

My father hums something in reply.

Simpering, she asks, "Why are we here?"

My father's hairy suntanned hand, it retrieves the PDA, and his voice says, "We're accompanying Camille's ghost hunter in room sixty-three fourteen." Encircling his finger, his gold wedding ring looks like a tiny dog collar. "You remember, the guy who Leonard told us to hire? From *People* magazine?" he says. "The one who takes boatloads of that animal tranquilizer?" The pace of his delivery slows, punctuated by the faint beeps of him pressing PDA buttons. My dad's still talking, but he's distracted, checking his messages. He proceeds to describe the out-of-body effects of tripping on some anesthetic, ketamine, what the counterculture hero Timothy Leary described as "experiments in voluntary death." He explains how this freelance ghost hunter triggers at-will near-death experiences by ingesting intentional overdoses of it. My father, Gentle Tweeter, can talk any subject into the ground. He describes what scientists call "emergence phenomena," wherein the ketamine abusers swear their souls take leave of their bodies and can commune in the afterlife.

Babette says, "You miss my point."

"Leonard told us to hire this freak and to camp out here, at the Rhinelander."

"But why am *I* here?" Babette prompts.

"I picked you up on Halloween—"

"The day *after* Halloween," Babette interrupts.

"I picked you up for the same reason I spit in the elevator on our way here this afternoon," my dad says. He talks even slower, as if he's giving orders to a stone-deaf, Somali-speaking maid. "*I want to get my wings, too,*" he says.

"Babs, honey, I'm only porking you because the tenets of Boorism command me to."

The bed creaks with his weight shifting. The shrieking mattress sounds begin anew, shrill arpeggios less like love-making than like the substitute screams in a movie where someone's getting stabbed to death in a motel shower.

Breathless, my dad's voice says, "Even if my daughter wasn't perfect, I love her." He says, "I'd lie, cheat, and kill to get my little girl back."

The incoming message on the PDA, it was from Camille Spencer. The "Brass Monkey" song is unmistakable; it's my mom's signature ring tone. And the message? It consisted of three words: "SHE IS RISEN."

A Tourist among the Dead
Posted by Madisonspencer@aftrlife.hell

entle Tweeter,

It was always my mother's coping mechanism to acquire far-flung *maisons*. In Stockholm and Sydney and Shanghai, a backup plan to every backup plan; that way she'd always have a refuge. Such was her fail-safe strategy: redundant places to retreat. If tax laws changed in one nation, or not-favorable publicity exposed her to public ridicule, my mom fled to sanctuary in Malta, in Monaco, in Mauritius.

For my father, girlfriends served the same function. In the same way my mother never fully committed to living in one domicile, my dad never favored one Miss Warty MacWanton. The subtle, largely unacknowledged appeal of extra homes and lovers relies on *not* making actual use of them. That unfulfilled longing, the idea of a gorgeous vacant home or a pining concubine, sustains the object's attraction. Picture *Playboy* centerfolds or the idle harem ladies painted by Delacroix or the vacant rooms depicted in the pages of *Architectural Digest*. All of them empty vessels waiting to be filled.

So upon shocked exposure to my dad's extramarital hanky-panky, I retreat. I bleed backward along the copper wiring of the Rhinelander hotel. Confronted, I quickly retrace my route back to the penthouse foyer and emerge like a bubble of my ghost self from the outlet I first entered.

The process involves expanding, inflating my balloon of ectoplasm to roughly my chunky thirteen-year-old size. My facial features solidify, then my horn-rimmed glasses, followed by my school cardigan sweater and tweedy skort. Last to take shape are my Bass Weejun loafers. At that, the remainder of my ghost self trickles from the outlet, intact but Ctrl+Alt+Disillusioned.

And it would seem I'm not alone. A man stands among the furniture, the chairs and tables humped beneath their white dustcovers. He stands below the chandelier in its cheesecloth shroud. Ghost me, my ghost eyes are locked with the eyes of this stranger. Perhaps here is the ghost hunter my nana tried to caution me about.

Gentle Tweeter, you may label me as a snotty elitist, but it still amazes me to see Americans in the United States. For most of my childhood I've trekked from Andorra to Antigua to Aruba, all of those glorious tax-haven states, in the constant migration of income tax exiles as they seek to shelter their gargantuan salaries in Belize and Bahrain and Barbados. My general impression was that the United States had shipped all of its citizens offshore and become largely operated and inhabited by illegal aliens.

Yes, you might occasionally see someone wearing a maid's uniform or driving a Town Car, but the man I find in our penthouse foyer, he's clearly no one's servant. For starters, he's glowing. Radiating a clear, blue light. It's not as if he contains a lightbulb; it's more as if he's something faceted, a jewel, collecting the ambient light. His face is hazy and indistinct, I realize, because I'm seeing both the front and the back of his head, his eyes, and his hair simultaneously. It's like holding the page of a book against sunshine so strong that the print on both sides is legible. It's dazzling, the way every angle of a diamond is visible at one glance. Through him I can see the buildings outside the window, the gray view over Central Park. His hair hangs down his back in a braid as long and thick as a moldering baguette. Each strand looks as clear and iridescent as Asian glass noodles. His neck is stretched cellophane, the skin pleated with tendons and veins. His suit coat, his pant legs, even his soiled running shoes are translucent as spit.

Standing there, his arms hanging at his sides, he trembles like a column of smoke. When he opens his lips they're as faint as the undulating form of a jellyfish swimming through some disgusting undersea documentary. His voice sounds muffled, as if I'm hearing a man whisper secrets in another room.

To CanuckAIDSemily, yes, before I died, this is how I'd imagined a ghost would appear.

Haggard and weary, he says, "You're that dead kid."

He sees me.

"Are you . . . ?" I ask. I gag on my own question.

His form sways a little from side to side. Just as he starts to topple in one direction, he stiffens with a jerk as if jarred awake. He overcompensates and begins to collapse in the opposite direction. Not quite standing straight, his fragile stance is a sustained series of barely arrested falls.

Gentle Tweeter, I may not know the much-touted womanly pleasures of menstruation, but I can recognize a junkie when I meet one. Life with Camille and Antonio Spencer meant rubbing elbows with a wide variety of the chemically dependent.

Dumbfounded, I swallow. My throat dry, I ask, "Are you God?"

"Little dead girl . . ." he seems to whisper. He's dissipating, and not in a metaphorical way. He's evaporating. His hands, dissolving like milk mixed into water. His words less than an echo, soft as a thought, he says, "Look for me in room number sixty-three fourteen. Find me." Only the trail of his voice remains as he says, "Come tell me a secret that only your mother would know. . . ."

My Parents Dispatch an Emissary

Posted by Madisonspencer@aftrlife.hell

entle Tweeter,

Here and now in the Rhinelander hotel, I trace the electrical lines from my parents' penthouse to room 6314. This, in response to the mysterious advice from the ghostly vision, the translucent man with his not-clean hair tortured into a hippie braid no less off-putting than the soiled tail of some incontinent upstate hay burner. My thanks to CanuckAIDSemily for asking, but yes, a ghost can be haunted by ghosts. My nana, case in point, she remains in my penthouse bedroom, smoking, loitering, by her very presence reminding me of our shared summer in the tedious Empire State, and the myriad horrors that were to occur there.

Skating along electrical circuits, past solderless connections and with a not-small number of wrong turns, I emerge from the slotted holes of an outlet in room 6314. The setting: a room in the back of the house, overlooking Barneys and the pond in Central Park South, two upholstered chairs near the window, a chest of drawers, a bed—every surface, no doubt, alive with blood-besotted bedbugs. Between the two chairs stands a small glass-topped table, and streaked across the glass are white trails of powder. A scale model of the Andes. The Apennines. The rugged Galápagos Islands, only rendered in peaks of crystalline white dust. A single-edged razor blade lies beside the heaps. Sprawled beneath the glass-topped table is my enigmatic visitor, chest down, his head twisted to one side. He lies there on the carpet, to all appearances dead. A tightly rolled tube of paper juts from one nostril. This tube is likewise dusted with the table's white residue.

Gentle Tweeter, life with my former-stoner, former-crackhead, former-snow-blind parents has left me too acclimated to this tableau. Even as I situate my ghost self on the edge of the bed, the sprawled denizen moans. His eyelids flutter. You'd mistake his torso and limbs for a not-fresh pile of sweat-stained laundry save for the gentle rise and fall of his breathing. His trembling hands push against the room's carpet, and the scarecrow ensemble of patched blue jeans, a plaid flannel shirt, a fringed suede jacket, it clutches at a chair and hauls itself to a standing position. No longer magically transparent, this not-appealing flesh-depleted person casts his gaze around the hotel room, asking, "Little dead girl?"

This, this must be the parapsychological private detective dispatched by my mom.

You'd be hard-pressed to guess his age. The skin of his face is pebbled and flushed as if it were a delicious crème caramel bombe frosted with a raspberry-ricotta streusel of festering boils. What at first I took to be a huge upper lip is merely a bushy lip-colored mustache. Creases web every trace of his exposed neck, his arms and hands, as if he's been folded over and folded over, like strudel dough, and now he can never again be smoothed flat. His bloodshot eyes sweep back and forth across the room, and he says, "Little dead girl, are you here? Did you come like I told you?"

As with so many of the chemically dependent, the man looks older than any cadaver.

It would seem that he can't see me. Yes, I could flick the lights or flash the television to confirm my attendance; instead I wait.

The rolled paper still protrudes from his nose and he plucks it out. "Send me a sign," he says. His hands unroll the paper, stretching it flat. It's a photograph of my mother hugging me, both of us smiling at the camera. It's the cover of an old *Parade* magazine. Gentle Tweeter, please understand that at the time this photo was snapped I had no inkling that they would superimpose the headline "A Movie Superstar and Her Afflicted Daughter Tackle the Tragedy of Childhood Obesity" across the top. Yes, there I am smiling like a happy toad, my beefy arms cradling a golden kitten. The deranged, pigtailed hobo rotates in place, showing the ragged clipping to the minibar, the bed, the bureau, the white-dusted table. "See," he says. "It's you."

Along its bottom edge the photo is darkened with damp from his nose. Fat as I am, my mom's arms go all the way around me. I smell the memory of her perfume.

Intrigued, I relent, slowly drawing the window curtains closed against the view.

The hobo's head swivels so fast, turning to stare at the moving curtains, that his loathsome pigtail swings in a wide arc. "Success!" he shouts, and pumps a stony fist in the air. "I found you!" As he stumbles in a circle, his eyes sweep the room. His fingers grope as if he could snatch my invisible form. "Your old lady is going to be so jazzed." He's not looking at me. He's not looking at anything as his eyes scan every corner. He's talking everywhere, saying, "This proves I am *the best*." His attention lands on the table, on the white lines of powder cut across the glass top. "This is my secret," he says. "Ketamine. You know, Special K." He rolls the photo of my mother and me and sticks it back into one nostril and mimes leaning down for a long toot.

"I call myself a 'psychic bounty hunter,' " he says. "Little dead girl, your old lady is paying me big bucks to locate you."

Yes, CanuckAIDSemily, you understood correctly. This much-eroded ragamuffin referred to himself as a *psychic bounty hunter*. I can surmise the worst.

The man's eyelids blink, open, blink, but they stay blinked too long each time, as if he keeps dozing off. Jerking awake, his eyes spring wide, and he says, "What was I saying?" He offers a handshake to thin air and says, "My name is Crescent City. Don't laugh." His outstretched fingers are palsied, trembling. "Before, my real name was worse. It was *Gregory Zerwekh*."

This, this is so the type of emissary my stone-ground, whole-grain mother would hire. Here is the winged Mercury meant to facilitate the exchange of our eternal mother-daughter bonding. He's smiling, showing an asymmetrical mismatched nightmare of bony teeth. His stretched lips quiver with the effort. When his smile fades and his twitchy, jaundiced eyes quit darting around the room, he slowly lowers himself into one of the chairs and leans his elbows on his knees. With the paper tube still stuck in his nose, he says, "Little dead girl? I need to get with you on your level." He draws a deep breath and blows it out to collapse his rag-doll chest. As he leans over the glass table he aligns the tube with a fat rail of powder and begins to anteater the white poison.

DECEMBER 21, 8:33 A.M. EST
Ketamine: A Brief Overview
Posted by Madisonspencer@aftrlife.hell

entle Tweakers,

If your parents failed in their duty to introduce you to a wide variety of controlled substances, please let me enlighten you. My own progressive mother and father left nothing to my childhood imagination. Not licking sun-dried toad skins. Nor sniffing oven-baked banana peels ground to a mellow yellow dust. As other parents labored to introduce their finicky offspring to raisin cassoulet or rutabaga goulash, mine were constantly admonishing me, "Maddy, sweetheart, if you don't drink your glass of Rohypnol you won't get any tiramisu for dessert." Or, "You may be excused from the table after you finish every bite of that PCP."

As children the world over might sneak their spinach or broccoli to the family pet, I was always sneaking my codeine tablets to ours. Instead of being boarded at a kennel, our poor dog was constantly being shuttled off to rehab. Even my angelfish, Albert Finney, had to be dried out because I was forever dropping Percodans into his aquarium. Poor Mr. Finney.

Ketamine, Gentle Tweeter, is a common trade name for hydrochloride. It's an anesthetic that binds to opioid receptors in brain cells, and is administered most often to prepare patients and animals for surgery. It comforts victims

54

trapped in terrible car crashes; it's *that* strong. To acquire it you can either buy ketamine for huge sums of cash via a covert network of third-world laboratories run by organized crime syndicates in Mexico and Indonesia, or you can just give Raphael, our gardener in Montecito, a hand job.

Ketamine comes as a clear liquid, but you can spread it on a cookie sheet and bake it to a grainy powder. Ah, the memories . . . how often did I walk into the kitchen of our house in Amsterdam, in Athens, in Antwerp, to find my mom wearing pearls and a flowered apron, sliding an aromatic tray of fresh-baked Special K out of the oven? To me the meth-lab reek of cat urine and battery acid evoke the same flood of comforting associations that my peers might find in warm Tollhouse cookies.

Once you've chopped the grains to a fine white powder, simply sniff it as you would cocaine for a euphoric buzz that lasts roughly an hour. *Bon appétit*. Not that I ever did. Again—our poor dog, Dorothy Barker, never knew a full week of sobriety.

In room 6314, as if to demonstrate all of the preceding, Mr. Crescent City leans over his cache of powdered K. One of his hands holds his braided pigtail to the side of his head lest it flop. His other hand squishes one nostril shut while the other nostril tracks the dusty trail. Like an upstate farmer plowing a dirt field, he completes one line and begins the next. When his nose has left the glass table clean, still bent double at the waist, Mr. Crescent City freezes for a moment. Not looking up, not standing upright, he says, "Don't be scared, little dead girl. . . ." His voice muffled near the tabletop, he says, "I'm a *professional*.

This is what I do for a living. . . ." His arms go limp. His braid flops loose.

"It's ironical," he says, "but I've got to die to make a living." At that Mr. Psychic Bounty Hunter pitches forward, crashing face-first through the glass.

entle Tweeter,

In room 6314 a dead scarecrow lies splayed in an explosion of broken coffee table. Strange as this admission may seem, this is not the first time I've stood alone in a room with a dead man on the floor at my feet, surrounded by shattered glass. Be patient, and a pattern will soon emerge.

How to describe what happens next? To date, I've suffered as an inmate of Hell. I've done battle with demons and tyrants and stood atop lofty cliffs overlooking majestic oceans of bodily fluids. Alive, I've been born aloft from Brisbane to Berlin to Boston in a Gulfstream as groveling minions plied my greedy mouth with peeled grapes. I've watched, albeit unimpressed, as my mother rode the back of a computer-generated dragon to a castle built of simulated rubies while drinking a Diet Coke in dramatic slow motion. Still, none of that has prepared me for the following. I step around the fallen Mr. Crescent City and crouch for a closer look. The floor is graveled in crystals of shattered safety glass. The rolled paper, the cover from *Parade* magazine, has slipped from his nose and slowly opens, blossoming against the sparkling nuggets. My mom, the perfect version of hair and teeth and human potential for everyone in the whole world. Me, the bane of her existence.

The naturalist in me—the *supernaturalist;* call me the

Charles Darwin of the afterlife—I take careful regard of what occurs. The heap of junkie-filled laundry begins to shine. Something as faint as a memory shimmers on the surface of the body. A glow as insubstantial as a thought begins to rise from the fallen figure. Please note, Gentle Tweeter, that memories and thoughts are the stuff of ghosts. For souls are nothing if not pure consciousness. This spirals up to shape the translucent form I first saw in the foyer of the Rhinelander penthouse. The wasted, wrinkled body remains on the floor, but above it stands a shimmering double. It looks at me and smiles, rapt. "Little dead girl."

Sitting on the bed, I say, "My name is Madison Spencer." I nod toward the photo of me and my mother unfurled on the floor.

The figure, I'll venture, is Mr. Crescent City's spirit. Anecdotal evidence suggests that ketamine users can depart their physical selves. The consciousness of the intoxicated person detaches. The soul leaves the sedated body and is free to travel, according to the not-exact testimony of numerous drugged-out Special K abusers.

The spirit glances from me to the photo and back to me. He drops to his ghost knees and touches his forehead to the carpet at my feet, his hairy braid flopping against my Bass Weejuns. His voice muffled by the carpet, he says, "Little dead girl . . . it's *you*!"

Out of pure meanness I put a ghost foot forward and step on his vile pigtail.

A foul sputtering noise rends the air.

A second trumpeting blast follows.

The prostrate underling, he's breaking wind. "Oh, great

Madison Spencer," he whispers. "Hear my prayer." He lets loose a fresh—fresh?—round of flatulence. "Hurry and accept my tribute and praise, okay? I need to make this quick, because I only have a couple minutes before I go back in my body, but I need to tell you about my holy mission. . . ."

And the vile monster, he lets another rip.

Boorism: The New World Disorder
Posted by Madisonspencer@aftrlife.hell

entle Tweeter,

The pigtailed phantom of Mr. Crescent City kowtows on the floor at my feet, clearly demented. His face pressed to the carpet, the ghost softly mutters the words, "Piss. Shit. Shit. Fuck. Pussy. Tits. Fucker . . ." A mantra of expletives. He's whispering, "Motherfucker. Butthole. Crap. Crap. Crap . . ." It's Tourette's syndrome suffered in an attitude of prayer. In time with his obscene utterances he lifts his open hands, stretching his fingers toward me, beseeching. Nearby lies the inert heap of his earthly body, starfished flat atop a sparkling sea of shattered glass.

From my position, sitting on the bed, I extend one chubby ghost leg and push the toe of a Bass Weejun against his supplicating head. Not kicking him in the skull, not exactly, I just push. I ask, "What's your problem?"

In response, Mr. Crescent City, his rude ghost, passes gas. A real honker, a real Canadian goose call. Tranced out, he's muttering, "Please accept the reverent song of my stale bunghole, dear Madison. Accept the humble praise of my 'Hail, Maddy. . . .' "

Hail, Maddy? Gentle Tweeter, these words form an instant blockage within my brain. Somehow, my name has come to be synonymous with making a stinky?

I say, "Let me confirm something: You're saying my mom hired you?"

"Accept my butt prayer," he says, "Sacred angel Millicent Spencer, I petition for your divine guidance."

I say, "You are disgusting." I say, "And for your information my name is 'Madison,' you pestilent worm."

"Forgive me, little pissed-off angel girl."

Me, an angel. As if. I ask, "How much is my mom paying you?" I stand and step closer, asking, "What did my parents tell you?" After all the Gaia agitprop my parents have spouted in *Vanity Fair*, my former-pagan, former-Buddhist, former-atheist mom and dad, I can't imagine what faith they espouse now. I snap my fingers to get his attention.

"Camille, great Camille," the kowtowing ghost says, "mother of the little messiah who will guide all mankind to paradise . . ." He belches. "Hear my prayers."

I lift one ghost foot and plant it on the back of his glowing phantom neck. "Let me get this straight. So you toot a fat rail of K and drop into a K-hole. Your soul leaves your body for, let me guess, an hour?" Through my clenched teeth, I warn, "If you break wind again, I'll rip that mangy pigtail right off your scalp."

"Thirty, maybe forty minutes," he says, still facedown. One of his outstretched hands tilts side to side, a gesture of hedging. "I found Marilyn Monroe this way. I found Elvis," says the spirit, tapping his breastbone, a note of pride in his voice. "I'm the best."

I say, "That's a lot of ketamine."

"Fuck. Fuck. Fuck," he says.

"Stop that!" I say.

"But it's how I pay tribute," he whines.

"To me?"

"We don't have much time," he says. "I pilgrimaged here on behalf of your old lady. My sacred duty is, I'm supposed to deliver you safely to the Pantages."

A theater?

"It's a big ship."

"Do you mean the *Pangaea Crusader*?" I ask.

He says, "What did I say? Whatever it is, you're supposed to follow me back there." The translucent figure pinned under my foot begins to fade.

"After your spirit goes back into your disgusting . . ." I gesture toward the pile of flesh and rags. "So I'm supposed to follow you?"

"Yeah," he says. "I guess." His brain-damaged attention is wandering. Already, his phantom self is vanishing the way it did in the penthouse. His soul is returning to his drug-ravaged body.

To hold him another minute I'm practically standing on his ghost neck. I'm shouting, "Tell me! I command you, you filthy cockroach!" That's me. That's just how I am: imperious. I demand, "What is my devious mother up to?"

Cutting cheese. The belching. *The path to redemption is swearing.*

I have a terrible premonition.

"You, glorious Angel Madison, you died and your flesh was buried, yet you spoke to your mother from beyond the grave. . . ." He's fading, Mr. Crescent City, seeping back to life. "You dictated the path for righteous followers to attain paradise. By farting in crowded elevators . . . by pissing in swimming pools . . . by going 'fuck' . . ."

Gentle Tweeter, my ghost self goes cold with dread.

"Since they were visited by your holy spirit," he says, "your parents have preached your teachings to millions all over the world. To follow in your steps zillions of your disciples are praying 'Hail, Maddys' as I do. . . ." He adds, muttering, "Fuck. Crap. Asshole . . ." He says, "The Supreme Mother Camille is our fervent harlot. . . ."

"Zealot," I correct him.

But it's too late. Mr. Crescent City is no longer under my shoe. Across the hotel room his scarecrow's body begins to stir.

A Rude Redemption

Posted by Madisonspencer@aftrlife.hell

entle Tweeter,

Passing gas. Belching. Picking your nose and flicking the boogers. Leaving your used chewing gum on park benches. These are the prayers of a new major world religion, and it's all my fault. My goal was just to reunite my little family, albeit in Hell. I told my parents to double-park and say the F-bomb and discard cigarette butts on the ground because I knew those acts would surely send them to Hell. And because they couldn't keep their mouths shut, now they've doomed a thousand million souls to eternal misery.

Gentle Tweeter, what I told my folks, *I was only kidding.* All I wanted to do was cheer them up.

Why do the impulsive notions of a would-be do-gooder always translate into the ideals of the next civilization? It's possible that Jesus and Buddha and Mohammed were just ordinary dead guys who simply wanted to say "howdy" and offer some comfort to their living-alive friends. This, this is why the dead don't talk to the future dead. Predead folks always misconstrue every message. Here I was only fooling around, and my mom's founded an entire theology on my practical joke.

Ye gods. Now we have "Boorism," an entire international religious movement founded on potty humor and rude behavior.

What can I do? I can try to set my parents straight. That, that's what I've got to do. As Mr. Crescent City drags himself to his feet, I resolve to follow him back to my deranged mother and set straight the flatulent, earthly world.

A World of Boors

Posted by Madisonspencer@aftrlife.hell

entle Tweeter,

Imagine a world where everyone goes about their daily lives with the absolute certainty that he or she is going to Heaven. Everyone has guaranteed salvation. This is the Earth to which I have returned. From room 6314 of the Rhinelander, I follow my derelict guide. Mr. Crescent City, he carries no luggage. With his every shambling footfall crumbs of shattered glass drop from his clothes, but he doesn't appear to have a cut or scratch after crushing the coffee table. As the elevator arrives at the lobby and the doors slide open, a waiting guest stands aside for us to exit. Nodding politely, this stranger says, "Eat shit, asswipe."

In response Crescent makes a little bow and says, "A merry faggot, cunt, nigger to you, too." And he spits a great wad of saliva on the stranger's shoes.

This is all my parents' doing! I should've known they couldn't keep their big traps shut. I'm willing to bet that the moment my mom was off the long-distance call with me she was telling her publicist to announce a press conference. No doubt she and my dad have been tirelessly disseminating the advice I gave them for getting to "Heaven." The Rhinelander lobby, once a sanctuary of reserved conduct and politely hushed discourse, has become a reeking locker room of stale vapors and toilet talk.

In jarring contrast, everyone's beaming. You've never seen so many people so happy. The guests, the concierges, the doormen, they wear the faces of joyous potty-mouthed children. As they glance at one another, theirs are the guileless, loving eyes of Renaissance cherubs gazing in adoration upon the Christ child. The desk clerk greets us with a smile so broad it suggests she's paid by the tooth. Her eyes shine with genuine rapture as she says, "How was your butt-fucking, dick-sucking stay, Mr. City?"

Crescent returns the rapturous smile, saying, "Fucking great, fuck you, you cunt lapper."

The clerk confirms that his room is being billed to Camille and Antonio Spencer. She accepts his room key and pleasantly asks, "It looks like your shit-eating car and jungle-bunny driver are waiting. Can I help you with any bullshit fucking, queer-bait thing else?"

"No, thank you," says Crescent. He shoves a hand into the front pocket of his tattered jeans and drags out some paper money. Between his drug-trembling fingers is a hundred-dollar bill. He folds this under his nose and blows it full of snot as if it were a tissue. Crescent hands this revolting cash across the desk to the clerk, telling her, "Why don't you finger this up your backside?"

Her smile couldn't be brighter as the clerk accepts the money and says, "I'll see you in Heaven, shit-for-brains."

"Kike," Crescent says gaily as he turns to leave.

Her voice trilling like a bird, the clerk calls after him, "Have a nice day, you butt-sucking turd."

A smiling bellman holds open the street door, tipping his cap smartly and bidding us, "Suck it, you stinking crap sandwich."

Crescent City palms the kid another snot-smeared C-note.

At the curb, a uniformed chauffeur holds open the door of a gleaming Town Car and asks, "To the airport, Mr. Jizz Guzzler?" The chauffeur is, as the desk clerk mentioned, of African descent. They shake hands amiably.

Settling himself in the backseat, Crescent says, "Yes, the domestic terminal, please, my porch-monkey friend."

Their bubbly, laughing conversation continues in this wretched vein all the way to the curb at the airport. No one takes offense. No slur seems to be off-limits. Even the people we drive past, walking on the sidewalks, seated in other cars, they all smile blissfully, as if immune to insults. If they catch Crescent's eye they smile and flip him a middle finger. The honking horns are deafening. The toothy smiles are blinding. Everyone is gloriously Heaven-bound, but only if they swear sufficiently.

Behind the wheel, the driver sneaks out a cloud of intestinal foulness, instantly filling the car with the fetid reek of his stagnant entrails.

"Good one!" Crescent City says, inhaling deeply. "The angel Madison must really love you."

"It's the smell of salvation, brother," replies the driver. "Breathe it up!"

In the airport terminal we pass a newsstand. The headline on the cover of *Newsweek* says, "A Rude Religious Revolution: The Boorists Have Arrived!" *Time* magazine announces: "The %&!?//$ Road to Redemption." On a television monitor mounted near the ceiling of the concourse a CNN news presenter says, "Boorists now claim their messiah has been resurrected. . . ."

As we walk toward our gate of departure, my chubby ham-hock legs hurry to keep pace with his long, zombie stride. Loping along, of course he can't hear me, not while he's sober, but he maintains a steady patter. To everyone in the airport he must look like an untreated schizophrenic, his not-clean shirt flapping open and untucked. Not that anyone seems upset by the sight of a lunatic dressed in rags yammering to himself. No, now that humanity is assured a permanent seat at the right hand of God, they're grinning with glee. Their eyes are misted with righteousness.

"Your timing, little dead girl, could not have been better," says Crescent. "We have bullshit laws about driving sober and laws about always wearing shoes and not owning giant boa constrictors, only we didn't have laws about the most important stuff: getting saved." He says, "People were starving to know those rules."

This new religion, Boorism, makes death look like an all-expenses-paid luxury vacation that lasts until the end of time.

"You created world peace! Nobody's a gay anymore, or a Jew or a person from Africa," he rants, forging ahead. "Look at us! We're all 'Boors'!"

It's simple, explains Crescent City. My parents staged a massive publicity campaign to announce that their dead daughter had contacted them from beyond the grave. They told the world that I was now an angel in Heaven, rubbing elbows with the Kennedy brothers and Amy Winehouse, and I had bestowed upon them a fail-safe, surefire blueprint for attaining salvation. They issued a blitz of press releases to blab that I was within the pearly gates, riding a cloud and strumming a harp. Ridiculous as this sounds, this is the milieu of Camille and Antonio.

"Boorism isn't the real name for our faith," Crescent says. "That's just a phony label the media vultures invented to pigeonhole us. Officially we refer to ourselves as apostles of Madlantis."

Realistically I can't slight my folks for getting so excited. Their previous theology of "Reduce, Reuse, Recycle" must've offered scant emotional comfort in the face of their only child being killed on her birthday. Yes, I expired on my birthday in an erotic-asphyxiation scenario that shames me to revisit here.

This is the death of angst. Forget Nietzsche. Forget Sartre. Existentialism is dead. God has been resurrected, and people have a road map for attaining glorious immortality. In Boorism, everyone who'd abandoned religion now has a path by which to return to God, and that feels . . . great. Just look at their strolling, patient gaits. In light of this new salvation, mortal life feels like the final day of school.

It's not the threat of Hell or jail or societal shunning that's brought this bliss. It's the complete assurance of paradise. It makes the inevitability of death shine like a final cosmic Friday preceding an infinite party weekend in Mazatlán.

As we wait in the jetway, Crescent says, "In Heaven the first thing I'm getting myself is a new liver. And a new body, and hair like I used to have." Clutching his boarding pass, he says, "I swear, once I'm in Heaven I'm never touching drugs. Never again."

"Amen," a voice says. It's a woman standing behind us in

line. She's shouldering a tote bag and thumbing the buttons of a PDA as she says, "In Heaven I'm eating steak and fries for every meal, and I'm still never weighing more than one hundred fifteen, maximum."

"Amen," says another voice waiting in line.

"In Heaven," says another voice, farther back in the jetway, "I'm going to reestablish contact with my kids and give them the kind of father those good kids deserve."

"Hallelujah!" someone shouts. Several "Praise bes" echo in the narrow jetway space. With that, everyone in line volunteers his or her aspirations for eternity.

"After I go to be with God, I'm going to finish high school."

"My car in Heaven is going to be bigger than anything you've ever seen."

"When I die, I'm asking for a dick bigger than your car!" someone spits.

Aboard the plane, in the first-class section, Crescent City finds our seats. He says, "You want the window or the aisle? I bought two tickets." He waits as if for me to choose. "I'll be right back," he says, and goes up to the toilet.

I take the window. The flight attendant makes an announcement. "As we prepare for takeoff, please fasten your fucking seat belts and make sure your cocksucking seat backs are in the full upright and locked position. . . ." The passengers laugh and applaud. Before the flight crew has finished its safety announcement, the familiar translucent form of Crescent City's spirit comes walking back down the airplane aisle and takes the aisle seat next to mine. His body must be near overdosed on ketamine, still occupying the locked toilet cubicle.

Watery, clear like a prism, but suggesting every color in the spectrum, the ghost smiles at me and says, "I can't wait to be an angel like you." At the front of the cabin, the flight crew is knocking, soon pounding at the locked bathroom door. Oblivious, Crescent's ghost asks me, "So, what was Heaven really like?"

An Abomination Is Born

Posted by Hadesbrainiacleonard@aftrlife.hell

nd what became of the latex thing-baby abandoned in the storm? In the account given by Solon, the Egyptian priests sang that the miniature idol will gradually come to be alive. Smeared with lipstick and chocolate, its body will circulate with the cooled seed expressed by a stranger.

And not for long does our soiled harbinger baby linger on the pink star beside Hollywood Boulevard, for the wind catches it and bears it a distance. The Greek statesman writes that the foul waters in the gutter collect and carry the babe. The tiny graven image, bloated with breath, faceless, it's borne along in the company of drowned rats and bloated strays. These the gutters of Hollywood channel underground. And the subterranean sewers of Los Angeles guide the little idol and introduce it to wayward bleach bottles and spent ketchup bottles. The storm-water tunnels and the weirs manage this flood of plastic discards, this downward migration of polystyrene. And the thing-baby ventures forth on the flood, not in a basket woven of rushes, but attended to by legions of used syringes. And swaddled in dry-cleaning bags it journeys among this flotsam of toothless combs and escaped tennis balls. They all flock together, routed through buried pipes and sunless catch basins. Swimming here are the mysterious ghost shapes of blister-packaged objects, those plastic cauls of products long ago given birth by consumers. And thus becomes the fate of all worldly treasures. And in due time the little thing-baby and all these earthly rewards, the immortal leavings of mortal humans, these are poured into the ditch of the Los Angeles River.

The way turtle hatchlings are baited by the moon's light, and each generation of salmon is compelled to find their destiny . . . so, too, will our thing-baby and its soiled host of man-made fragments be lured. A receding tide compels this entire generation of shapeless, useless castoffs to venture forth into the Pacific Ocean.

A Sexual Predator in the Animal Kingdom

Posted by Madisonspencer@aftrlife.hell

entle Tweeter,

Not to boast, but no adult mind could ever be as depraved, as perverted as that of an innocent eleven-year-old virgin. Before one absorbs the boring facts about reproductive anatomy, while still free of tact and mechanical knowledge, children can envision sexual goings-on with sea urchins . . . zebras . . . flamingos.

As a predead girl I dreamed of giving birth to babies with wings. I would seduce a porpoise and our offspring would swim across oceans. Puberty enticed me with the possibility that my own children could roar with the huge heads of lions or run on hoofed feet. Why no one had done this before, who knew? I couldn't wait.

Inspired by my stuffed menagerie, my diary grew fat with such carnal hijinks. Needless to say these adventures, they were all fictional. I'd only invented them and carefully put pen to paper in meticulous handwriting for my mother's inevitable consumption. "Dear Diary," I'd write, "today I daubed hallucinogenic jellyfish toxin on my exposed woo-woo. . . ."

In response to CanuckAIDSemily, yes, I could've started a blog, but my plan would be effective only if my parents believed I was hiding the details of my sordid vices. "Dear Diary," I'd write, "Mother must never know, but today I sipped the *most divine* absinthe using a dried monkey din-gus as a drinking straw. . . ." I'd shelved the imaginative diary among the Regency potboilers on my crammed bookshelves, and not a week after my initial entry my parents began their hostile spying.

Not that they announced their campaign. I merely guessed as much because, apropos of nothing, during breakfast conversation my mother mentioned that sucking on monkey ding-dings was an excellent high-risk practice for contracting HIV.

"Really?" I asked, nibbling my toast, secretly thrilled to know she'd taken my bait. "Does that go for all monkey ding-dings?" I licked the butter from my stubby fingertips, asking, "Does that include the *Saimiri sciureus*?"

My father sputtered his coffee. "The *what*?"

"The adorable squirrel monkey," I said. My eyelashes fluttered. A coquettish blush suffused my cheeks.

My father said, "Why do you ask?"

And in response I shrugged. "No reason." At that age I was so obsessed with monkeys that I wanted to marry one. College would come first, of course, but after I graduated with my degree in comparative postmodern marginalized gender studies I wanted to become mommy to a cuddly monkey baby.

My parents exchanged pained looks.

"What about the enticingly thick ding-ding of the *Calli-thrix pygmaea*?" I asked. I spread the buttered fingers of one hand and counted them off as if remembering past trysts. "The pygmy marmoset?"

My mother gave a long sigh and asked my father, "Antonio?" one eyebrow arched as if to demand, *What went on at the Tiergarten, mister?* They were both loath to impose restrictions on my behavior, but clearly some acts needed to be declared off-limits. Nevertheless, after all the free-love ideology they'd thrown at me, the most they could counsel was that I engage only in safer-sex practices, no matter what the species. Smiling wanly, my mom asked, "Would you like a Xanax, sweetheart?"

"What about . . . ," I asked, pretending anxiety, *"Chloropithecus aethiops?"* Indeed, my father had taken me to the Berlin Zoo the previous month, and the outing had made for an excellent research opportunity.

The curdled expression semidistorting my mom's Botox-saturated features was the exact one she made at the Oscars when Tom Cruise was given a Lifetime Achievement Award, just moments before she leaned over and upchucked into Goldie Hawn's A-list swag bag, ruining a small fortune in pricey chocolates and Gucci sunglasses.

At best they could gift me with a multispecies set of variously sized disposable condoms and deliver a lecture about demanding respect from my simian sex partners.

From that point I knew they would never fess up to reading my diary. However, now that I was exposed as an eleven-year-old sexual sociopath they would always be *forced* to read it. They couldn't risk *not* reading my diary, and through my calculated faux-confessions I could manipulate them. They were my slaves.

"Dear Diary," I'd write, "today I sucked mind-altering lungfuls of Maui Wowie through a bong filled with bubbling, lukewarm elephant semen. . . ." It saddens me, in retrospect, how easily my parents accepted the reality of my wanton bestiality. "Dear Diary," I'd write, "today I ingested LSD and gave loving hand jobs to a herd of wildebeests. . . ."

Yes, on paper I was a libertine. However, secret repressed snob that I truly was, while my mom and dad imagined me in sticky twosomes and threesomes with donkeys and capuchin monkeys, I was in fact nestled in some dirty laundry hamper, reading historical romances by Clare Darcy. Most of my childhood consisted of this sort of double-entry behavioral accounting.

"Dear Diary, what a hangover!" I wrote. "Please remind me to never mainline stale hyena urine with a dirty needle ever again! I was awake all night, standing over my sleeping parents with a Wusthof butcher knife in one hand. Had either of them stirred I'm certain I would've hacked them both to bloody ribbons. . . ."

Me? In hindsight I'd made the same strategic mistake Charles Manson made. I should've quit while I was just a garden-variety animal-sex-and-drug addict, but, no, I had to escalate my status to potential knife-wielding psycho. . . . Small wonder that it was shortly after that particular diary entry that my folks sent my eleven-year-old sexually incorrigible self packing to tedious upstate.

A Prelude to My Exile

Posted by Madisonspencer@aftrlife.hell

entle Tweeter,

I wasn't always a great, fat pudding of a child. As an eleven-year-old I was rail thin. A mere sylph of a girl, with a body-mass index that hovered just above all my major organs failing. Yes, I'd once been a willowy pint-size ballerina with the metabolism of a hummingbird, and as such I gave good value. My job was to serve as the child equivalent of arm candy, proof of my mother's fertility and my father's glorious genetic legacy, smiling beside my parents in paparazzi photographs.

And then they sent me to live upstate. The distant memory curdles in my brain.

Upstate. Tedious upstate. It's one of the few places my parents don't own a home. Picture a million-billion wounded trees weeping drops of maple syrup into the snow, and—voilà—you have upstate. Envision a billion-billion ticks infected with Lyme disease and waiting to bite you.

And not to speak in unkind generalities, but using my mom's laptop, the eleven-year-old me found a satellite photo of the location. Seen in its entirety, upstate is exactly the same mottled green-on-green as army surplus camouflage. From outer space I could trace the line of State Route Whatever forging a vital transportation link between nowhere and nowhere. I read the names of towns, looking for anyplace famous, and the truth hit me. . . . There on the map was Woodstock.

Woodstock, NY. Vile Woodstock. Forgive me for what I'm about to admit. For my part I shudder to broach the topic, but my parents first met at Woodstock '99, where everyone rioted over the price of pizza and bottled water in the center of those thousand noxious acres of overpopulated mud. My mom was just a naked farm girl encased in sweat and patchouli. My dad was a pale, naked dropout from MIT with long greasy dreadlocks, who'd shaved off his pubic hair to look more like the Buddha. Neither of them owned a single pair of shoes.

They fell into a puddle and did the Hot Nasty. His wiener got mud in her woo-woo and she got a UTI, and they got married.

Who says magic doesn't happen?

Nowadays they tell the story, switching off in tag-team fashion, making strangers laugh at wrap parties and in television green rooms. They stress the mud detail because it gives a self-effacing verisimilitude to the sordid episode.

And, yes, I know the meaning of *verisimilitude*—I can even pronounce it.

As a Somali maid had packed my suitcases, my mother checked each article of clothing for any dry-clean-only labels. Apparently people upstate did laundry by beating their dirty Vivienne Westwood basques between flat rocks on riverbanks. They didn't have sashimi, either. Nor did they have Internet access, my mother explained. At least, my grandparents did not. Nor did they own a television. Instead, they harbored livestock. Not animals in some distant, abstract sense, like the downward-spiraling number of polar bears or the baby harp seals that lolled on some arctic ice floe, ripe for the Eskimo clubbing; no, these would be nanny goats and chick-chicks and moo-cows that I would tend as part of a daily chore regimen.

Ye gods.

No amount of pleading could stay my banishment, and I was summarily placed in the back of a Lincoln Town Car and whisked off, the whole of one smallish suitcase dedicated just to carrying my ample provisions of Xanax. That summer, at the tender age of eleven, I would learn to swallow my fear. To choke down my pride and my anger. And that would be the last time my mother could boast a skinny daughter.

entle Tweeter,

Early on, my papadaddy conscripted me in his ongoing campaign against biodiversity. His strategy was that we two crouch in the harsh upstate sunshine and excise every trespassing native plant from a portion of my nana's vegetable garden, leaving only the nonnative green beans. While we labored shoulder to shoulder, plucking, uprooting, endeavoring to create a questionable monoculture of legumes, he asked me, "Maddy? Dumpling? Do you believe in fate?"

I made no reply.

Still he pressed his topic. "What would you say if every iota of your life was predestined before you was even born?"

I continued to not engage. Clearly he was trying to enroll me in some demented existentialist worldview.

He paused in his weed pulling and turned his wrinkled face to regard me. "What do you know about God and Satan?" An upstate breeze ruffled the strands of his gray hair.

Without meeting his gaze, I killed a weed. I spared a bean plant. I felt like God.

"You know, don't you, that God and Satan got themselves a feud going?" He glanced around as if to confirm we were alone. No one would overhear. "If I told you a secret, do you promise not to tell your nana?"

I yanked another weed. I promised nothing. Instead, I girded my girlish loins for some hideous revelation.

"What if I told you," he continued, unbidden, "that you was born the greatest human being who'll ever live?" He asked, "What if your destiny was to patch things up between God and Satan?"

A Politically Incorrect Feast
Posted by Madisonspencer@aftrlife.hell

entle Tweeter,

If you must know, my papadaddy and nana's isolated upstate farmhouse consisted of a book-lined parlor ... two cramped bedrooms ... a primitive kitchen ... none but a single bathroom. Of the two bedrooms one had been my mother's, and now it would serve as mine. As I'd been warned, they did not own a television nor any sort of a computer. They did own a telephone, but only of the most rudimentary rotary-dial sort.

A typical luncheon would find me seated at the kitchen table, confronted by a plate filled with my worst eleven-year-old's nightmare. Veal, for example. Or cheese sourced from nonunion, slave-labor Central Americans. Factory-farmed pork. Gluten. I could taste the spores of Creutzfeldt-Jakob disease. I could smell the aspartame tested on lab monkeys. When I ventured to ask whether the beef had come from cattle raised on slash-and-burn-decimated Amazon rain forest, my nana merely looked back at me. She lit another cigarette and shrugged. To buy some time I dropped my fork to my plate and launched into a droll recounting of what had happened to me the previous month at Barbra Streisand's house party, really the most madcap mishap at Babs Streisand's lavish beachfront villa on Martha's Vineyard—

The telephone rang in the parlor, and Nana rushed to answer it. Her voice as thin as an odor, from the next room she said, "Huh-lo?" The springs of the sofa squeaked as she took a seat. She said, "Well, I don't ever buy the cotton balls. I'm more likely to buy the cotton *swabs*." She fell silent, then said only, "Blue." After a beat of quiet listening she said, "Mint." She said, "Married, for some forty-four years, now." She said, "One child, our girl, Camille." She coughed the words, "I was sixty-eight June last." Adding, "Assembly of Brethren in Christ."

Alone in the kitchen with my truncated Streisand anecdote, I didn't eat a bite. I flung my tortured cutlet through the open window above the sink.

Likewise, dinner revealed a plateful of dolphin-unsafe tuna casserole. The piquant flavor of Japanese drift nets was unmistakable. Not ten words into my droll yarn about Toni Morrison, the telephone rang yet again.

My nana went to answer it, and from the parlor I heard her say, "Babette, ain't it? Yeah, I'd be happy to answer a few questions. . . ."

As before, I tossed the offensive meal out the kitchen window, making it a present to some less scrupulous rural mammal. The world was crowded with attractively starving children my parents could adopt, and I was not going to twiddle my thumbs upstate, guzzling gravy and getting too fat to be anything but a handicap to my mother's public image.

That became the pattern of our meals. My Nana Minnie would serve me some creamed corn of politically dubious origin—obviously loaded with butter containing conjugated linoleic acid—and I'd tell a shaggy-dog story about

85

Tina Brown until the phone rang with some telemarketer or survey taker. Dinnertime meant my nana sitting on the parlor sofa saying the word "radiation," saying "chemotherapy" and "stage four" and "Leonard" into the telephone receiver. Where she couldn't see, in the kitchen, I'd be sailing my fattening meal, meatball by meatball, mushroom by mushroom, out the open window. Thinking: *Leonard?*

Papadaddy Ben was seldom home, always running some errand that took longer than you'd expect. At times I thought my nana raced to the phone because she hoped he would call. Or that my mother would. But the caller was never anybody; it was merely some market research slave named Leonard or Patterson or Liberace phoning from God knew where.

Just once I beat Nana Minnie to the ringing phone. She was washing dishes, both hands plunged into sudsy sink water up to her elbows, and she asked me to pick it up. Giving a labored sigh, I left my plate of not-fair-trade, nonsustainable pecan pie and went to the parlor. I put the telephone receiver to my ear, and it smelled like cigarette smoke, like my nana's coughing, and I said, *"Ciao!"* A silence followed. For an instant I thought it might be my mother calling to check up on me, but a voice asked, "Madison?"

It was a male voice. A young man, possibly a teenager. Definitely not Papadaddy Ben. Half laughing, he said, "Maddy? It's me, Archer!"

He was nobody I knew, and I froze him out. As my nana followed me into the parlor, drying her hands on a threadbare towel and slinging it over her shoulder, I asked the phone, "Have we been introduced?"

"Give it a couple years, killer," the boy said, adding, in the deeper tone of a conspirator, "Did you tear off anybody's dick today?" And then he laughed outright. He laughed and laughed and laughed.

And as slow as tai chi, I handed the smoke-smelling receiver to my nana.

entle Tweeter,

On another occasion my papadaddy enlisted me as his accomplice as he plundered the not-hatched offspring from beneath the feathery bottoms of domestic poultry. We made the rounds of a ramshackle hut where the chickens were quartered, and ruthlessly stole their future generations. All the while he grilled me: "You ever stop and consider how your ma and pa got themselves so rich so fast?"

My hands burdened with the basket of looted eggs, I merely shrugged.

He pressed his point. "How come every investment they make pays off?" Without waiting for a response, he explained, "Well, Sunshine, when your ma was your age she got herself a guardian angel named Leonard. Regular as clockwork he called her on the telephone." Talking, he continued to loot nests. "She come to me and said as much. She was just a teenager when she told me her angel gave her the lucky number for a lottery ticket. She asked for me to buy it. Some stranger calling from gosh knows where . . . what was I to believe? Her ma believed her."

Unthwarted by my failure to engage, he continued. "Her guardian angel, Leonard, even today he still calls her up. Angels can do that. It don't matter where in the world she's at; he finds her. Calls her direct. Calls your pa, too."

I busied myself by inspecting a particularly speckled egg-shell.

"It's that Leonard," my Papadaddy Ben insisted. "He's the one who demanded they send you to us for the summer."

That detail, Gentle Tweeter, arrested my eleven-year-old attention. I returned his rheumy gaze.

"You're not supposed to know," he said. His voice dropped to a whisper. "But you got a big showdown this summer with the forces of evil."

My eyes must've betrayed my confusion.

"You didn't know, did you, Honey Bun?" His complexion testified to a lifetime of neglected skin care.

No, I did not. A showdown? With evil?

"Well," he stammered, "now you know." His gnarled hands foraged in the straw of a nest and brought forth another egg. This new plunder he set in my basket, saying, "It's best not to worry your little head about it too much."

Embarking on a Bon Voyage
Posted by Madisonspencer@aftrlife.hell

entle Tweeter,
   The summer I spent on my nana's
farm upstate offered no end of diversions.
Amusement could be found in, for example,
shelling peas or shucking corn. A scintillating plethora of
cherries offered themselves for the ready pitting. I breathlessly complained that I simply did not know where to begin.

A lurching husk of weathered human skin, her jawline
and upper arms replete with flapping wattles, my Nana
Minnie stood over her electric stove. She fiddled with the
appliance's complicated heat controls while the lid of a pot
vented so much steam that the kitchen air shimmered, as
sweltering hot as that of any Turkish hamam. Scads of local
fruits had been slaughtered and arrayed about the counter-
tops in differing stages of being skinned and dressed, and
every work surface felt sticky with the dried blood of their
flesh. Peaches, disemboweled of their stones, filled a large
crockery bowl. Other fruits, apples, had been dismembered
and embalmed in glass jars for their root-cellar interment.
The aforementioned steam condensed on the walls, collecting into rivulets. It dripped from the ceiling. Busy amid all
this butchery, my nana squinted at her grim labors, and,
talking around the cigarette clamped between her pale lips,
she told me: "Sweet Pea, darling, you're underfoot. Go and
entertain yourself."

Entertain myself? My nana must've been insane. As nicely as possible, grasping her not-clean apron strings and giving them a tug with my own smooth child's hand, I said, "Nana, my darling, you might want to get screened for age-related dementia. . . ."

Entertain myself! As if I could possibly use the sticks and dirtied rocks readily available to assemble a television receiver, then construct a distribution network and a local broadcast affiliate, then launch the production companies and stock the pipeline with a season of programming content. Such a venture, I told my nana, undertaken by a pre-adolescent girl over the course of a single summer, seemed highly not-likely to succeed.

"No," my Nana Minnie said, tugging her apron free of my stubborn hold. "I mean you ought to read a book." At this she abandoned her boiling fruity corpses. Nana turned to face me, grasping my shoulders, and ushered me from the kitchen, down a short hallway to the parlor, where bookshelves ranged from floor to ceiling, filling an entire wall. There she bade me choose from among the aged leather-bound tomes.

It must be noted here that I was not yet as passionate a reader as I would soon become. My Swiss school, although appallingly expensive, was largely weighted toward awareness of flashpoint environmental issues and the squelched civil rights of oppressed indigenous peoples. On the basis of these ethical priorities I protested that I couldn't consider reading books which had been bound in the dead hides of factory-farmed, no doubt highly stressed cows.

My nana merely shrugged her weary, apron-yoked, farm-wife shoulders in response. Saying, "Suit yourself, little missy," she exited the living room, returning to the dreary pastime of canning tomatoes or pickling field mice. Doing so, she called back to me over one calico shoulder; she warned, "You can read a book or you can beat the rugs. Take your pick."

Such are my morals that I couldn't fathom inflicting any form of violence, even upon an insensate floor covering. Nor did I fancy the other forms of stooped, agrarian fieldwork suggested by my nana: another weed pogrom . . . confiscating more warm ovum from poultry nests . . . Strictly as a political compromise I chose to select a book. My fingers trailed the dead leather of the various spines. *Moby Dick*? No, thank you. For once I was thankful for my mother's famed Greenpeace affiliation. *Little Women*? Ye gods, too monstrously sexist an option! *The Scarlet Letter*? *House of Mirth*? *Leaves of Grass*? My nana's shelves sagged, burdened with obscure, long-forgotten titles. *Tropic of Cancer*? *Naked Lunch*? *Lolita*? Fie. Nothing racy here.

Gentle Tweeters, in response to your charges that I'm too precocious for an eleven-year-old, please accept the fact that people do not change over time. The elderly are, in reality, aged tikes. Conversely, the young are juvenile codgers. Granted, we might develop some skills, achieve some profound insights over a lifetime, but by and large who you are at eighty-five is who you were at five. One is either born intelligent or not. The body ages, grows, passes through near-lunatic phases of reproductive frenzy, but you are born and die essentially the same person.

That . . . that is proof of your deathless soul.

Standing in my nana's parlor, at last I resolved to shut my eyes. Thus blinded I pirouetted a full three rotations and extended an unseeing hand in the general direction of the shelved library. My fingertips brailled their ribbed bindings, the titles embossed there. The cracked grain of the leather felt soft, even crepey, not unlike the skin of my nana's calloused hands. After stroking them all, my touch settled on the one I could sense was my destiny. Here was the book which would deliver me from my immediate impoverished circumstances, my long television-deprived days, my Internet-starved boredom. My blind fingers closed around the book and pulled it from among its brothers. I opened my eyes to this new future.

Printed across the worn cover in gilded type was the author's name: Charles Darwin. Here was a book to shelter me. A story I could hide within for months.

My Nana Minnie's voice, hollering from the recesses of the farmhouse kitchen, called, "Time's up, Pumpkinseed. Them peas ain't going to shell themselves. . . ."

I called back, "But I *found* one!"

"One what?" she called.

Putting a child's happy smile into my voice, I called, "A book, Nana!"

A silent pause elapsed, broken only by the mating cries of icky out-of-doors birds trying to entice one another to engage in avian sexual hijinks. Indoors, the air smelled of cigarette smoke and the steam from my nana's tireless torture cooker.

"What book?" my nana asked warily. "How's it called?"

I turned the book sideways, searching its spine for the title. "It's about a dog," I said. "It's about a cute little dog that travels on a maritime adventure."

In response my nana's voice sounded jolly, her tones

rounded almost to laughter, the voice of a younger woman. In almost a girl's voice she shouted, "Let me guess. It's *The Call of the Wild*!" She shouted, "When I was your age I loved Jack London!"

My hands cracked open the book, and the pages smelled like a room where no one had walked for a long time. This paper room smelled enormous, with varnished wooden floors, and stony fireplaces filled with cold ashes, and dust motes swimming in the sunlight that fell through the room's tall windows. Mine were the first eyes to peer inside this paper castle for generations.

No, the book's title wasn't *The Call of the Wild*, but— Gentle Tweeter—my Nana Minnie was happy. I was excused from shelling peas. That's what mattered most.

The author was not Jack London, but who really cared? If I were to read slowly enough, this book would fill my entire desolate summer holiday. To tedious, odious upstate it would deliver all the joy and excitement of a bygone canine universe. Already, my head was nodding over the open volume, engrossed in the words and perceptions of some long-deceased narrator. I was seeing a vanished past through the alien eyes of that dead man.

Flipping to the title page, I read, printed there: *The Voyage of the Beagle*.

Papadaddy Three
Posted by Madisonspencer@aftrlife.hell

entle Tweeter,

To help alleviate my tedium, Papadaddy Ben suggested we construct a housing unit for the indigenous birdlife. A sort of avian Habitat for Humanity, minus Jimmy Carter and his ilk. Actual architectural planning played a very small part in the project. We sawed boards to fashion rudimentary walls, floor, and roof, cobbling these together with nails. A not-unsatisfying process. Last, we applied a coat of sunny yellow paint.

Brush in hand, my papadaddy asked, "You remember me telling you about Leonard? Your ma's guardian angel."

I feigned deafness and concentrated on my painting technique, avoiding leaving brush marks and drips. I worried about the paint smell, concerned that I might be contributing to the birdhouse equivalent of sick building syndrome.

Oblivious, my papadaddy forged on. "What if I was to tell you the angels call your nana as well?"

I dipped my brush and dabbed yellow around the invitingly round door of the house. I wondered whether the birds who'd set up housekeeping would migrate, as did my parents, between similar dwellings in Nassau and Newport and New Bedford. Likewise, would their migratory patterns be determined by the income tax rates of each location?

Papadaddy took my silence as encouragement. "I don't want to scare you none, but do you remember how I mentioned your big showdown? From what Leonard tells your nana, the forces of good and evil will be testing you."

My Chanel playsuit felt snug in the hips.

"On some island," he added. "Your big test will come on an island."

Despite Ctrl+Alt+Hurtling my nana's cuisine out the kitchen window, I was gaining weight as if by osmosis. Genetics or environment, I worried that my body-fat percentage was nearing double digits.

"According to your nana, somebody's going to die pretty soon." Papadaddy dipped his brush and resumed his work. "Just so you know to be careful, the one who dies might be you."

Charting a Course for Glory
Posted by Madisonspencer@aftrlife.hell

entle Tweeter,

Contrary to its merry title, *The Voyage of the Beagle* is not a picaresque yarn about a small, plucky dog who embarks upon a madcap over-the-waves maritime adventure. If I were compelled to write the CliffsNotes summarizing the book, that distillation would go as follows: *Stupid wild fish . . . dumb wild bird . . . big rock . . . Snake! Snake! Snake! . . . slaughtered animal . . . another rock . . . turtle.* Imagine such a series made long enough to fill almost five hundred pages and you've more or less written the *Beagle* book for yourself. In half a thousand pages hardly a dog is mentioned, and nothing exists in the spotlight for longer than the duration of Mr. Darwin's ten-second attention span. Instead of evolution, Charles Darwin seems to have invented attention deficit disorder, and his focus is constantly distracted by a different fungus . . . a novel, new arthropod . . . a brightly colored pebble. Reading along, one hopes to see a pretty señorita catch the narrator's eye. The reader expects a romance to blossom among the pampas followed by a lover's quarrel and the introduction of a romantic rival, kissing, fistfights, drawn swords—but it's just not that kind of book. No, *The Voyage of the Beagle* seems more akin to watching five years' worth of vacation snaps, shown by an Asperger's sufferer compelled to narrate incessantly.

The title of the tome is a blatant misdirection. The *Beagle* cited is actually the ship upon which Mr. Darwin and Co. are sailing, apparently christened by some long-ago dog fancier. Nonetheless, it's within these brittle old pages that I found my destiny.

It takes but a single remarkable victory to cement the reputation of a budding scribe. For my nana's favorite, Jack London, it required only six months of mucking about in the gold-rush towns of the Klondike. For Mr. Darwin the transformative episode in the Galápagos Islands lasted at most four weeks. Both men had begun their adventure in resignation: London had been unable to secure gainful employment in San Francisco; Darwin had dropped out of college, failing to earn his degree in theology. Both men returned to their ordinary lives while still young, but milked inspiration from their short-lived adventures until they died.

There was no reason why the summer of my eleventh year need be wasted. I had only to find some as-yet-undocumented species of disgusting creature—fly, beetle, spider—and I could write my own ticket back to civilization. Scientific acclaim would be mine. I'd reinvent myself as a world-renowned naturalist who need never kiss and hug her evil, heartless parents ever again.

The morning I'd resolved to begin my fieldwork, I sat at the table in my nana's kitchen. The dawn light shimmered, brown-orange, through the jar of stagnant water and sodden tea bags that she kept on the windowsill above her sink. I feigned spooning some vile porridge to my mouth, tasting nothing except the bovine growth hormone in the milk.

Still, I smiled winningly, my *Beagle* book open beside my breakfast, and asked, "Nana, *dearest*?"

My Nana Minnie turned from her stovetop chore—stirring a wooden spoon in some simmering glop—and considered me coolly. Her eyes narrowed with suspicion, she said, "Yes'm, June Bug?"

Keeping my voice laconic, my tone breezy and nonchalant, I asked whether there were any tropical islands within a walkable distance.

Her stirring hand lifted the spoon from her witch's cauldron and brought it to her crooked mouth, where a darting, furtive tongue tasted the concoction. Smacking her lips with great gusto, my nana said, "Did you say 'islands,' baby girl?"

My mouth fixed in a smile, I nodded my head yes. Islands.

Her requisite cigarette smoldered between the fingers of her free hand. This morning as every morning the sunrise found her gray hair wrapped around curlers and pinned tightly to her pink scalp. Papadaddy Ben remained abed. From the world outside the farmhouse resounded the racket and squawk of fowl announcing their successful ovulations.

My Nana Minnie continued to muse over the bubbling production of her noxious cookery. One could almost discern the click and whir of cogs within her head. The *tick-tock* of gears meshing was nearly audible as she searched her memory for any facts concerning a local island. Giving a short cough, a snort, she said, "No *real* islands," adding, "not unless you count the traffic island out in the middle of the highway."

What she proceeded to describe was a nearby traveler's comfort station which was sandwiched between the numerous traffic-choked southbound lanes of a major highway and the equally congested northbound lanes. I had seen the place: a squat building of concrete blocks cowering in the center of a parched, lemon-yellow lawn spotted with the dried feces of domesticated dogs. I'd glimpsed the place only in passing, from the tinted window of a Town Car en route to my exile on Nana's farm, but the concrete hovel seemed to shimmer with the acrid stink of human waste. A small number of cars and trucks had occupied parking spaces along the edge of the ragged lawn, abandoned by the various persons who rushed to void their bowels and bladders.

This place qualified as an "island" because it was isolated, cut off from the surrounding upstate countryside by the slashing rivers of high-speed vehicles. In lieu of a more conventional island, perhaps this one might serve my purpose.

I lingered over my breakfast. Regarding *The Voyage of the Beagle*, I'd read up to the point where Darwin drinks the bitter urine of a tortoise. Clearly I was not the first reader challenged by the idea of our hero quaffing a frosty mug of turtle pee, for a previous reader had underlined the entire passage in pencil. In the outer margin of the page a different reader had used blue ballpoint pen to write, *Pervert*. Occasionally these comments seemed fortune cookie–cryptic. Occluded and coded. For example, listed in a column down the outer margin of one page, noted in pencil were the words *If I ever have a baby girl, Patterson says to name her Camille.* Elsewhere, jotted in blue ink were the mysterious words: *Atlantis isn't a myth; it's a prediction.*

These two fellow travelers—the pencil scribbler and the blue-ink vandal—had become my reading companions, always present to share the *Beagle* book with me. Their snide, insightful comments leavened my own reaction to the many otherwise tiresome depictions of lizards and thistles.

In what was clearly a child's hand, another penciled notation read, *Patterson says to start collecting flowers for my husband's funeral someday.*

A squiggle of blue pen said, *Leonard wants me to pick some flowers for my dad.*

As if to illustrate these notes, pressed between the pages were buttercups. Yellow buttercups. Purple violets. Proof of long-ago free time and long holiday strolls and fresh air. Brown ribbons of ancient grass. A record of sunshine. Bits of physical evidence documented a vanished summer. And not just the colors of summer . . . here were the smells as well! Dried sprigs of rosemary, thyme, and lavender. Rose petals still pungent! These layers of paper and words had preserved them, like an armor. Each primrose and morning glory I came across I was duly careful to leave intact.

From her station at the stove, my nana said something, her words ending on a high note, a question.

I responded, "Excuse me?"

Taking the cigarette from her lips, exhaling a plume of smoke, she repeated, "How are you liking that *The Call of the Wild*?"

I looked at her, my eyes wide with incomprehension.

"The novel?" she prompted, nodding at my book opened on the kitchen table.

Obviously she hadn't seen the cover closely enough to know its actual title.

She asked, "Did you read to the part where the dog gets himself kidnapped and took to Alaska?"

Yes, I nodded. My eyes returning to my reading, I agreed that the dog lived a very exciting life.

"Did you read to the part . . . ," she asked, ". . . where the collie dog gets took by Martians in a flying saucer?"

Again, I nodded, saying the scene in question was quite thrilling.

"And," my nana prompted, "was you scared when the space aliens impregnated the Irish setter with radioactive chimpanzee embryos from the Crab Nebula?"

Automatically I agreed. I said that I simply could not wait for the film version. I glanced up just to check the sincerity of her expression, but my nana merely stood there, her dour peasant body garbed in the usual calico apron worn over a shapeless gingham Mother Hubbard, the latter liberated from all style and color by a lifetime of launderings. I made a mental note that this *Wild* book must be a real humdinger.

As she dipped a second taste from the bubbling pot, lifting the spoon to her pursed lips and blowing to cool its steaming contents, the telephone in the parlor began to ring. As she'd done countless times, my nana set aside her dripping utensils and waddled out the kitchen door and down the short hallway. The springs of the divan squealed as she settled herself. The ringing stopped, and she coughed the word "Huh-lo?" Her distant voice dropped to a conspiratorial hush, and she said, "Yeah, she went and grabbed the evolution book, all right. That Maddy's a pistol." Between coughs, she said, "Yeah, I told her about the island. . . ." Choked and breathless, she said, "Don't you fret none, Leonard. That girly is more than ready to do battle with evil!"

Here, Gentle Tweeter, I turned a page in my *Beagle* book and discovered more ancient words. Handwritten down the margin in blue ballpoint pen, they said, *Leonard promises that one day I'll raise a great warrior as my daughter. He tells me to name her Madison.*

Now, Voyager!
Posted by Madisonspencer@aftrlife.hell

entle Tweeter,

So it was, that summer of my exile to tedious upstate, that now-vanished sunny yesterday, I found myself standing at the fraying asphalt margin of State Route Whatever, the outer edge of six northbound lanes packed densely with horn-blasting, gear-grinding tractor-trailers. The morning air smelled wretched, polluted with axle grease, tar, hot oil, and the smoke of burning dinosaur juice.

No explorer had ever set forth to ford more dangerous seas.

My own path would lead at cross-purposes to the flow of automobiles, their momentum, the hiss and growl of their radial tires, the stuttering thunder of exhaust brakes. Through this deadly parade of speeding metal I could see the opposite shore, my destination: the island where vehicles parked to void their occupants, and those occupants hurried to the cinder-block restrooms to deposit their own excremental contents.

With one step I would be committed to cross the entire roadway. A single step, and I would be fully invested in taking the half hundred additional strides needed to deliver me to safety on the distant restroom isle. There, pet dogs strolled, leisurely staging their feces in small piles, as judiciously as any endangered tortoise laying its precious eggs.

How strange I must've appeared to the drivers, an eleven-year-old girl wearing denim trousers and a blue chambray workshirt, the tails of which hung to my knees, the too-long sleeves rolled back to my chubby elbows.

My arms were crossed over my chest, hugging the *Beagle* book and a frail, unwieldy gallon-size jar of my nana's windowsill tea. The murky tea sloshed and shifted, heavy inside its fragile glass. Prior to requisitioning the tea I'd dropped untold sugar cubes into the golden liquid, and as it leaked along the jar's ill-fitting lid my hands and forearms grew sticky. The skin of my fingers gummed together as if they were webbed, as if I were evolving for some new aquatic purpose. So thusly was I glued to the heavy jar that even if my grip failed I suspected the sloshing glass vessel would remain fixed to the chest of my blue chambray shirt.

Once I entered the flow of traffic the smallest pause would place me dead center in the path of pulverizing impact, to be hurtled through the hazy, torpid summer air, my every bone broken. Or to be overridden, the girlish blood crushed out of me and tracked for miles down the highway in the zigzagged, lightning-bolt tread patterns of mammoth black-rubber tires. Any hesitation would mean my death, and in those bygone days I was still highly prejudiced against being dead. Like so many living-alive people I aspired to stay breathing.

Drawing one deep breath, quite possibly my last, I plunged forward into the chaos.

My Bass Weejuns slapped the hot pavement as garbage trucks raged by on every side. Sirens wailed and horns blared. Vast tanker trucks brimming with flammable liquids . . . roaring log trucks . . . these behemoths blasted past me, buffeting my tiny self with such force that I spun like a cork in heavy seas. Dragging their great waves of stinging grit, humongous Greyhound buses peppered me with a buckshot of sharp gravel. In the wake of flatbed trucks, blistering siroccos tore at my skin and hair.

People with happy home lives do not board ships bound for Alaska and the Galápagos. They do not take leave from their loving families in order to sequester themselves in lonely workshops and studios. No psychologically healthy individual would expose herself to X-rays, Marie Curie–style, until they poisoned her. Civilization is a condition which unsocial misfits impose on the rest of popular, easygoing, family-oriented humanity. Only the miserable, the failures, the outcasts will crouch for days to observe the mating habits of a salamander. Or to study a boiling teakettle.

The avant-garde in every field consists of the lonely, the friendless, the uninvited. All progress is the product of the unpopular.

People in love—with nurturing, attentive non-movie-star parents—they would never invent gravity. Nothing except deep misery leads to real success.

The preceding observations steeled my spine even as tractor-trailer combos hurtled past, not a hand's length away. If my mother had been happy living as Rebecca of Sunnybrook Farm she'd never have become a glorious icon for the moviegoing world. If my life's dream were to boil innocent apricots into a vile jellied condiment, alongside my nana, I wouldn't now find myself dashing across the hostile congested lanes of State Route Whatever.

My chubby legs scampered, advancing and retreating in

106

the flurry, dodging lest I be run down and tatters of my chunky childish flesh be pasted to an assortment of chrome bumpers and radiator grilles, bound for Pennsylvania and Connecticut, my denim-chambray ensemble reduced to sodden rags ironed flat against the searing blacktop. One stumble and I'd perish. One forward misstep led to two backward steps. My burden of tea shifted, heaving me off balance. I reeled sideways into the path of an oncoming long-haul monster. Blaring its mighty air horn, the looming tires squealed and skidded. A cargo box of doomed cattle slid by my side, so close I could smell their bovine musk, too close. Their thousand large brown cow eyes stared down piteously upon me.

Without pause other trucks bore down, herding me, prompting my stubby legs to scurry hither and yon, my mind blind with frenzied self-preservation. I darted. My eyes squeezed shut, I raced, ran, flitted, and cowered. I pivoted, slid, and dived with little idea of my direction, mindful only of the howling automobile horns and swerving near misses. Pursuing headlights flashed their indignant high-beam strobes at my jiggling belly fat.

Sopping with perspiration, I was chased. My flabby monster arms flapping, I was intercepted. My progress thwarted, my meaty love handles bounced as my direction was redirected. An onslaught of irate motorists succeeded in elevating my heart rate higher than would the next two years of costly personal trainers.

At last I stumbled. The toe of my shoe kicked an obstacle, and I tumbled and rolled, ready to be slaughtered by the next pursuing conveyance. My arms and torso were collapsed forward, crumpled to protect the fragile glass jar and *Beagle* book. However, instead of hard pavement I landed on something soft. The obstacle which had arrested my foot, I opened my eyes to find it was a concrete curb. The soft place where I'd fallen was a lawn of mown grass. I'd reached the traffic island. The grass itself flattened and yellow-dead, the yielding cushion where I now lay was a warm mound of squishy dog poo.

A Tortured Nontortoise Bladder Driven to Near Madness
Posted by Madisonspencer@aftrlife.hell

entle Tweeter,

To avoid the sometimes soporific pace of Mr. Darwin's travelogue I'll not describe every molecule of the upstate traffic isle. Suffice to say the island was ovoid in shape, bounded along all sides by maniacal drivers operating their motor vehicles at breakneck speed. As is so typical of the upstate region, the island's terrain was boring. The view in every direction was uninteresting. The geology ho-hum. A scanty layer of lawn blanketed the island, and every surface—the grass, the inoperative drinking fountain, the concrete pathways—radiated heat at a temperature comparable to the surface of the sun. To be more exact: the surface of the sun *in August*.

The object of my quest was to locate some insect trapped here and specifically adapted to this sordid environment. I needed only to collect a specimen and name the new species for myself. My discovery would launch my new future as a world-renowned naturalist, and I'd need never again be claimed as a dependent on the tax returns of Camille and Antonio Spencer.

Not that my parents ever paid taxes.

Hulking at the center of the island, like a dormant South Seas volcano ripe with the gaseous stench of brimstone and methane, stood the cinder-block public toilets. To attract exotic insects I uncovered my jar of highly sugared tea, and I waited. Dared I hope for a blaze-colored butterfly? If such a unique species appeared, it would be my own: *Papilio madisonspencerii*. My clothing hung drenched with perspiration. My neck itched. My thirst grew.

Instead of unique aboriginal butterflies, I was beset by houseflies. Rising as a dark haze, migrating en masse from the reeking public toilets, sated from feasting on fresh human bowel movements, wet with the excrement of strangers—these flies migrated straight to the sweetness of my lips. Fat, buzzing black flies as large as twelve-carat diamonds swarmed in a teeming fog around me. Mr. Darwin, my invisible mentor, would be ashamed, for I was unable to summon up even a distanced scientific curiosity about these loathsome vermin as they alighted on my arms, my sweaty face, crawling upon my damp scalp and specking me with their poo-tinged feet. Parched and frustrated, I flailed them away and drank greedily of the tea. The sweetness begot more thirst, and soon I drank again.

Besides the vile houseflies, the only evidence of animal life thereabouts was dog doo-doo. In the same way seabirds have deposited millennia of guano on certain remote islands, thus making those nations wealthy with quarries of nitrogen-rich fertilizer, I posited that future upstate residents would someday mine their traffic islands for the vast accumulations of dog poo. No butterflies arrived. Nor did any neon-colored dragonflies. Stymied by the day's suffocating heat, I partook of more tea. Between the heat and the vigorous exertion required to ward off poop flies, I soon found I'd drunk most of the gallon.

So well irrigated by tea, I found myself compelled to make number one. Painfully compelled.

Please, Gentle Tweeter, do not take what I'm about to say as elitist. If you'll recall: You are alive and most likely eating a nice buttered snack, while my own precious body is providing craft services for earthworms. Recognizing our relative statuses, in no way can I really high-hat you. But, plainly put, until that tedious upstate moment I'd never before made use of a public toilet. Oh, I'd heard tell they existed, these shared spaces where one and all might venture to donate their wee-wee to a community sewer, but I'd simply never been forced to exercise so desperate an option.

My clenched woo-woo howling in wordless distress, I abandoned my empty tea jar—the sticky glass at present paved with black houseflies. I carried my Darwin and went in search of relief. The landscape offered nothing in the way of cover. No options existed save for the ominous cinder-block bathrooms, their exterior walls painted a dull ochre. So advanced was my condition, so distended my bladder, that I had no hope of successfully retreating to my nana's spartan albeit semihygienic commode.

The beckoning public toilets seemed to boast two doors, each door occurring on a side of the building opposite the other door, both doors painted a dismal brown. Mounted at eye level beside each was a sign lettered in an alarming sans-serif, all-caps typeface. These read MEN and WOMEN, respectively, suggesting the genders were segregated in their public-toilet-going pursuits. I waited for confirmation, hoping to follow a woman into what seemed the appropriate door. My plan was to mirror some stranger's behavior, thus avoiding any major faux pas. I especially worried about under- or overtipping any attendant. Etiquette and protocol constituted no small part of my Swiss boarding school education, but I remained oblivious as to how one ought to comport herself while tinkling among bystanders.

Even at school I eschewed using the shared lavatories, preferring always to return to my room's en suite water closet. Among my worst fears was that I might suffer from a shy bladder and find my pelvic muscles unable to sufficiently relax.

My skills as a naturalist determined my course of action: I waited for a female with full bowels to arrive. Initially, none did. After a few agonizing minutes, even more women didn't arrive. I racked my brains for any teachings about how such facilities did business. For example, was a patron compelled to take a paper slip printed with a number and wait for her turn to be called? Or perhaps a reservation was needed. Were that the case I was determined to cross the maître d'hotel's palm with silver and secure myself an immediate piddle. The idea of money chilled me with terror. What *did* the natives of tiresome upstate use for currency? A quick rifling of my denim pockets yielded euros, shekels, pounds, rubles, and several credit cards. Still, as no butterflies had arrived, no widdle-burdened women arrived. I wondered if such public pooping establishments accepted charge cards in payment.

Eventually a stranger obviously brimming with caca hurried from a parked sedan to the WOMEN door. I readied myself to follow her lead, by now almost knock-kneed with my rapidly accruing wee. As the poo-burdened stranger reached toward the door handle, I stood so close at her heels that I could've been her shadow. Grasping the handle she pulled—but with no result. She braced her shoulder against the door and pushed, then again pulled, but the brown-painted door refused to budge. Only then did my eyes follow her gaze toward a paper card affixed to the door with adhesive tape. It bore the handwritten legend *Out of Order.* And, hissing a genital expletive, the woman turned on one heel and stalked back to her car.

Unbelieving, I seized the door handle but succeeded only in rattling some unseen bolt which held it fast. Ye gods!

During my vigil several men had entered and exited the MEN's bathroom on the opposite facade of the building. Now, confronted by the options—to express my wee-wee like a base house pet on a scratchy dooky-laden lawn, fly-menaced, in full view of all the leering truck drivers and lead-footed soccer moms in tedious upstate . . . or to waddle back to my nana's farm, my denim slacks drenched like an infant's . . . offered those two humbling choices, I availed myself of neither. My alternative would be to abandon every tenet of civilization, to surrender every moral and ethic I held dear. I'd violate humanity's most fearsome taboo. I felt a stray drop of wee-wee trickle down my leg, wetting my denim slacks with a small dark spot. Thus, clutching my *Beagle* book as I would a shield to cover my shame, I lowered myself to the depth of an outlaw, a heretic, a blasphemer.

I, an eleven-year-old girl child, crept off to use the MEN's room.

Entering the Labyrinth of King Minos
Posted by Madisonspencer@aftrlife.hell

entle Tweeter,

As I sat in the toilet stall of a long-ago upstate public restroom, my worst fear was not of being grabbed and manhandled by some drooling Mr. Pervy McPervert. No, the reason my lungs contracted and my heart thrashed like a netted Galápagos finch—even as my bladder unleashed its torrent of scalding widdle—owed more to the terror that I might be arrested. My presence in the MEN's bathroom violated sacred societal taboos. It seemed certain that I would be severely punished—and, on some level, I prayed for it.

Don't ask me why, but that terror felt as exciting as Christmas Eve, and I anticipated that unknown punishment as if it were a solid-gold pony.

Not that my parents ever celebrated Christmas.

If I were caught here, dared I hope that I'd be pilloried? Some stone-faced magistrate would lash me to a post in an upstate village square. My tender child's budding form would be stripped of its protective clothing, and I'd be flogged. Not merely the lash would fall upon my tender skin. The lustful gaze of drooling oafs would also ravage helpless, captive me as they greedily fingered their reproductive organs through the ragged holes worn in their peasant britches.

Gentle Tweeter, if I may be honest, I found such a prospect infinitely exciting. How glorious it would feel to be smote a great blow and return to my Swiss boarding school with the raised welts and ruddy contusions that proved to those coddled children how much someone Ctrl+Alt+Loved me. Oh, to be so proved a stoic!

As a fledgling naturalist, here was my first expedition into the dark continent of masculinity. The sound of dripping faucets echoed around the room in bright, subterranean notes, like someone plucking harp strings at the bottom of a deep cave. The real world existed elsewhere. The tuberous dog doo, the careening trucks. The harsh, humiliating daylight. Within this space dwelled something well beyond my naive schoolgirl experience.

No Turkish prison could appear less enticing. Scaly curls of filth-colored paint peeled down from the ceiling. Leprous patterns of mildew, like black-flocked wallpaper, crept in arabesque designs across the cinder blocks. All herein was unclean, corrupt, rusted. Aggressively sullied. A row of sinks hung along one wall, the faucets dripping beneath a mural of menacing graffiti and gouged telephone numbers.

Facing the sinks was a wall of piddle-spattered urinals. Near those, a trio of flimsy sheet-metal partitions separated three caca-scented toilet cubicles, and it was in the third-most of these that I hid myself to make water. These partitions were in no manner opaque; hoodlums, perhaps hungry upstate woodpeckers, had assailed the sheet metal and torn holes of differing sizes. Through those sordid rents I had a limited view of my surroundings.

Seated as I was on a hideously stained and battered commode, my lungs shrank away from inhaling the toxic air. My hands recoiled from any contact.

A fellow student at my Swiss boarding school, some Miss Trampy von Trampton once told me how Catholics would forget their sins. According to her they'd sit alone inside a darkened little booth and they'd talk dirty to God through a hole in the wall. Sitting here, shut inside a toilet stall, I could see how that might take place. About halfway up the wall of my cubicle a hole opened in the metal, and I could see a little tunnel through to the next toilet. The hole was only about eye-size, edged with jags of torn steel metal like a small mouth of snarling teeth. I wanted to peek through, but it felt too scary to put my eyeball so close to those knife-sharp metal points. Even with my eyeglasses on.

Pretending to seek divine forgiveness, I put my mouth to the frightening hole. To test God's love in the same way my false diary tested my parents', I whispered about committing fake murders and shopliftings. I whispered the make-believe details about bearing false witness.

Every inhale smelled, in the words of that same aforementioned Miss Von Trampton, like a bag of sweaty armpits.

Human sexuality is by no means limited to genital reproductive functions. I'm safe in saying The Erotic covers a broad spectrum of behaviors which create and manage and eventually resolve accumulated tension. Even as I loosed my pent-up wee-wee, that gushing pleasure was my model for how an orgasm might someday feel. My mother had openly discussed orgasms with me, as had my father, but my knowledge of sexual matters remained piecemeal and theoretical.

With the commode seat framing my childish buttocks, I looked to be sure the stall's door was locked. I sat with the *Beagle* book open across my lap, idly turning the pages, scanning for handwritten memories from my predecessors. Noted in blue ink in the margin of one page were those words: . . . *one day I'll raise a great warrior* . . .

A noise interrupted my reading. A squeal, the squawk of rusted hinges, told me the bathroom door was swinging open. I was no longer alone. My tinkling complete, I squirmed into my denim pants and made ready to take flight; however, frozen by heat and fear, I sat on the commode fully clothed and leaked sweat from every pore in my skin. Through the holes in the partition I could discern very little, merely a flash of untidy clothing, a hirsute knuckle. The stranger entered the toilet stall beside my own and slammed the flimsy door.

The brute sounded enormous. With the wet, sucking sound of a bathtub drain he hawked up a massive wad of saliva. I could hear it rattling from his cheeks and throat into his mouth, followed by the spit-bullet splat of his robust mouthful hitting the floor. Flecks colored brown with masticated tobacco sprayed my way under the partition, and I stepped my Bass Weejuns back as far as the tiny space allowed. A great hulking ogre had taken up residence on the toilet next to mine. This thought infused my fear with a hunger, but not for food. As the tedious upstate sun had filled me with thirst, the looming sense of some hairy giant spurred a tenuous new physical need. A *true* scientist dedicated to studying nature, I reasoned, would remain motionless and silent. The cubicle made a suitable "blind" from which to spy; Mr. Darwin had endured worse. I heard the buzz of a heavy zipper parting. That ominous sound was followed by the clank of a metal belt buckle striking the concrete floor.

In the stealthy manner of Mr. Darwin I remained toilet-bound, but leaned forward from the waist, lower and lower, so as to peek beneath the bottom edge of the partition. What I saw baffled me: The beastly monster's feet were shod in rather louche shoes of the type called "cowboy boots," and his low-quality, prêt-à-porter gabardine slacks were collapsed to rest around his booted ankles. The two ends of a belt dangled from his open waistband, flanking the yawning zipper, and the buckle was a hammered oval of tarnished silver embedded with faux turquoise and engraved with the legend WORLD'S BEST DAD. What piqued my professional curiosity was how his toes ought to have been pointing forward. They were not. Both tips of his boots were pointed toward me, facing the metal wall that separated us.

The flimsy sheet metal bowed and groaned as if some leviathan pressed against it from the opposite side.

Alarmed, I slowly sat upright. There, the real horror awaited me.

What appeared to be a stubby boneless finger now protruded through the snarling mouth hole in the stall partition. This short, thick cylinder was mottled brown, fading from a red-brown at the blunt terminus to a soiled beige where it disappeared through the wall. Infinite tiny wrinkles carpeted the finger's spongy surface, and several short, curling hairs clung to it. The finger gave off a sour, not-healthy odor.

Before I could make a closer inspection, mercifully, my eyeglasses chose that moment to slip from my sweat-slicked face. Their tortoiseshell frames clattered against the concrete floor, skidded through the field of expectorated tobacco juice, and spun out of my reach. I grabbed at the air, desperate, but caught nothing. Everything in the world smeared together. Minus my corrective lenses nothing had an edge. This place was already as dark as wearing ten pairs of Foster Grants and ten pairs of Ray-Bans at the same time, and now everything looked mixed-up as well.

Squinting, I leaned so near the finger that I could feel its animal heat. I peered from so close up that my breath stirred the short, curled hairs. I sniffed at it tentatively. As my brain whispered that the "finger" was not an actual finger, I was shocked by the true nature of this encounter. The scent was unmistakable. This apparent psychopath . . . this sexual deviant . . . he was attempting to menace me with a longish lump of dog poopie.

I was seated in close proximity to a deranged masher who'd armed himself with a longish, brown dog boo-boo.

Some unbalanced Mr. Lechy Vanderlech, most likely an escapee from a lunatic asylum, had traveled to this location for the specific purpose of collecting a discarded dog dooky. In all likelihood he'd lingered over his selection, scouting for a dried pet poo nugget with sufficient length and tensile strength to be so brandished, but with not so much girth that it wouldn't fit through an existing hole in this partition. I was merely the unlucky target of his deranged attentions. Only a breath away from my look of dumbstruck horror, the poo log emerged from the battered metal and drooped at a steep angle.

It was the downward angle of my nana's cigarette when she was subject to a serious emotional depression; however, as I watched, the mood of the drooping poo finger began to improve. Like some horrid, soft-focus miracle it began to inflate. The hideous mud boo-boo rose until it jutted straight out from its rough hole in the metal wall. Its ruddy color shifted from red-brown to pink as its angle slanted upward. Before I could blink my eyes it was pointed at the ceiling. By now it had swollen so large, and it thrust up at such a steep incline, that I doubted my assailant could easily retract his hostile doo-doo probe.

Even seen, vague and unfocused, through my crippled eyes, the transformation was astounding. The nascent naturalist within me began to formulate a strategy.

Wary, I lifted the heavy tome of Mr. Darwin. For as long as I could recollect I'd been the victim of schoolyard bullies, those giggling Miss Skanky Skankenheimers who'd misled and tormented me. No longer would I tolerate similar forms of demeaning abuse. Tensing the slight muscles of my youthful arms, I took aim. My plan was to swing the heavy book and swat the menacing poop with such force that it would fly the full extent of the room. After that, I'd bolt, running full speed, and return to the bright outside world before my lunatic harasser knew I'd so destroyed his sad, ridiculous toy.

Besting the Minotaur
Posted by Madisonspencer@aftrlife.hell

entle Tweeter,

Those long years thence, seated astride a stained toilet bowl in an upstate public bathroom, I tightened my grip on the *Beagle* book. With both hands I held the heavy, leather-bound volume. Like a golfer preparing to hit a drive down the fourteenth fairway at St. Donats, or a tennis star rearing back to hit a scorching serve over the net at the French Open, I slowly aligned the book with the offensive dog dooky. The magically swollen pet doo-doo jutted eagerly toward me, oblivious to my imminent violent actions. The cinder-block room echoed with the *plink-plunk* musical notes of dripping water, but otherwise a silence had settled, so intense it proved my harasser and I were both holding our respective breaths. The muscles of my frail shoulders and shoestring arms flexed, rigid as iron, focusing the strength garnered from my mom's spacey yoga gurus in Kathmandu and Bar Harbor. A wild karate yelp took shape at the back of my throat. Squinting my nearsighted eyes, I told myself: *Exhale.* I told myself: *Lean into the swing.*

Steeling myself, I was Theseus about to do battle with the Minotaur in the dank basements of Crete. I was Hercules girding my loins to fight Cerberus, the fierce two-headed watchdog of the underworld.

I told myself: *Now.*

Wielding the heavy volume from above my head, swinging it diagonally, down and sideways simultaneously, I rendered the threatening doggie poo a mighty *thwack*. Without hesitation, my backswing landed a second, resounding smack against the loathsome doodie-caca, but it refused to detach and go flying as I'd hoped. Trapped by its own magically increased size, the menacing poo finger appeared to be wedged within the jagged metal hole. The awful dooky bobbed and flopped wildly, flailing and twisting in every direction. From behind the sheet-metal partition a sharp gasp of breath preceded a howling scream. The pressure which had bowed the partition in my direction now reversed, and some great force seemed to tug against the metal wall. The scratched, mutilated barrier pulled away from me, dragged backward by the efforts of the trapped dog boo-boo attempting to escape.

Flogging with the hardcover book, I pummeled my foe's vile puppy poop with one savage blow after another. In response, the unseen opponent bellowed and shrieked. These were animal sounds. The wailing which might occur on the killing floor of a slaughterhouse. This senseless keening might be a suffering horse or cow as likely as it was a human male.

Striking a hail of blows upon the struggling caca, I likewise found myself howling great screams of rage. Mine was the vengeful whoop of every child ever tormented by cruel bullies, a combination of fury and weeping and sheer hysterical laughter. The concrete room felt flooded, swamped with the outcries of two combatants, the fetid air vibrating with the multiplied echoes. So fiercely did I scream that frothy spittle ribboned from my lips.

Even in the throes of my fury, my naturalist instincts held sway. Even with my soft-focus vision, sans eyeglasses, I saw how the beaten dooky had begun to shrink in size. The noxious boo-boo was recoiling, becoming smaller, shorter, until it seemed about to retract itself back through the ragged hole. To prevent its impending escape I opened the *Beagle* book to roughly its midpoint and placed the opened volume so that the gutter would cradle the wilting poo. As my colleagues, the Pencil and the Blue Pen, had pressed samples of leaves and flowers, preserving those ferns and grasses for posterity, so would I press my own shocking discovery. At the moment before the poopie-doo-doo might flee, I slammed shut the huge tome. All of upstate trembled with the resulting scream. Kuala Lumpur, Calcutta, or Karachi, wherever my parents were sunbathing, watching their navels fill with sweat, they must've heard the outburst. All the world shook with the force of that howl.

Thus I held captive the shrinking tortured number two: sandwiched in the paper middle of Mr. Darwin's voyage, by my estimate clamped somewhere within his account of Tierra del Fuego. I retained possession of the evil poopie by squeezing the book shut, and continued my efforts to pull it free, yanking from side to side, pulling with all my strength. Getting jerked this way and that meant the poochie-poo-poo was snagged and chewed by the hole's jagged, snaggletoothed edge. By this point the flimsy sheet-metal toilet cubicle swayed, its bolts rattling loose, and readied itself to collapse.

It happens on rare occasion, Gentle Tweeter, that natural phenomena occur for which we've no ready explanation. The role of the naturalist is to take note and to record

123

a description of said occurrence, trusting that eventually that rogue event will make sense. I mention this because the oddest thing happened: As I held fast, gripping my book with the boo-boo-caca shut snugly inside it—me yanking the book on its short tether—the book appeared to vomit. A thin stream of vile sputum jetted from between the pages. This viscous off-white vomitus erupted from the depths of Mr. Darwin's journal. My memory slows the moment, stretching the seconds so as to depict the finer details: A pulse followed by a second and third pulse of colorless sputum burst from the book clasped in my hands. Not a large quantity, nonetheless it presented itself at such a velocity that I'd no time to react. Before I could move aside, the jelly's trajectory landed it upon the chest of my blue chambray shirt. Here, my professional demeanor failed me. The spoutings of mysterious phlegm still clinging to my meager child's bosom, I abandoned the fight. I deserted the *Beagle* book and the dog boo-boo it still held prisoner. I burst from my toilet stall, and I ran squealing at the top of my lungs.

I Flee the Scene

Posted by Madisonspencer@aftrlife.hell

entle Tweeter,

When I burst from the brown-painted door of that hellish public toilet in tedious upstate, the lackluster sun had dropped to late afternoon. Where I'd sated my thirst with too much tea, the empty glass jar still lay in the scorched grass. Soon my deranged attacker would emerge from the MEN's restroom behind me, perhaps not deterred by our struggle, perhaps only enraged and bent on the single purpose of seizing me and rending me limb from limb and completing a frenzied sexual act upon my lifeless, beheaded torso within full view of a million speeding upstate motorists.

That endless stream of tailgating tanker trucks and logging trucks and minivans continued to roar around the edges of this shunned traffic island. To my naked face, with my eyeglasses still abandoned back on the bathroom floor, the vehicles layered and overlapped each other until they became the solid wall of their growling tire tread sound. No space existed between them. I stooped to retrieve the gallon-size tea jar, distracted by my impending doom.

Perhaps I had brashly overreacted to the proffered dirty-poo finger? After all, I was a stranger in upstate. Perhaps thrusting doo-doo sticks through holes in toilet stalls constituted a local backwoods custom akin to a mild flirtation. My Nana Minnie once told me, "Boys only tease the girls they like." In response, I'd quoted Oscar Wilde, saying, "Yet each man kills the thing he loves."

Nonetheless, upstate being upstate, it's not impossible that I'd just now thwarted an amorous country swain. If, indeed, waving caca logs at young girls was some rural prelude to romance, then I'd lost myself a potential suitor.

Whether I'd foiled a rustic courtship or escaped a murderer, my heart still struggled high in my throat, and the cold sweat of shock washed down from my forehead. The mysterious ejaculate that had sprung from the *Beagle* book hung heavily, in coagulated lumps, on the bosom of my shirt. Sans my eyeglasses, everything in the world was either too close or too far away for me to see it clearly. I was in no good condition to fling myself into the clockwork tangle of dense traffic, but if a poo-wielding madman were to emerge from the cinder-block building, I felt I'd have precious little choice. Here my bleary gaze fell upon the glass tea jar I'd grasped and lifted, the walls of which now showed themselves to be studded—nay, fairly paved—with black houseflies trapped by the thick residue of sugar. Recoiling from these vermin, I dropped the jar and watched it bounce in the grass. As it had before, the cunning naturalist within me formulated a plan. Carefully, I once more stooped and lifted the empty jar, gingerly avoiding its carpet of gluey bug life. With a few steps I carried it to the margin where the parched lawn met the asphalt parking lot; there, a curb awaited, the white concrete fairly shimmering in the day's heat. Granted, my nana needed this jar to brew her windowsill tea, but my self-protection seemed a higher priority. In the future, if my Nana Minnie missed her homemade swill, I'd simply telephone Spago and have them FedEx a single serving of their delicious blend. For now, using both hands, I lifted the sticky, insect-laden vessel over my head. With a cathartic yelp, I hurled it against the curb, where the glass burst into countless shards. The largest, cruelest, most daggerlike of these jagged glass pieces I selected as my weapon.

Lest my course of action seem overly dramatic, please understand that I'd written my name within the end pages of the *Beagle* book. Even if I quickly fled the scene, that book—and my eyeglasses—remained with my foe. The psychotic fiend would see my name. A poop-brandishing nutcase would discover my name and begin stalking me to exact his revenge. To protect my hand I wrapped the hilt of my glass dagger in euro notes. Thus armed to retrieve my book, I crept soundlessly back toward the dingy cinder-block toilets.

Scattered around me on the grass were doodie dog logs so like the one that had recently been thrust at me, and I could tell that for the rest of my life the sight of a dog boo-boo would make my heart stumble with terror. My eyes would see inflating doodie-cacas lurking in every shadow. Every future nightmare would be an echo of today.

At the building's entrance I turned my head sideways and placed a listening ear to the brown-painted door. No sounds emerged from within. From that stance my flawed peripheral vision included the rest-area parking lot, the sun-toasted lawn, the endless riptides of motor vehicle traffic. Only a single automobile waited, unoccupied, in the lot. It was a dented, rusted truck of the type known as a "pickup." A crack bisected the windshield lengthwise. My poor eyesight might've been mistaken, but a taillight appeared to be repaired with layers of red-colored adhesive tape. My deranged nemesis, I deemed, had arrived here in that sad, mud-dappled, well-scratched truck.

World's Best Dad . . .

My brain belched up something I refused to taste. I choked back the possibility, the as-yet-unrealized horror that lodged itself within my throat. This new idea was like seeing an Asian person speaking Spanish. It was too impossible a concept.

Without question, I was in a state of shock. As an animated zombie, clutching my glass knife, I shouldered open the door and reentered the reeking public toilet. The movement from blazing day to dim interior blinded me, but I could hear the *plink-plunk* of dripping water. In that catacomb echo I heard a man's raspy breathing. My eyes beheld, in the next blink, a figure sprawled on the filthy concrete. It was a man, his head resting on the floor. His wrinkled skin and gray hair had matted together until you couldn't, in surety, vouchsafe where his face ended and his scalp began. At first I wouldn't swear whether he lay faceup or -down, but then I saw his knees were together, pulled to his chest in a fetal pose. His slacks were still wadded around his ankles, and his belt with its WORLD'S BEST DAD buckle was splayed open. Of his naked legs, the exposed flanks were so white they glowed, pearlescent, hazed with small, black hairs. Between his knobby pink knees stretched the empty hammock of his dingy underbriefs, and one of his hands disappeared into his crotch, where it appeared to be cupping his shame. His other hand had reached the full length of his extended arm and clutched the air near my dropped book. As bright as a spot of sunlight in this stony traffic island tomb, a gold band circled the base of his ring finger. It was, to my handicapped vision, nothing better than nine-carat.

Even my bad eyes could see a stream of crimson running from the man's withered loins. This rivulet of red rolled down the slight slope of the floor, collecting his discarded flecks of tobacco spit and edging toward the rusted central drain. There, all of his various fluids were disappearing in sizable amounts. Following his gaze, his reaching hand, my worst fears were confirmed, for he certainly intended to examine the book.

With my next step my Bass Weejun foot found my lost glasses. Under my baby-fat weight they weren't anyone's glasses; they weren't even eyeglasses anymore. A loud pop and the crunch of glass and plastic turned the old man's head in my direction.

The *Beagle* book had fallen, facedown and open, so its precious pages were pressed flat to that awful floor. A pathetic assortment of dried flowers and leaves had fallen from their hiding places deep inside Mr. Darwin's narrative. After being safely preserved for decades, these tiny blossoms were scattered and sprinkled over the body of the fallen pervert. In a panicked impulse I lunged forward, closing the short distance, and leaned down to seize my paper property.

As my fingers closed around an edge of the book, likewise did the hand of the psycho grasp the volume. For a terrible eternity he held fast. We endured a dark tug-of-war, me and this anonymous Other. I still could not see his face, masked as it was by the disarray of his hair. As his arm strength failed, his grip did not, and my efforts dragged the man closer. He was old, an old man with gaunt sunken cheeks and glazed, rheumy eyes. His cheekbones and chin were as craggy as the totem sculptures people carved with chain saws and sold in vacant lots next to upstate gas stations. The dried flowers, ancient violets and pansies, age-old foxgloves, sprigs of lavender, desiccated marigolds, and fragile four-leafed clovers, all of these still retained their colors from long-vanished summers. From summers before I'd been born. These preserved daisies and asters formed a bier under his body, and a final, fading breath of their long-ago perfume sweetened the fetid air of that profane setting.

My arms tugged the book free, and I backed away a step but could not bring myself to take flight. Strewn among the flowers and broken eyeglass lenses was a scarlet butterfly, dead and pressed flat. It was the blaze-colored butterfly of my greatest naturalist dreams. My own species: *Papilio madisonspencerii*. But on closer examination it was neither scarlet nor a butterfly. It was merely a white moth newly saturated in this stranger's rapidly issuing blood.

The man, shrouded with flowers, resting upon flowers, he lifted a quivering hand toward me. His old lips twitched with a single word, but no voice emerged. His pale lips moved again, this time saying, "Madison?"

Involuntarily the hand holding my makeshift knife relaxed—that longish shard of glass with a handle of tightly wrapped currency notes—and the dagger fell. The room's hardened walls, scarred with their layers of graffiti, resounded with the fragile ringing sound of something brittle breaking into infinite fragments. Shattered glass sparkled, and the paper money fluttered to land in the escaping blood. My nose could smell air I didn't want inside my mouth.

The familiar dented pickup truck parked outside. The World's Best Dad.

Leonard wants me to pick some flowers for my dad.

The old lips hissed the words, "Little Maddy?"

My heart overcame my brains, and I inched closer, close enough that I could see the red was soaking his pants and the front of his shirt. He reached a trembling hand, and my hand, now empty of its weapon, met his halfway. Our fingers laced together, his skin feeling icy cold despite the summer heat. The stranger was my mother's father. He was Nana Minnie's husband. He was Papadaddy Ben, my grandpa, and his failing lips worked softly, saying, "You have murdered me, you evil child. . . . Don't think you won't burn in hell for this!" He hissed, "Forever are you condemned to the unquenchable lake of fire!"

His bony grip crushed my fingers. And like the repeating song of a finch . . . like waves lapping at a Galápagos beach, he kept saying, "You are a wicked, despicable girl. . . ." He rasped, "Your mama and grandma will hate you for breaking their hearts!"

On and on, with his every dying breath my papadaddy cursed me.

entle Tweeter,

As an actor my mother hates sitting for still photographers. Fashion models, she says, are able to communicate themselves in a fixed expression, but an actor needs to use the pitch and volume of her voice, the motion of her gestures. Limiting an actor to a still, silent image is a reduction, as flavorless and aroma-free as a perfect snapshot of the most delicious mesquite-roasted, Cajun-rubbed tofu. That's how absurd this feels: reducing Papadaddy Ben's death to a blog entry. Mere words. To make you experience the scene fully I'd need to smear his warm dying blood on your hands. Instead of just reading this, you'd have to sit next to him on that concrete paved with dirt until his fingers felt nothing but cold. You'd need to take the biggest chunk surviving from my busted eyeglasses and hold it over his gaped-open lips while you prayed to see the glass fog even a little bit. Not that my parents ever taught me how to pray. Spurred by your gigantic panic, your feet would launch you out through the brown-painted bathroom door, sprinting down pathways across soft steps of dead grass, your soles slapping parking lot until you were waving for somebody's attention from the edge of freeway traffic. Crying all the way. Hearing nothing except the loud sound of your lungs yelling air in and out. Without thinking twice you'd do jumping jacks between lanes of air-horning, headlight-flashing trucks and cars, and you'd perform all these verbs without seeing anything clearly. You'd be fluttering your blood-painted hands like red flags for some grown-up to please stop.

You'd need to go back, defeated, and see a warped scratched reflection of yourself in that belt buckle given to him by my mom in an earlier life, from back before she was a movie star. To really appreciate that long afternoon you'd need to see the dried flowers wicking up his blood. No longer faded, now flushed. Those daisies and carnations, reviving decades after they'd been picked, you'd watch them come back to life, blooming again in various shades of red and pink. Tiny vampires.

Even if my nana only boiled water in a pan, she'd scrub the pan before putting it away in the cupboard. That's my Nana Minnie in a word: fragile. I couldn't tell her the truth about anything.

Imagine being an expert witness to something you could never, ever tell anyone about. Especially not anyone you loved. I was going to hell. It's why I know I'm evil. That's the secret I've kept hidden from God.

The Dog Doo-doo Defense

Posted by Madisonspencer@aftrlife.hell

entle Tweeter,

Eventually, the state patrol officers called what happened a hate crime. I wanted to correct them and politely explain that my grandpa Ben's death was actually more of a hate *accident*. Maybe a *hate misadventure*. But I didn't dare. Before anybody called the death anything, nobody called at all. My Nana Minnie had to issue the opening volley of tentative telephone inquiries.

The first night my Papadaddy Ben was dead, my nana stayed awake, waiting for his rusted pickup truck to pull into the driveway. I pretended to go to bed but my heart stayed alert, listening to her make restless sounds in the parlor. My thinking stomach ached with the hunger of not knowing my next action. I knew I could fix all her worries but that would involve telling her a truth that would make her feel even worse. Lying in that weird upstate bed without even security cameras watching me, I pictured her pantry and root cellars, where wooden shelves were lined with bottles of pickles that had lived and died before I was ever born. Their labels, like tombstones for stillborn babies with one year telling the whole story. Cucumbers floated in brine, their skin rubbery and see-through, like a homemade circus sideshow. Like biology, these pickles were so translucent you could see the dead seeds of future generations embedded within them. I imagined all the rows of preserved bottles so that I wouldn't fall asleep and relive my awful day. I had only to close my eyes to see my papadaddy dragging his bloody pantless self across the bedroom floor, ranting and shouting that I was evil and damned forever.

This same bed had been my mom's about a hundred years earlier, only she'd been stuck in it for her whole childhood. Her threadbare, Chinese-slave-labor-made stuffed teddy bears sat around my pillow, smelling like her. Not merely like her Chanel No. 5, but like her real skin, how she smelled when she wasn't slaving away as a big-time movie star. My fingers half expected to encounter loose strands of her farm-girl hair.

Tomorrow I'd have to pretend to be devastated. If my mother could be a famous actor, I could at least fake sleeping. Later on, I'd fake shocked bereavement. Every day I already had to pretend that I didn't feel hurt and abandoned, but for tonight, pretending to be asleep seemed like good practice.

In bed, I wondered whether my papadaddy's dead outline was marked in chalk or masking tape next to the drain where all his blood had trickled away. I pictured a scene like in a movie starring my mom as a plucky private detective hot on the trail of a ruthless serial killer. This imaginary version made me the serial killer, but even being some Jeffrey Dahmer tasted better than being some idiot kid who'd mistakenly bled her grandpa to death by carelessly slicing his amorous wiener against daggers of sharp metal. My mind wandering, too tired to sleep, I wondered whether I could kill again. I worried that I might develop a taste for murder. By killing a larger variety of victims, possibly

I could establish a pattern and look less like a hapless amateur at my eventual prosecution.

The alternative was to swear to tell the truth and look totally ridiculous at my trial for one klutzy half-baked manslaughter. Any little Miss Hottie Hot Pants could tell an erect penis from a regular dried-out dog poop. I imagined my Swiss classmates following my trial live by satellite. Even getting the electric chair would be better than going back to boarding school with everybody giggling behind my back. In Locarno, girls would chase me down hallways, forever menacing me with their fecal-looking candy bars.

Nobody would believe my side of the story. My explanation would be endlessly joked about as the "Dog Doo-doo Defense."

Every direction I could see to go was just a different nightmare.

My nana's voice came down the hall, around a couple corners, faint from where it started in the parlor. First came a tickling sound: a fast dash followed by a quiet rattling of tiny clicks. This I recognized as a finger dialing their old rotary telephone. Yes, my grandparents had a telephone, but just barely. It was a phone like the Pilgrims might use to check their voice mails from Plymouth Rock, connected to the wall by a cord you couldn't unplug. The rattling dial sound went on for seven long times, and my nana's voice said, "Admitting, please." I imagined her toying with the curly cord that held the receiver to the ringer part, trapped on the parlor sofa by the short length of that cord. Her voice said, "I'm sorry to bother you . . ." and it was light, singsong, the tone you might use to ask a stranger on a street corner for the correct time. She said, "My husband ain't come home yet, and I wondered if there'd been any accidents reported?"

She waited. We both waited. If I shut my eyes I saw my fingerprints dotted on a dirty toilet behind stretched-tight Day-Glo crime-scene tape. In my fantasy, state patrol detectives in wide-brimmed Canadian Mountie–style hats held walkie-talkies alongside their lantern jaws and barked all-points bulletins. Stripes ran down the outside legs of their uniform pants, leading to polished shoes. I envisioned a forensics expert wearing a white lab coat as he lifted a thumbprint using a piece of clear tape; holding the print between his face and the upstate moon, he studied the whorls, saying, "Our suspect is an eleven-year-old girl, four-foot-six, pudgy, a little dumpy, a real fatty-fatty-two-by-four, with hair that never does what she wants it to. . . ." He'd nod sagely, reading the finer details. "She's never even kissed a boy, and no one likes her."

At that, a police artist standing nearby and sketching wildly on a large pad would say, "Based on the evidence I think I have your killer." The artist would whip his pad around, and drawn on the white paper would be a portrait of me, my eyeglasses restored to my nose, my freckles, my giant, shiny forehead. Even my dreaded full name would be written across the bottom: *Madison Desert Flower Rosa Parks Coyote Trickster Spencer.*

From down the hallway my nana's voice said, "No, thank you." She said, "I'll hold the line."

Covering my tracks hadn't occurred to me. It wasn't until lying there that I thought about the *Beagle* book and my stained shirt. My murder weapon. Moonlight stretched a white rectangle into my bedroom, the shape of it flaring from my windowsill to almost fill the far wall. Under the moon's scrutiny I scrambled from the quilts and covers and donned my second-best pair of eyeglasses. I knelt beside the bed and wedged an arm between the mattress and box spring, feeling until my fingers dug out the book wrapped by the incriminating chambray shirt. Even in just moonlight you could see the stains had set in the fabric. They made larger and smaller blob shapes across the front of the shirt, trailing but close to one another, like a cloth map of the Galápagos Islands. In the middle of the *Beagle* book, around Tierra del Fuego, the pages were stuck together. With my fingernails I picked at their edges. Like a forensic investigator lifting a fingerprint, I pinched each of the two center pages and slowly peeled them apart. The paper felt heavy, gummy, and the pages came apart with a sound like a Korean aesthetician waxing my mom's legs, ripping out all her hairs by the roots. The sound of incredible pain.

From down the hallway my nana's voice told the telephone, "I see." She said, "Yes'm."

My hands spread the book's pages like you'd part curtains, and spattered there was a psychology test in dark splotches. Made more or less symmetrical by the book's being shut, the dark parts looked like a butterfly . . . or a vampire bat. While my eyes were trying to decide, the rest of me saw the white shape down the middle of the book where the two pages met. There, still white and printed with Mr. Darwin's thoughts, a longish narrow shape pointed straight at me. Under the moonlight the blotchy black parts you could tell would be red in other light. Tomorrow they'd be blood. The ghost shape in the middle, the void where nothing was, that was an outline.

Still kneeling there beside my bed, I heard a breeze that was really my nana gasping, loud. With the air of that same inhale she told the telephone, "Thank you." She said, "Give me twenty minutes to get there."

The shape at the heart of my book was my papadaddy's dead wiener. As heavy footsteps approached down the hallway, I slammed the book shut. In less than two footsteps I buried my stained shirt deep in the dirty-clothes hamper. In another two approaching footsteps I stashed the book under my pillow and leaped back into bed among the Mom-smelling teddy bears. By the last footstep my eyes were closed and I was faking a deep, peaceful slumber when the truth came knocking at my door.

Grand-patricide

Posted by Madisonspencer@aftrlife.hell

entle Tweeter,

That first night my Papadaddy Ben went missing, my nana had to drive us to the hospital to find out something the police refused to reveal over the phone. Something that I already knew. In her car she lit each new cigarette off the last. She dropped the butt of the smoked cigarette out her window, a tiny meteor flaring orange sparks into the dark. The way a falling star foretells a death. Mostly, back then, it felt weird for me to ride in a front seat next to where a chauffeur should go. Thusly, we followed our headlights into the grim future.

I wanted to impress upon Nana the social stigma of secondhand smoke and littering, but decided to swallow my gripe. This chore-haggard woman was about to become a widow. No doubt the melodramatic reveal would take place in front of a crowd of strangers in the autopsy suite of some medical examiner. Probably she would collapse into a dead faint still wearing her calico apron getup paired with a faded gingham housedress, a smoldering butt pinched between her careworn lips.

Farm fields lined either side of the highway, and our headlights skimmed over an occasional soiled upstate cow garbed in distressed, low-quality leather.

For our midnight foray I chose to wear flannel pajamas, pink flannel, under my junior-size, stroller-length chinchilla coat. The feeling was glamorous, like posing as a Miss Hooky von Hooker, with my bare feet in bedroom slippers made of pink fuzz sewn to look like floppy-eared bunnies with black button eyes. My nana hadn't given my snazzy ensemble a second glance. Her attention had a ten-mile head start and was waiting impatiently at the emergency room for the rest of her to catch up.

Our route skirted one side of the infamous freeway traffic isle, and as we passed I saw police cars nosed up close to the cinder-block bathrooms, all their spotlights aligned to bathe the squat, ugly building like a stage. The uniformed officers who stood in that glare looked like actors drinking coffee out of paper cups and underplaying the drama of their scene. Papadaddy's pickup truck with its cracked windshield and patched taillight still sat in the parking lot, but now it was roped off with sawhorses and twisting swags of police tape. People stood outside those barricades and stared at the truck like it was the Mona Lisa.

As we drove past I pretended not to look. My feet didn't reach the car's floor. I bounced my pink bunny slippers and tried to resolve the toilet wiener flasher with the Papadaddy who'd taught me how to paint a birdhouse yellow. My memory tried to keep the poopie finger a poopie finger, but keeping a lie alive in my head was wearing me out. It's exhausting, the energy it takes to unknow a truth. It didn't help that this was two in the morning.

That holiday in tedious upstate, everyone kept a secret: I'd killed someone. My papadaddy was a restroom lurker.

My nana had cancer the size of a cherry, a lemon, a grape-fruit, growing inside her like a garden, but I didn't know that as yet.

Just in case the police found a witness, I planned not to look like myself for a while. That's one reason I got truly obese: camouflage. Becoming a fatso turned out to be a very clever disguise.

Otherwise it was only my nana and me and drunk drivers on the late-night highway. She motored past the traffic island without a glance. A cigarette puff later, after a couple hacking coughs, she asked, "How are you liking the book?"

I choked back the memory of a squashed, dead wiener outlined in people blood between two pages. That *Beagle* book, squirted full of some juice I told myself wasn't sperm. "It's fine," I said. "That book is a literary tour de force." God only knew what she was rambling on about. I reached to turn on the radio, and my nana slapped my hand away from the knob. Just that tiny smack reminded my stomach of the Darwin tome thwacking that wrinkled menacing . . . whatever.

Now I'd never know how evolution ends.

The way my nana talked, with her lips clamped onto the brown part of a cigarette, the white paper burning part bobbed in front of her face like a blind man's cane. Red-tipped, even. She was feeling her way along, asking, "Have you got to where the collie dog helps stick up a bank?"

Of course, she meant that *The Call of the Wild* book. The saga of some animal implanted with radioactive chimpanzee embryos from the Crab Nebula. If I'd chosen that Jack London book we'd all still be alive. Even with my eyes shut

I'd picked the wrong option. I told her, "Bank robbery?" I said, "I loved that chapter."

Nana Minnie's chin tilted up a little, lifting her eyes off the road a smidge. She stared in the rearview mirror, watching the bright toilet crime scene shrinking from a real place, smaller and smaller, until it was just another night star. She said, "How about the part where the dog sees the crazy person murder the old fella in cold blood?" She asked, "Have you got that far?"

Our headlights zoomed ahead, skimming over a stretch of upstate highway, and I watched the steady horizon without giving her any answer. Instead, I imagined peaches, apricots, cherries, tomatoes, beans, even watermelon pickles preserved in clear glass bottles. Sapphire pink and ruby red and emerald green juices. A treasury of food, this bounty steeped in too much sugar or too much salt, to keep bacteria from setting up shop. My Nana Minnie had blanched, boiled, and canned a long future of meals for her and Papadaddy, and now it was only her. The best way to support her would be to help her eat. Maybe between the pair of us we could justify all those years of peeling and coring.

My nana asked, "You know, I always felt sorry for that collie dog." She said, "If that dog could've just told the truth, you know, folks would've still loved it."

Whatever she was talking about, it was no book I'd been reading. Instead of answering her with more lies I sagged my head to one side on a limp neck. My hands snuggled in my chinchilla pockets. My eyes drifted shut and I made a fast snore like I was asleep, only it sounded more like I was just reading the word *snore* off a thousand cue cards.

Nana Minnie said, "Everybody knew that collie dog was just defending herself," but then she had to take a break from talking in order to catch up on her coughing. For my part, the car was jam-packed with everything I didn't want to say. If my nana was going to be hurt, I wouldn't be the person to do it.

I couldn't spit out my secret any easier than she could cough up her tumor.

At the hospital she pretended to wake me, and I pretended to be groggy, mostly blinking my eyes and acting out yawns. One unintended outcome was that we'd no doubt have to hold a funeral, and my parents would have to come. They'd have to collect me and take me away with them, and that rescue seemed almost worth killing someone for. We walked, me and my nana holding hands, up a hospital sidewalk and into bright light behind sliding glass doors. The linoleum floor was waxed so shiny it seemed as bright as the fluorescent ceiling, and the waiting room seemed sandwiched between these two forms of light. There, she left me to sit with the magazines, in a hard-plastic chair that would've been avocado-chic in Oslo but in upstate read as just plain shabby. Among the magazines were three old issues of *Cat Fancy* with me cuddling my kitten, Tigerstripe, on the cover. Poor Tigerstripe. Beginning with *People, Vogue,* and *Time,* I began to leaf through every copy in search of scenes from my other life. My real life.

Suddenly, I worried my papadaddy might be alive in a bed nearby, tubed to a saggy, hanging-down bag of second-hand blood, laughing and eating Jell-O as he told the nursing staff how his roly-poly, spoiled-rotten grandbaby had tried to hack off his wiener when all he'd been doing was playing her a practical joke. Then I heard a police officer walk past saying the words "hate crime" to a doctor, and I guessed I was in the clear.

Within my earshot the officer said how my grandpa's wallet, watch, and wedding ring were missing, and I fumed that someone would rob an old man lying dead on a toilet floor. It's true I'd killed him. That goes without saying. But I was his Baby Bean Sprout. That made it different. From their talk it was clear the police didn't have anything right. It irked me to let their theories stay so totally wrong, but there was no pressing reason my nana had to be a widow *and* know she'd outlived a sex pervert.

No one said anything about finding my dropped euros and rubles soaked in blood, or about finding my busted eyeglasses or the dagger of shattered glass from the tea jar. The policeman said, "Insane thrill killer."

The doctor said, "Ritual mutilation." Suggesting space aliens, I hoped.

The policeman let slip with, "Satanic cult."

All along I thought they were bad-mouthing my Papa-daddy Ben, but then I realized they meant me. At best they were referring to some crazed, at-large killer, but that was still me, sitting here in my bunny slippers and fur coat. Just by being a dead body with no wallet or blood, his wiener half torn off, that made my grandpa the innocent injured party. It didn't seem fair. Yes, it hurt to have authority figures call me a "sadistic bastard," but if I tried to defend myself I'd wind up in the electric chair, and that wasn't going to improve the situation for my nana. Or help my already unruly, flyaway hair.

A New Book and a New Beau

Posted by Madisonspencer@aftrlife.hell

entle Tweeter,

It was at papadaddy's funeral that I noticed my nana started to cough in a new, more intrusive way. Among infants, one might cry, but another will cough to attract loving attention. Other babies will drink vodka and gobble down illicit drugs. Other babies will date abusive men. Or overeat. Even negative attention beats ending up some Baltic orphan ignored in a crib, warehoused in a forgotten ward filled with castoff urchins. Coughing through Papadaddy Ben's funeral, coughing and hacking at the graveside, this was my nana's bid for sympathy. I never dreamed she'd escalate her emotional neediness all the way to cancer.

Despite my pleadings, my parents didn't come upstate for the memorial service. They contracted for a video crew with a satellite truck that narrowcast the event in real time to their home in Tenerife. The paparazzi, however, flocked to attend. The *New York Post* ran the headline "Dad of Star Found Dead in Toilet Torture."

In lieu of flowers or sympathy cards, my mother sent my nana and me lavish gift baskets of Xanax.

Each time the telephone rang I expected the police to call me in for death by lethal injection. For the funeral, I wore a black Gucci veil over black Foster Grants. I wore a stroller-length vintage Blackglama junior mink and black gloves, just in case some crafty sleuth would attempt to acquire my fingerprints from the communion rail. To answer CanuckAIDSemily, little Emily, the actual church was a rustic clapboard structure where a dead body did not seem out of place, juxtaposed as it was with paper plates of peanut-butter cookies. The congregants seemed genuinely distressed by Papadaddy's tragic demise, and they displayed their aboriginal upstate empathy by presenting me with a gift: a book. Unlike the *Beagle* book or the *Call of the Wild* book, this tome was freshly printed, a new title, bound in handsome almost-leather. It seemed to be this summer's beach read, for everyone present also carried a copy. Here was the moment's mega–best seller, the *Angela's Ashes* or *Da Vinci Code* du jour. A quick perusal suggested a postmodern work told from multiple viewpoints—very Kurosawa in structure—plot-driven, a sword-and-sandal epic filled with magic and dragons, sex and violence. I accepted it, their rustic offering of condolence, as graciously as my mother would an Oscar.

Printed in gold leaf along the spine was the title: *The Bible.*

As fanciful as anything penned by Tolkien or Anne Rice, this new tome presented an elaborate yarn about creation. In my heart, it would easily displace the *Beagle* book, with Mr. Darwin's somewhat didactic nineteenth-century flavor. His saga depicted existence as a one-shot endeavor, a desperate struggle to endure and procreate. It's no comfort when confronted by death to be assured that you're merely some flawed variation of life reaching the end of its evolutionary blind alley. Whereas the *Beagle* book depicted a narrative of death after death, endless adaptation and failure—all history literally glued together with sperm and blood—the Bible book promised a happy life everlasting.

Survival of the fittest versus survival of the *nicest*.

Which author, Gentle Tweeter, would you choose to read at bedtime?

This homespun church even held a weekly book club to discuss their newest literary sensation. To present the book, these simple upstate denizens coaxed forward a young boy child. As I was leaving the church with my nana, this darling towhead stumbled forth from their patchwork ranks. In both hands before him he carried this Bible book, and to my world-weary, eleven-year-old eyes he appeared an earnest sort, clad in his freshly laundered rags, a minor player destined to milk cows and sire similar agrarian laborers and ultimately die in not-undeserved obscurity, the probable victim of some future combine mishap. He, a rural David Copperfield, and I, a glamorous globetrotting fashion plate, we appeared to both be the same tender age. Some brutish farmwife pushed him toward me with her calloused hand, saying, "Give it to the poor girly, Festus."

That was his name, Festus. He placed the book in my black-gloved palms.

While I was not immediately smitten, Festus did pique my romantic curiosity. A spark, most likely statically electric in nature, jumped between his person and mine, so strong that I felt the tiny shock through my elegant handwear. I accepted his gift with a simple nod and a murmur of gratitude. Feigning emotional distress, I pretended to collapse against him, and his sturdy farm urchin's arms caught my fall. In our clinch, Festus's prepubescent hands seized me bodily; only the Bible book lay between the full contact of our sensitive groin areas.

Festus, holding me an instant, whispered, "The Good Book will sustain you, Miss Madison."

And, yes, Gentle Tweeter, Festus was an uncouth primitive, fragrant with the poultry manure lodged beneath his fingernails, but he did use the word *sustain*.

Ye gods. I was thrilled. *"Au revoir,"* I breathlessly bade my hardy swain. "Until we meet in . . ." I covertly checked the book's title. ". . . in 'Bible' study."

His ardent child's lips whispered, "Fierce wristwatch . . ."

And from that moment forward I was putty in the young farm laborer's hands. My fertile mind immediately began to spin romantic scenarios set in his world of subsistence agriculture. Together, we would scratch our daily bread from the hardscrabble upstate landscape, and our love would be the unvarnished stuff of a Robert Frost poem.

For comfort after the funeral, Nana Minnie had baked apple tarts and Bundt cake with lemon drizzle and apricot flan. Spiced crumb cake, maple bars, cherry grunt, peach cobbler, pear Betty, raisin slump, coconut crisp, walnut pandowdy, cinnamon buckle, plum trifle, and hazelnut fool. She built pyramids of pecan sandies on plates. Platters of gingersnaps and shortbreads. Busy frosting cupcakes and glazing doughnuts, she wasn't much more of a widow than she'd been before. You never know the complicated deals two people negotiate in order to stay married beyond the first ten minutes. It could be she knew about Papadaddy's traffic island antics. For my part I found the Jack London book on the parlor shelf and carried it back to my bedroom with a plate of cupcakes and read it, waiting for the chimpanzee embryos. By the middle of the novel I decided that what two people don't say to each other forges a stronger bond than honesty.

Nana's strawberry cupcakes were bribing me not to tell the truth. It might be the cupcakes were punishment for my lies. On my nana's farm you could see only as far away as the next tree. That made it hard to think of the future. Any future.

Not the day of my papadaddy's funeral, not the day after, not even the day after *that*, but a week after the funeral I was still eating. My Nana Minnie broke eggs, poured milk from a paper carton, knifed a yellow square of butter off a plate she took from the refrigerator. She sprinkled flour. Coughed. Spooned sugar. Coughed. Showing me all of the terrible things that go into making food: vegetable oil, yeast, vanilla extract, she dialed the oven temperature and ladled foamy batter into muffin tins, coughing the words, "When your mama was your age she was always bringing home head lice. . . ."

Nana Minnie told her life backward while she cooked, reciting details like ingredients. Like how my mother used to wet her bed. How one time my mom ate cat poop and Nana pulled a tapeworm as long as a spaghetti out of her bottom. Even that image didn't stop my eating.

She went on—at length—about how my mother had bought a lottery ticket and won the fortune that was to be her grubstake as an aspiring movie actor.

At night, the *Beagle* book stuffed between my mattress and box spring made sleep impossible. I'd lie awake with the book's lump lodged in my spine, certain the local district attorney would knock at my bedroom door to serve a search warrant. The investigators would grill me under a bare lightbulb, insisting they'd found several words printed in reverse on my papadaddy's dead wiener, printed backward in mirror writing. It was obvious those words had rubbed off or been transferred from the murder weapon. Those words were the fingerprints they needed to convict a suspect. The reverse words included *Wollaston, wigwam, guanaco, Goeree, Fuegians, scurvy,* and, most damning of all, *Beagle.* A team of police goons would toss the bedroom and discover the stashed book.

In the rare event I drifted off, my dead Papadaddy Ben would roll a hot-dog vendor's pushcart into the room and serve me boiled kielbasas smothered in sauerkraut and blood. Or a plate of steaming cat poop tapeworms smothered in marinara sauce.

As bad as any nightmare, one day my nana was sorting dirty laundry and came into the kitchen carrying something blue. I was seated at the kitchen table eating a cheesecake. Not a *slice* of cheesecake—I was paddling with a fork, halfway across an ocean of cheesecake, not tasting a bite, I was cramming it down so fast. Open on the kitchen table was the Bible book. I stopped reading and chewing, midswallow, when I saw my blue chambray shirt wadded in her hands, and I worked hard not to gag.

Not that I actually chewed my food. The way I ate, it was more like the reverse of vomiting.

Poised in my face, as close as the next hovering forkful of cheesecake, were the mysterious dried sputum spatters.

Her face bland and guileless, my nana asked, "Raindrop?" She coughed the words, "Can you remember what's this mess so I know how to pretreat it?"

First, I wasn't sure I actually knew. Second, I was sure she wouldn't want to know. Edging my tasty cheesecake away from the moldy, yellowing blotches, I said, "Dijon mustard."

To my horror, Nana lifted the crumpled fabric near her face, peering close. She scratched at a crusted patch with her fingernail, saying, "It don't smell nothing like mustard. . . ." The scratched spot sprinkled down specks like powdered dust. Specks landed on my fork. On my unfinished pan of cheesecake. Nana Minnie brought the besmirched shirt closer to her face and reached toward it with the tentative point of her tongue.

"It's not mustard!" I shouted. My fork clattered to the kitchen floor. I stood so quickly my chrome chair teetered and fell over behind me. The crash brought my nana's full attention to my face. I said, calmly now, "It's not mustard."

She stared, her tongue pulled safely back inside her mouth.

"It's sneeze," I said.

She asked, "Sneeze?"

I'd needed to cover a sneeze, I explained. No tissues were at hand, so I'd been forced to use my shirt.

My nana's shocked, round eyes surveyed the sizable Galápagos archipelago of stiff deposits. "This is all your boogers?" she asked, as if I were the person about to die of some gruesome cigarette-induced chest condition.

I shrugged. I'd stopped caring. As long as I didn't hurt her, I would let her think I was a dirty, disgusting animal. I was eleven years old and bloating like a blue-ribbon sow.

As if on cue she coughed, and coughed and kept on coughing, embarrassed and hiding her red face behind the knot of blue shirt still in her hands. Coughs that rattled like Papadaddy Ben hawking the tobacco spit from far down in his throat. The veins stood out in her neck like Darwin's maps of major river systems. These were coughs so bad she couldn't stop even when we both saw the bright red she was coughing all over the already-there dried sputum stains.

Between wiener juice and lung blood, I'd say that chambray shirt was a goner.

What I learned is, it's never too late to save anybody. And it's always too late. And what are the chances you'll make any difference? And instead of declaring to my nana that her grandbaby was a liar and that her husband was an inverted sexual pervert and that her own movie-star daughter didn't like her very much, instead I told her she made the best peanut-butter cheesecake in the whole wide world. And I held my empty plate up to her and begged for yet another helping.

My Countdown to Good-bye

Posted by Madisonspencer@aftrlife.hell

entle Tweeter,

Late at night, in my upstate bed, I once again became the naturalist. Settling into sleep I sucked a sugary sweetness from under my fingernails, and stared up into the darkness where I knew the ceiling to be. And I listened. I listened and counted. I could always tell where my nana was— the kitchen, the parlor, her bedroom—by the sound of her coughing, like the regular call of a bird, but a sound both reassuring and terrible. That coughing. Those coughs. Simultaneously, they served as proof she was still alive, but that she wouldn't be forever. Nights I learned to cling to the sound of each cough, each volley of hacking and wheezing, and to find comfort in the noise. Despite the hard lump of the *Beagle* book stabbing me in the back, I could eventually fall asleep with the Bible book open against my heart.

The same way people will count the seconds between lightning and thunder, I counted the seconds between coughs. One-alligator, two-alligator, three-alligator. Hoping the longer I could count the better Nana Minnie might feel. Hoping at least she'd fall asleep. If I could get to nine-alligator I'd tell myself that all she suffered was a chest cold. Maybe bronchitis, but something curable. By twenty-alligator I'd be dozing, seeing my dead, half-naked nightmare Papadaddy Ben claw at my blankets with bloody hands. But finally the coughs would come back, the choking and gasping for breath, so rapid I couldn't squeeze even one alligator between them.

In bed, I sucked my fingers clean. My nana and I had been making popcorn balls all day, and the smell of popped corn filled the house. Did I say how the next day was Halloween? Well, this was the night before Halloween, and we'd been cooking popcorn balls to distribute to trick-or-treaters. Like offshore sweatshop laborers, we'd combined the popcorn with corn syrup and drops of orange food coloring, then shaped the corn in our buttered hands to make knobby miniature pumpkins. We'd pressed triangles of candy corn to make them orange-colored Jack-o'-lanterns with pointed eyes and vampire teeth. As packaging, we'd wrapped them in waxed paper.

And did I mention that I'd secretly laced all of our Halloween treats with my ample, unused supply of funeral Xanax? *Well, waste not . . .* I'd reasoned.

A cough came from my nana's bedroom, and I counted: *One-alligator . . . two-alligator . . .* , but another cough came too fast. With the detachment of a Darwin I began to categorize the coughs by their qualities. Some rasped. Others gurgled wetly. A third type amounted to only a species of breathless hiss. It might've been the first cough of a baby learning to breathe, or the last failed breath of someone dying.

Listening closely, lying in bed, my fingertips tasted like buttered pancakes smothered in syrup. When the last cough came, I counted: *One-Mississippi . . . two-Mississippi . . . three-Mississippi . . .* until a new cough sent me all the way back to counting from zero.

My parents didn't celebrate Christmas or Passover or Easter, but how they celebrated Halloween was compensation for a million ignored holidays. To my mom it was all about the costumes and adopting alternative archetypal personas, blah, blah, blah. My dad was even more boring on the subject, waxing on about the inversion of power hierarchies and subjugated children recast as outlaws in order to demand tribute from the prevailing hegemony of adults. They'd dress me as Simone de Beauvoir and parade me around the Ritz in Paris to beg for gender parity in the workplace and snack-size Hershey bars, but really to demonstrate their own political acumen. One year they dressed me as Martin Luther, and everyone I met asked whether I was supposed to be Bella Abzug. Grown-ups, fie!

In my upstate bed no coughs came for so long I'd counted up to sixteen-alligator, and I crossed two sticky fingers under the covers, hoping for luck. I considered, briefly, dressing as Charles Darwin this year, but didn't want to have to explain myself on every hillbilly front porch in this tedious missing-link neighborhood.

I hit twenty-nine-alligator. I got to thirty-four-alligator.

The bedroom door swung open, soundlessly, and a withered hand reached toward me from the shadows in the hallway. A figure began to crawl into the room, desiccated and skeletal, its face a leering skull stained with tobacco juice. Instead of ghostly chains it dragged a silver belt buckle. One bony hand stretched forward, offering a long, dried dog boo-boo nestled in a hot-dog bun. The poo-poo log was garnished with a golden squiggle of Dijon mustard. This same monster I saw every night, or some version of it, and it came as good news lately, because it meant I'd finally fallen asleep. No more counting. I was having a nightmare, but I was asleep. It meant my nana had fallen asleep.

The bed that had once been my mother's bed felt deep and soft. My nana had changed the sheets today, and these smelled airy and fresh from a sunny afternoon on the clothesline. Nothing hurt.

The cadaver of my Papadaddy Ben swam across the floor, its gabardine pants wadded around its anklebones. The grinning skull hissed, "Ye murderer!" And as it crept closer, the corpse left a trail of blood smeared on the floor behind it.

Nothing hurt.

As fast as a cough, the thought hit me: the *Beagle* book. I couldn't feel it. The painful lump of it. The grinning monster of my dead papadaddy disappeared, and I was awake. Scrambling from under the blankets I found no blood on the floor. The door was shut. I plunged both arms under the mattress, all the way to my shoulders, and felt around. I found no book. I crawled along the bedside, feeling everywhere between the mattress and box spring, still no book. A nightmare beyond my worst nightmare. I knelt beside the bed and prayed to still be asleep and only dreaming. Not that I believed in God back then, but I'd seen my mom play a pious nun in a film one time, and her character had spent half her screen time on her knees muttering demands into clasped hands.

When pretending to pray didn't work, I tiptoed out of my room, down the hallway, to the bookshelf in the parlor. In the dim light I finger-walked from spine to spine, and here it was: *The Voyage of the Beagle*. It was making the other books stand tight again, stuck back in the place where

I'd first found it, looking the same as if nothing had ever happened. As if every gory detail of the past weeks had taken place in a dream. Maybe that's why I couldn't pull it from the shelf, because I didn't want to open it and find the bloody wiener-shaped reality. Because I didn't want to think my nana had possibly found that same secret truth.

I stood in the dark parlor until the world turned to Halloween at midnight, counting, *Seven hundred eight–alligator, seven hundred nine–Missisippi . . .* , my hand hovering between me and the book so long my shoulder ached. My hand extended like my papadaddy's rotting hand had been extended. My fingers dyed orange from food coloring; the orange looked dark red in the shadows.

I counted that way, not touching the truth until something broke the spell. My nana coughed. The comforting, terrible sound came from her bedroom, the proof of life and death, coughs overlapping coughs, so fast I stopped counting. I left the book and went back to bed.

Halloween
Posted by Madisonspencer@aftrlife.hell

entle Tweeter,

The only thing that makes autumn a tragedy is our expectation that summer ought to last forever. Summer is summer. Autumn is autumn. Neither do grandmothers last an eternity. On Halloween my Nana Minnie had laid open my suitcases on the bed in my room, and she spent the day packing. The next day, November, a car would collect me for the drive to Boston, for the jet to New York, for the jet to Cairo, for the jet to Tokyo, for the rest of my life. While packing my clothes, it occurred to me that I lived a perpetual journey home, from Mazatlán to Madrid to Miami, but I never arrived.

While she ironed and folded underwear, my nana recited, "When your mama was your age, she used to pick her nose and wipe it under the chairs." Reciting, "She bit her own toenails." Reciting, "Your mama wrote in books. . . ."

That summer in tedious upstate had been the longest stretch of time I'd lingered in one place. In a way I'd gone back in time, had lived my mother's childhood. I could see why my mom had rushed off in such a frantic hurry, out to the world, to meet everyone and proceed to do everything wrong.

I hovered around my half-filled luggage and asked, "She wrote in *what*?"

As my nana plucked my freshly laundered items from the clothesline, she repeated, "Your mama used to write in books."

The Pencil and the Blue Pen. The ferns and thyme and rose petals.

I did not, Gentle Tweeter, inquire about the ultimate fate of my ejaculate-spoiled chambray shirt.

Patterson says to start collecting flowers. . . .

Leonard wants me to pick some flowers. . . .

These had all been my mother's and my nana's thoughts when they had been my age. I studied my nana as intently as I'd study my own reflection in a mirror. For there was my nose, my future nose. Hers were my thighs. How her shoulders stooped forward when she walked was how I'd someday walk. Even her cough, ragged and constant, would likely be part of my inheritance. The liver spots on her hands I'd someday find on my own. It looked like such an impossible task: growing old. It scared me how I'd ever manage to achieve all those wrinkles.

My nana never asked about her missing tea jar. She didn't seem to notice me always wearing my second-best eyeglasses. And in turn I went from not eating anything to scarfing down everything. In Toulouse, cooks say the first crepe is always *"pour le chat."* For the cat. The first crepe is always flawed, scorched, or torn, so they let the cat eat it. Somehow I decided that I could do the same with my nana's flaws. The more she cooked and baked, the more I ate. I could absolve her sins by eating them. And, if not forgive them, I could carry them around my hips as my own burden.

160

With every bite I swallowed my fear and grew older. And fatter. In every mouthful I choked down my bilious guilt.

The *Beagle* book had taught me about turtle eggs, but the Bible book taught me about Jesus Christ, and Jesus seemed like the greatest ally I could ever gain in the battle against my do-gooder parents. What a summer this had been. I'd gotten plump . . . chunky . . . just awful, in fact. And I'd begun to love reading. And I'd killed a man. I'd killed my grandfather. And I'd learned discretion.

Yes, I might've been eleven years old and a secret grandpa killer, an upstate-hating, passive-aggressive snob, but I learned what *discretion* meant. That summer I learned discretion and reserve and patience: qualities my former-hippie, former-punk, former-everything parents would never acquire.

On Halloween day, I didn't speak up when I spied my nana sneaking on tiptoe. I was pretending to take a nap on the parlor sofa when she crept to the bookshelf, and from the wall of books she untucked one I'd never noticed. Hiding the book in the folds of her apron, Nana Minnie carried it back to where she was packing my luggage.

Exhibiting enormous willpower, I did not eat the basket of orange-colored popcorn balls we'd prepared for the night's trick-or-treaters.

When she wasn't looking, I peeked into that same suitcase. Buried under my neatly folded sweaters in the bottom was the book. *Persuasion* by Jane Austen. A book I would cherish for the remainder of my own short life.

As the sun set on my last day in tedious upstate, a trickle of monsters staggered out of the dusk. Skeletons emerged.

Ghosts appeared. They came carrying pillowcases and paper shopping bags. They took form from out of the shadows, their not-clean faces smudged with graveyard dirt, and their clothes shredded. Their hands smeared with blood, these zombies and werewolves stumbled toward where my nana and I stood in the farmhouse's front doorway.

These lurching, swaying corpses, they shouted, "Trick or treat!" And my nana offered them popcorn pumpkins from a big wicker basket she held in front of her in both hands. Then a cough came, and not even two alligators later, another cough. She handed the basket to me and lifted her apron to cover her face. As the monsters picked through the orange balls, she stepped back into the parlor and settled on the sofa, gasping to catch her breath. In my arms the basket felt lighter and lighter.

Among that first wave of ghouls was a towheaded angel, a boy child whose placid face looked as smooth as fresh-baked bread. A lightly freckled brioche. His wispy halo of blond hair shone as pale yellow as butter melting down his forehead. False wings were tied to his back with a hank of rough twine, but their whitewashed cardboard was layered quite meticulously with the castoff quills of some indigenous farmyard goose. His cherubim hands carried a rude three-string lyre, and this he strummed as he bade, "Trick or treat, Miss Madison." He held a pillowcase already bulging with red licorice and gummy bears. "Has the Good Book helped you in your time of loss?"

Standing before me on the porch was the ragged youth I'd met at Papadaddy's funeral. My upstate version of David Copperfield. As before, I sensed my flesh calling to his. On that, my final night in my nana's house, I yearned to cleave my eleven-year-old self unto him, but subverted the carnal impulse by offering, "Popcorn ball?" As added enticement I whispered, "They're loaded with Xanax." He looked confused, so I added, "It's a drug, not an Old Testament king." Gravely said I, "Do not operate farm machinery while under the influence of this popcorn ball."

My rustic beau helped himself to several. Taking great lusty bites of sweet Xanax, he lingered a moment to ask about my summer. We discussed the Bible book. Finally, he bade me good night and took his leave.

To answer CanuckAIDSemily, no, I did not get his e-mail address; I rather doubt he'd have one. But while his feathered wings were retreating, dwindling in size as he departed down the dusty country thoroughfare, I called out, "It's Festus, right? Your name is Festus?"

Without turning back, he waved his harp above his head in a lighthearted salute. And with that gesture of farewell he was gone.

Coughing out the words, my Nana Minnie said, "Don't fret, Tiny Sweet." From the sofa she coughed, "Everything is going to be all right."

And I forgave her for telling her biggest untruth to date.

I stood alone on the porch in the gloaming dusk. That's why my nana didn't see someone new arrive: a scarecrow figure. Stopping at the foot of the porch steps was a gaunt old man. His cheekbones and chin were as craggy as the sculptures people carved with chain saws and sold in weedy vacant lots next to upstate gas stations. My worst nightmare made real, here was Papadaddy Ben standing at the ragged edge of the porch light. His eyes stared from behind the mess of his gray hair. Even as harpies and witches swarmed around him and climbed the steps, his eyes held mine.

The naturalist in me knew this was impossible. The dead didn't come back. It happens, on rare occasion, that natural phenomena occur for which we've no ready explanation. The role of the naturalist is to take note and to record a description of said occurrence, trusting that eventually that rogue event will make sense. I mention this because the oddest thing happened next. . . .

A smirking voice asked, "Popcorn balls?"

The question broke my trance. Standing at my elbow was a teenage boy dressed as an ancient Egyptian something. Nodding his head at the basket, he asked, "Not *popcorn balls* again. What's up with this place?"

A Marie Antoinette of the ancien régime, gowned and bewigged, ascended the steps, demanding, "Yeah, what's the deal with popcorn balls?" She was wearing fake Manolo Blahniks and carried a fake Coach bag.

Also in the Egyptian's company were a Roman legionnaire . . . and a Sid Vicious punk with a safety pin poked through one cheek. . . . The four of them smelled faintly of sulfur and smoke. The punk's hair was dyed electric blue and shaped into a Mohawk. He dipped his black-painted fingernails into the basket and lifted out a popcorn pumpkin, asking, "You have anything better, Maddy?"

Screening my mouth with the side of my hand, I whispered, "They're loaded with Xanax."

These people were strangers to me, but something about them seemed familiar. But not *known*. They were more like *inevitable*.

The Roman legionnaire winced at the sight of the orange balls and asked, "Do you know what these are worth in Hell?" He made a fist and knocked at his forehead, saying, "Hello? Earth to Madison Spencer . . . these are worth jack shit!"

Indignant, I asked the group, "Do I know you?"

"No," the girl said. She was wearing blue eye shadow, and her white nail polish was chipped. Crassly oversize dazzle-cut cubic zirconia hung from her earlobes. The girl said, "You don't know us, but you will soon enough. I've seen your file." Her eyes fixed on my wristwatch, the girl asked, "What's the time?"

I twisted my arm enough to show her it was after eleven o'clock. My nana's coughs came between every sentence, between every word. And when I looked again for the scarecrow Papadaddy, he was gone. Vanished. None of the four teenagers took popcorn pumpkins. As they turned their backs on me and started down the porch steps, I asked, "Aren't you a little old for this?"

The coughing stopped.

Without turning back, the Egyptian shouted, "Only by about two thousand years."

Shaking his fist in the air, his index finger pointing skyward, the punk rocker shouted, "Remember, Maddy, Earth is Earth. Dead is dead." Walking into the night, he shouted, "It won't help the situation for you to get all upset." And as they receded into the dark, I thought I saw another figure join them. This new person wore a calico apron wrapped around a gingham Mother Hubbard. The lady smoked a cigarette without coughing. The punk touched her elbow and she extracted a pack from her apron pocket and shook him out a butt. As she smacked her lighter against the palm of her hand and flicked it, the tiny flame showed her careworn face. She waved back at me, and the group of them disappeared down the road and into the Halloween night.

Eventually, when I stepped back inside the parlor door, only my nana's body was left on the sofa. The best of her—her laugh, her stories, even her coughing—was gone.

The Abomination Gains Strength

Posted by Hadesbrainiacleonard@aftrlife.hell

t was from Solon that great Plato learned of the eventual end times. In turn Plato taught the Doomsday mythos to his student Xenocrates, who taught it to his student Crantor, who taught it to Proclus, and thus was the advent of the thing-baby prophesied before synthetic polymers ever existed.

Minute traces of human saliva still cling to it, our inflated idol. Wearing a war paint of chocolate and lipstick muck, it rallies its forces of polystyrene and polypropylene in the waters of Los Angeles Harbor. As foreseen by the visions of the ancients, reinforcements will arrive steadily from the north, from the Yukon River and Prince William Sound.

And what had been a trickle of Styrofoam packing peanuts, adrift in the tributaries of Puget Sound, the Skagit and Nooksack rivers, these are present to welcome the thing-baby to the Pacific Ocean. More constant and numerous than the salmon and steelhead, these plastic emissaries will converge off the temperate coast of Long Beach to await the birth of the thing-baby. Far exceeding the birds of any flock or the fish of any school, these objects are baked by the sun and degrading to become a rich soup of plastic corpuscles. These nurdles. These mermaid tears. Fluoropolymers and malamine-formaldehyde. They create a simmering broth not unlike the murk isolated within the skin of the thing-baby.

Thusly do the unresolved fragments of the past linger, according to Plato, and in that manner do they coalesce to create the future. And off the shores of Long Beach one infinitesimal speck of plastic comes into contact with the thing-baby and remains, stuck. And a second fleck of plastic cleaves itself unto the graven image until the infant idol is coated in a layer of such specks. And that first layer accumulates a second layer, and the thing-baby begins to accrete layer upon layer, and to grow. And the larger the whole of it grows, the more specks it draws, becoming a fledgling. Becoming a thing-child.

And in that manner, Plato foretold that plastic will be fed plastic. A skin accrues atop its skin. Fed an ample diet of juice boxes and disposable diapers, the ordinary grows to become an abomination.

Saint Camille: A Theory
Posted by Madisonspencer@aftrlife.hell

entle Tweeter,

CanuckAIDSemily asks, "Do ghosts sleep?" My experience as a supernaturalist attests that no, they do not. As the occupants of this aircraft doze or peruse a wide selection of films featuring Camille Spencer—my mother is inescapable—my ghost self updates my blog. I check my texts.

The longer I consider my parents' new role as global religious leaders, the less I'm surprised by this sacrilegious turn of events. For a decade I've watched my mother in filmic roles where she was China-syndromed while investigating melty overheated nuclear power stations . . . ax-handled by strike-breaking Pinkerton thugs who resented her efforts to organize the loomy weavers of a Deep South textile mill . . . poisoned Erin Brockovich–style with groundwater tainted by Republican plutocrat Christians allied with the military-industrial complex. Even at this airborne moment, the jetliner passengers surrounding me nibble peanut snacks while watching Alsatian police dogs and racist Klansmen tear the clothing from her flawless bosom.

A career of cathartic martyrdoms. Date movies. She's died a thousand deaths so the members of her audience can live happily ever after.

Yet despite the piercing arrows and savage biting wolves, she returns to us . . . ever more ravishing. The woman we watch die horribly, she reappears on the red carpet at Cannes looking divine in an Alexander McQueen ball gown. As the spokeswoman for Lancôme cosmetics she's reborn, glowing with diamonds and good health.

My point is that Camille Spencer is the closest thing our world has to a secular martyr. She is the saint of our modern era—nothing less than our Moral Compass—ritualistically sacrificed time and time again. She and my dad are the social consciousness of a generation, saving endangered species from extinction, curing pandemic plagues. No famine exists until my parents call it to our international attention and record a hit song, with all the profits going for food relief. This woman whom we've seen suffer and survive every cruel atrocity, for years she and my father have determined what's good and bad for the entire globe. No political figure holds higher moral authority; thus when Camille and Antonio Spencer renounce their nondenomi-national lifestyle and embrace a single true faith, Boorism, three billion rudderless agnostics are bound to heel to.

Thrilled as I am to have the world's attention, I wish it wasn't for an ill-considered lie. My blog followers in the underworld advise me that living conditions—living conditions?—in Hades are in rapid decline. Already my calls for more expletives, more belching, more coarseness are resulting in a steady uptick in the number of inbound souls. According to CanuckAIDSemily, these newly dead are arriving with the expectation that they'll be in Heaven. Not only are they disappointed—but they're ticked off! Everyone blames me. Everybody's going to Hell, and they're all going to hate me. Even worse, they're all going to hate my parents in every language. Perhaps my dad could handle that, but my mom's going to hate being hated. She's a skinny beautiful lady with perfect hair; she's just not equipped to deal with hate.

It breaks my heart to imagine my folks killed by Japanese harpoons or a freak bong explosion, and then getting their skin flayed by demons because I sold them a bill of goods.

Outside my little airplane window, the sun is blazing away, half sunk in a tufted mattress of clouds. There are no angels. At least, no angels that I can see.

A Birthday Offering

Posted by Madisonspencer@aftrlife.hell

entle Tweeter,

The work of a supernaturalist never ends. As my flight begins its initial decent into Calgary or Cairo or Constantinople, you find me worming my ghost self into the port provided at my seat for stereo earphones. I'm shimmying deep into the electronic innards of the airplane. Tracing wires. Bridging relays. By satellite, I'm hacking into the various servers which control the security cameras ogling my parents' far-flung abodes. Not so much to spy on them; no, I'm accessing the archived history files. By referencing the time codes I locate video footage of myself celebrating my tenth birthday, that long-ago, clothing-optional kids party where my parents hoisted a heavy piñata poured full of prescription pain medications and recreational hallucinogenics. There I am, that prepubescent me, mortified, clutching pastel-colored napkins to cover my exposed fleshy shame even as the naked adults disembowel my festive papier-mâché burro with their bare hands. These former-punk, former–New Wave, former-grunge scenesters, they squirm together on the littered floor like a mass of sweaty, drug-hungry eels.

It's for the comfort of perspective that I seek out video of the most demeaning, most humiliating events of my former life. To all you predead people, please take note.

Whenever you're feeling depressed about being dead, duly remember that being alive wasn't always a picnic. The only thing that makes the present palatable is the fact that the past was, at times, torture. For further solace I retrieve the cringe-inducing video files of my six-year-old, living-alive self Morris dancing, naked, around the base of an old-growth pine tree. I review footage of my four-year-old backside splayed to the camera as I gingerly utilize the shared bamboo toilet stick at ecology camp.

Ye gods, my childhood was atrocious.

Scanning through random video time codes, I glimpse my mother. In Tashkent or Taipei, she's telling someone over the phone, "No, Leonard, we have yet to identify the right assassin. . . ."

On a different time code, I watch my dad on the phone in Oslo or Orlando, saying, "Our last would-be executioner ran off with Camille's credit cards. . . ." Both tiny flashbacks occurred in the final few months of my life.

To savor the unhappiness of someone other than myself, I retrieve the video of my brother, Goran, on his last birthday. If you must know, Goran was my brother for about fifteen minutes. My parents adopted him from some tragic refugee-camp situation, largely as a publicity stunt. Said adoption was not, shall we say, a success. In the video they've rented Disney's EPCOT Center and populated it with the outlandish players of a dozen Cirque du Soleil productions. Members of the media outnumber the guests, making sweet, sweet public relations hay for my mom and dad. Cameras and microphones broadcast every smidgen of the magic as my folks proudly trot out their birthday gift: a pretty Shetland pony. What was Goran to make of this situation, he who'd only recently arrived from some veiled post–Iron Curtain regime? Surrounding him were crowds of capering French Canadian clowns and nymphlike Chinese ribbon dancers. Here, he was clearly the guest of honor, and his hosts were presenting him with this young, tender animal. The pony's mane and tail were braided with blue satin ribbons, its fur dusted with silver glitter. My father led the pony with the reins of a silver bridle, and a silver bow the size of a cabbage was tied around its diminutive neck.

Not that I, movie-star scion that I am, have ever seen an actual cabbage.

On the video, every eye is glazed with happiness. Or serotonin-reuptake inhibitors. Goran has been handed an ornate antique knife for the purpose of slicing and serving a mammoth birthday cake. His sinewy gulag body is decked out in Ralph Lauren togs, to fulfill the legal obligations of a commercial tie-in contract. Like an anarchist's mask, his dense hair hangs down to hide his stone-colored, disdainful eyes. The casts of a dozen Andrew Lloyd Webber productions swing into a rousing rendition of "Happy Birthday," and the horror ensues.

It was not entirely Goran's fault. In many cultures an animal so merrily presented would read as a blood sacrifice. It's the equivalent of, say, blowing out birthday candles before ritualistically butchering the cake and handing portions of it 'round to guests. In such lusty, throwback cultures fresh meat amounted to the greatest tribute. Recognizing that, we shouldn't have been so stunned to see the huge knife blade lash forward. Using the same effort that an American child would to extinguish every flaming candle with a single breath, Goran gripped the knife's handle and swung it as would a hale gladiator: to execute a hearty feast. Here, I slow the video to a frame-by-frame analysis. The prancing clowns are fixed in their manic attitudes. The silver reins are wrapped twice around my father's hand. In moaning slow motion my mother says, "Make . . . a . . . wish. . . ."

There's no blood, not at first. What follows comes in slowed strobes of tragedy. Goran wields his weapon in a wide, gleaming arc, and the tip of the blade passes cleanly through the furred throat of the startled pony. Even before it drops, before a hot fan of blood bursts from its nicked artery and bisected windpipe, exploding in every direction, the animal's eyes roll backward until only the whites show.

Like a matador's crimson cape, the curtain of equine blood sweeps over the massive birthday cake, melting the sculpted sugar flowers and dousing the tiny flames of its thirteen candles. The pony's flailing heart casts thick gobbets of blood that splash the rainbow sequins and spandex of the Cirque clowns. Even as network cameras continue to roll, hot pony gore assails the elegant Xanaxed facades of my parents' placid smiles. Even now, watching this on video, I see myself in the background as the poor little horse collapses on the lawn. The assembled multitudes shield their faces with their upraised forearms and duck their heads for protection; fainting or dodging, this vast field of onlookers appears to be bowing in humble awe. As the pony slumps to the ground, everyone falls, everyone but Goran and myself. Only my brother and I remain upright. The pair of us stand alone in the center of what looks like a battlefield, a massacre of blood-smeared victims.

This, despite the counsel of my mother and Judy Blume,

this forceful red spouting is how I'd always imagined my first menstruation would present itself. Therefore, I remain steadfast.

Judging from our calm expressions, it's clear that Goran and I have both borne witness to far worse atrocities. Me, in an upstate restroom. He, in whatever war-torn hamlet he'd originated. Neither of us is a stranger to the cold reality of death. Neither of us will be stopped by it. Despite our youth, we've been tempered by secrets and suffering that these goofy clowns—the real clowns, I mean, not our parents—could never surmise. The Shetland pony sputters the last drops of its wet life into the grass at our feet, and the ancient kingdoms of the world surround us: Europe, Asia, Africa, and the Americas, albeit crafted in quaint Disney microcosm.

Such a grisly panorama this presents. A tableau of Armageddon. Countless populations bowing, subjugated, baptized in hot blood, and at the center a freshly slaughtered beast is flanked by a young Adam and Eve, unfazed, examining one another's blood-streaked bodies with newfound curiosity and admiration. Through the blood-spattered lenses of my horn-rimmed eyewear, I recognize a kindred spirit.

I'd never really fit in the world, not easily, not like coffee fits into a cup. However, seeing Goran's cold assessment of his own mistake, I realized that I was not entirely alone. Even on low-resolution security video, my living-alive self was clearly and unmistakably in love.

Meet the Devil
Posted by Madisonspencer@aftrlife.hell

entle Tweeter,

Please take note, you predead persons: as former-cynical, former-snarky former nihilists, you've eschewed all forms of religious faith for years. Woe unto you, for it leaves you primed for a false prophet. This spiritual anorexia has left you starved, poised to gorge yourself on whatever newish theology is set before you. Witness my escort, the "psychic bounty hunter" sent to corral my ghost and wrangle me home to my parents. Walking through the arrivals level of LAX, Mr. Crescent City believes he's hugging me close, but he embraces an armful of air.

"Little dead angel," he says, loping along, "first we need to find our chauffeur. Then we need to catch the helicopter to get us to your mom's boat."

We stride past a young mother who leans over her toddler, cooing and coaxing it, "Say 'fuck,' sweetheart. Say 'fuck' so you and Mommy will never be separated, in this world or the next. . . ."

It goes without saying that I am following at a distance well outside his distasteful grasp. Even the slightest contact with Mr. Crescent City means a comingling of his earthly form and my spiritual one, a union more intimate than even the most passionate goings-on of an earthly marriage.

His touch is, well . . . imagine huffing a vast toke of vaporized depression. Or guzzling a tall glass of bitter regret.

"When I get to fucking Heaven," says Crescent, "I'm teaching kids that drugs are a detour for the rest of your fucking life."

As Crescent leads me through the crowds, LAX looks more tragic than I'd ever noticed. Among these milling hordes I see human beings so racked with hunger that they're reduced to eating triple-bacon cheeseburgers dripping with a sauce identical to the loathsome fluid which once spurted from between the pages of the *Beagle* book. I see whole families forced by global inequalities of wealth to wear prêt-à-porter Tommy Hilfiger. A glance in any direction reveals such scenes of hardship and deprivation. It's one thing to hear that such grinding poverty exists in the modern world, but it's heartrending to actually see people compelled to carry their own luggage.

An ancient crone, almost my mother's age, not an hour younger than thirty-two, walks past wearing last season's Liz Claiborne, and the pathetic sight brings a flood of ghost tears to my eyes. One has only to see the damage wrought by home hair coloring and carbohydrates to feel the same passionate empathy that spurred the progressive likes of Jane Addams.

These sullied throngs of travelers—who, unlike my parents, are not being paid to wear their clothes—they must be crazed. Either crazed or intoxicated with drugs. Because? Because everyone is grinning the same exaggerated clown's leer. They're poor and pimpled and clutching coach tickets to Sioux Falls, and still—they're smiling. They stroll along as if ambling through the Jardin du Luxembourg listening to the splash of the Medici Fountain. This is no 6th arrondissement. There's nothing but thin plastic carpet laid atop airport concrete. Inexplicably, these apparent strangers coalesce into groups. They join hands while they wait for flights, forming impromptu prayer circles in sterile gate areas. Once assembled, they close their eyes. In somber unison they chant, "Fuck. . . ." Their eyes closed, they make church faces. With their heads tilted back, they sing hymns of "Fuck . . . fag . . . nigger . . . cunt . . . kike . . . ," their words slow and deliberate as a NASA countdown.

Gentle Tweeter, how peaceful is a world where everyone gives offense but no one takes it. Within my circle of vision everyone is littering and spitting, and no one seems put off by those uncivil acts.

What's more, I shudder to say, fat people are holding hands with thin people. Mexican tongues share ice-cream cones with white tongues. Homosexuals are being nice to other homosexuals. Blacks are happily rubbing elbows with Jews. My hero, Charles Darwin, would be so ashamed of me. My meddling has so destroyed the entire natural order of living things.

"The whole fucking world loves you, little dead girl, for showing us the righteous fucking path." As Mr. Crescent City says this, we're gliding down an escalator. We've no luggage to collect. Below us, our chauffeur waits among a bevy of other uniformed chauffeurs. One snaps his fingers, drawing our focus. He holds a clipboard hand-lettered with the name *Mr. City*. Even indoors, this chauffeur wears mirrored sunglasses and a brimmed cap. No name tag. He wears old-school black riding boots with gray-wool jodhpurs. Despite the Los Angeles heat he wears a double-breasted coat, like a driver right out of Agatha Christie sent by way of the Western Costume Company circa 1935.

"This is us," says Crescent to the chauffeur, gesturing to nothing and then to himself. "We're going to the chopper."

The chauffeur turns to look his sunglasses directly at me. "Why, if it isn't the angel," he says, his breath scented like a hard-boiled egg. He drops to one knee. "Our most glorious redeemer." With one gloved hand he sweeps the cap from his head and brings it to cover his heart. A mocking tone in his voice. That familiar methane stink to his words.

For my part, I don't need to see a name tag. As he kneels before me I can see the twin tiny points of his horns buried deep in his thick blond hair. The crowd of chauffeurs surges forward to meet their respective passengers, and a jolly Falstaff wearing a blue serge uniform stumbles over the man kneeling. Both drivers sprawl. The mirrored sunglasses tumble, and I get a glimpse of yellow goat eyes. The bumbling Falstaff climbs back to his feet while our malodorous, supplicating driver scuttles on his belly to retrieve his fallen hat as it rolls away. Standing now, the Falstaff offers the fallen driver a hand up, saying, "Sorry, buddy." He laughs and says, "Can you fucking forgive me?"

Another driver stoops to rescue the sunglasses, but their lenses are shattered, already broken by the tread of a scurrying air traveler. Yet another driver catches the rolling hat and returns it to the crawling man, who yanks it firmly over his head and pulls the brim low to hide his strange eyes. He reaches up to accept the Falstaff's helping hand. Their two hands touch, like something depicted on the ceiling of the Sistine Chapel or the floor of an upstate public toilet, and the fallen man says, "I forgive no one." His voice a hiss.

His uniformed body moving against the LAX carpet like a serpent.

With his free hand the oafish assailant is already slapping dust from his accidental victim. His mitt swats the shoulders of the wool coat, brushing the sleeves. "No harm done," he says, but as the fallen man stands, the larger man sinks to his knees. Their hands unclasp. "Fuck," says the Falstaff. Drops of sweat appear along his hairline and run down as if his forehead were a corn-based biodegradable plastic cup containing an iced soy latte. His goofy smile turns to gritted teeth, and so much blood rushes to his cheeks that he looks sunburned with agony. Clawing at his chest, he topples to make the shape of a fetus on the floor, and his legs run sideways against nothing, going nowhere fast. His Falstaff mouth stretches to turn his red face inside out while his hands dig at his jacket like a dog digs, like he can't wait to rip out his own heart and show us. The brass buttons of his uniform pop and fly. His fingernails are through the skin, digging up blood, before he shudders and stiffens.

And yes, Gentle Tweeter, I may occasionally confuse dog excrement and male genitalia, but I can recognize when a man is suffering a massive heart attack on the floor at my feet. By now this is a familiar sight.

Under fluttering eyelids, the dying Falstaff looks back at the gawkers who surround his final suffering, staring down upon him with their eyes of awe and jealousy. He's hemmed in by the toothy chrome zippers of all their roller bags. This bon voyage crowd, their envy is undisguised. No one dials 911. No one steps forward to administer heroic measures. The dying man whispers, *Crap.*

Some voice among the assembled passersby shouts, "Hallelujah!"

The dying man whispers, *"Shit."*

Everyone present, including Mr. Crescent City, whispers, "Amen."

Like a chime, a small voice calls, "Bye." It's a little boy with a saddle of pink freckles across the bridge of his nose. With his whole arm extended straight out from the shoulder, he wiggles his wrist to flop his small hand. At the same time, he says, "We'll see you in Heaven!"

Following his lead, other hands wave. Slow waves. Beauty pageant waves. The crone wearing outdated Liz Claiborne blows a kiss. A choir of sphincters tootle sadly, a chorus of lamenting "Hail, Maddys." Onlookers belch in solemn respect.

The gasping man goes still. The blood stops flowing from the hole he's torn in his chest. Here's my chance to set things right, to return the Earth to its natural unhappy order. It's only when the paramedics finally arrive that I make my move.

DECEMBER 21, 10:22 A.M. PST

Returned to Life!

Posted by Madisonspencer@aftrlife.hell

entle Tweeter,

 By now I'm well accustomed to men falling dead in front of me. I'm not thrilled, not about seeing grown men wither and die at my feet, but neither am I paralyzed by the event.

To comprehend what happens next at LAX, you future-dead people need some fresh insight into the nature of your physical being. Until now you've largely conceived of your earthly body as a human-shaped utensil you use for having sex. Or for gobbling up Halloween candy. Yes, your fleshy self is the application which allows you to interface with automobile steering wheels, teams of oxen, embroidery hoops, trained dolphins, hair spray, cricket bats, rectal thermometers, hot-stone massage therapists, saltine crackers, Chanel No. 5, poison ivy, contact lenses, prostitutes, wristwatches, riptides, tapeworms, electric chairs, chili peppers, oncologists, roller coasters, tanning beds, meth, and cute hats. Without a corporeal self, all the preceding would be rendered moot. In addition your body is the canvas needed to express yourself in the world. At the very least, it's the only avenue that allows for acquiring a truly rad tattoo.

 Besides being a tool and a means of expression, the third truth is that a fleshy corpus acts as a cuddly, warm security blanket. Imagine a comforting suit of armor, i.e., you as your own teddy bear. A body is the Marc Jacobs shoulder bag that contains all the junk that constitutes you. And at this moment, an unoccupied body lies dead on the airport floor right in front of me. No, as bodies go this would not be my first choice—a largish lumpenprole chauffeur, a middle-aged male whose last meal was a take-out lunch of beef curry—but beggars can't be choosers. Dead on the LAX carpet, he wears a driver's uniform of worsted serge, and it appears that he's been killed by clasping the hand of Satan. He's rolled onto his back and frozen into a still photograph of a massive heart attack victim. His entire face, moments before, it was the color of a tongue. Now his face, his hands, all of his skin is the pale color of chrome. His desperate fingers have clawed open his coat and shirt, and his panicked fingernails have torn his chest into a vivid pizza margarita of shredded skin, red glop, and tangled black body hair. Dashed with hemoglobin red, his chrome name tag sags near his armpit. It says, HARVEY.

Dismal as he looks, it's no worse than I looked dead on the floor of a Beverly Hills hotel suite surrounded by left-over room service meals. Do not, Gentle Tweeter, imagine that you'll look any better.

I watch the spirit rise from his corpse, but not the way your eyes see smoke or mist. It's more the way your nose sees a smell. It's the inside way your whole head feels a headache. The way blood has poured from his chest, pooling on the floor, his soul drains upward in a flood of blue as thick as liquid, collecting in the air against the ceiling. At first the blue forms a lump, a clump, a cloud, but that quickly takes the shape of a textbook embryo, then a fetus. It hangs there. The blue is the blue your tongue sees when you eat whipped cream. Not an instant passes before a full-size blue version of the man is staring down at his dead self.

He gapes at his own mortal remains, working his mouth like someone choking on a fact too large to swallow. The assembled mob of airport strangers, for their part they study his final moments as if a quiz will follow. Only I see his ghost leak away and balloon into the air. I watch, and Satan watches. One of Satan's hands, sheathed skintight in a leather driving glove, reaches toward the puzzled spirit. The bystanders, their eyes follow the gloved hand into the air, but can't see why. We all hear Satan say, "Harvey, is it? Harvey Parker Peavey?" He says, "If you'll come this way, please . . ."

The ghost's eyes find the offered hand. His ears find the question. "You're my ride to Heaven, right?"

Satan sneers. His eyes eclipsed behind the visor of his cap, he says, "Tell him, Madison."

The newbie ghost's eyes turn to find me, and he asks, "Madison Spencer? *The* Madison Spencer? Madison Desert Flower Rosa Parks Coyote Trickster Spencer?" He smiles as if he's meeting God.

"Tell him about Heaven, Maddy," taunts Satan. Everyone present, our audience of living-alive busybodies, they all follow Satan's voice in my direction, but they can't see me. My escort, Crescent, looks as well, muttering, "Little dead girl?" A team of paramedics comes crashing through the crowd.

Oh, Gentle Tweeter, the road to perdition is paved with short-term, stopgap mercies. Even as Satan's grip closes around the man's blue ghost wrist, I say, "Yes." As the Devil begins to drag his smiling victim away, I assure him, "It might take a smidgen longer than you expected, but yes, I promise, you'll get to Heaven, Harvey." Satan tows the floating bulbous blue form as if it were something in the Macy's Thanksgiving Day Parade.

Poor Harvey, even as Satan is dragging him into the distance, he's saying, "Thank you, angel child!" His blue head lolls happily on his neck as he sings my name, *Madison. Madison Spencer.* The messiah who returned from death to lead mankind to joyous salvation.

My papadaddy was right. I am cursed and despicable. I am a coward.

As the paramedics squat beside the abandoned body, I seize my opportunity. As they peel the backing from sticky electrodes and paste them on the messy fingernail-clawed torso, I step forward and kneel beside the head. I cup my girlish hands over the glassy eyes. In the posture of a snake-handling, strychnine-swilling faith healer, I gingerly touch the icky forehead skin of this dead stranger. At the same instant, one of the paramedics shouts, "Clear!"

To you future-dead people, do not attempt this at home. If you're familiar with the custom of saying, "Bless you," when someone sneezes, you might understand what's taking place. The electric shock from a defibrillator doesn't startle one's failed heart back to life so much as it opens a portal for the lingering spirit to return. Picture pulling the plug from a bathtub in the Hotel Danieli, and the way the accumulated Venetian bathwater spirals into the drain. The momentary charge from a defibrillator opens such a route and allows the departed's spirit to reenter.

In the event the soul has taken permanent leave—as Harvey's clearly has—any spirit making contact may take up residence. Thus, when I open my eyes my perspective is that of someone sprawled on the not-clean carpet of LAX, corralled by the bovine gaze of curious passersby, hemmed in by the steady drone of tiny wheels as roller bags eddy in a stream past my sweat-chilled face. I reside within the damaged body of a stranger, the taste of curry still in my strange new mouth, but I am alive.

Ye gods, Gentle Tweeter, I had forgotten how awful it feels to be alive. Even when a living-alive person is in good health, there's the torment of dry skin, ill-fitting shoes, scratchy throats. As a child on the cusp of puberty, I have not been much troubled by what an adult body entails. However, from this instant I'm abraded by coarse under-arm hairs. I'm suffocated by my own pungent endocrine musk, so like the masculine reek of an upstate public potty. As a girl, I'd always imagined the joy of having a pee-pee: like having a best friend and confidant, only attached. The reality is that I'm no more aware of my newfound wiener than I am of my appendix. I twist my impossibly thick neck and cast my glance in every direction. A female voice asks, "Mr. Peavey, can you hear me?" It's a paramedic leaning over me, the one who administered the shock, shining a pen-light into my eyes. She says, "Mr. Peavey, may I call you Harvey? Don't try to move."

The beam of the penlight is a searing agony. My bowels roil and ache. My newly acquired chest throbs where the torn skin begins to leak fresh blood, and my ribs burn where the sticky electrodes are still plastered. My intention is merely to brush the attending paramedic aside, but the gesture, a robust sweep of my arm, knocks her over backward. Imagine being Venetian water sucked down a drain and taking the shape of some strange, new plumbing. I don't know my own strength. Nor do I fully realize my size. I'm inside a colossal fleshy robot, trying to make the arms and legs function. These arms and legs are huge. To stand upright takes a skillful feat of engineering; I overcompensate and stagger a step. Pinwheeling my arms for balance, I scatter paramedics and security guards like tenpins. I'm upright and stumbling, staggering stiff-legged. This is my nightmare: I'm a demure schoolgirl who finds herself stripped half-naked in one of the world's busiest air travel crossroads. Realizing that my breasts are exposed—also, they're hirsute and padded with muscle—I squeal and tuck my beefy elbows tight to my ribs to hide my mortified, large brown nipples. My massive hands flapping frantically around my stubbly face, I squeal and take off running. "Golly, I'm sorry," I chirp, lumbering through the horrified airport masses. "Excuse me," I shrill as my considerable spurting of man-blood dapples the recoiling gawkers.

Despite my linebacker size I gallop along like a gamine, clutching my bosoms, my shoulders shrugged up to my hairy ears. My steps splayed. Every stride crashes against wheelchairs, baby strollers, luggage carts. In my attempt to pussyfoot I barge and bulldoze my way through the stunned airport malingerers while a team of peace officers sprints after me, their walkie-talkies crackling with static and officious chatter.

I stagger after Satan and his latest hostage, crashing into

innocent travelers and trilling, "Golly, gosh, darn . . ." I try to speak in cheerful peeps, but blast out the words in a strange, blaring voice: "Sorry . . . my fault . . . sorry . . . oops . . ."

In my pants now I can feel something bobbing and jiggling. My pee-pee feels less like a faithful compadre and more like something gross falling out of my pelvic floor. Like a dangling, pendulous rupture. Like a strangulated hernia several inches long. Ye gods! It's like taking a poop from the front! How can men tolerate this vile sensation? My vision begins to frost inward from around the edges, and I can guess this is because I've lost so much blood. My heart is speeding up. My heart feels the size of a revving Porsche 950. In the near distance I can see Satan dragging his captive through an emergency exit.

My years of sexual assault prevention training come to mind, and I shout, "Rape!" My size-twenty feet clumping along, I bellow, "Help me! Rape!"

My pursuers are a dozen powerful police hands reaching to grab me from behind.

My feet stumble, my blood pressure failing, and I begin to sink to the floor.

Satan observes my humiliation, laughing as soundlessly as any character from Ayn Rand. The blue ghost tethered to him looks back in confusion.

And I shout, "Someone stop him!" I shout, "He's the Devil!" Hands grab my arms and yank them away from my chest, cruelly baring my hairy, muscular prepubescent breasts, and I shout, "Madison Spencer didn't tell you the truth! She's lying!" Woozy now, with hardly sufficient blood to blush modestly over my bared titties, my naked nipples peaking in the frigid LAX air-conditioning, I squeal, "Everyone, please, stop saying the F-word!"

The agony, Gentle Tweeter, is excruciating. Even Satan's laugh smells like methane. Especially Satan's laugh. At last, mercifully, my massive giant's heart fails once more, and all is plunged into darkness.

DECEMBER 21, 10:29 A.M. PST

A Gruesome Setback

Posted by Madisonspencer@aftrlife.hell

entle Tweeter,

The next time some sensitive, inquiring person asks you whether you believe in life after death, take my advice. That pompous question—which smarty-pants, intellectual Democrat types use to winnow the idiots from their own ilk: Do you believe in an afterlife? Do your personal beliefs include a life after death?—no matter how they phrase their snotty test, do the following. Simply look them in the eye, snort derisively, and retort, "Frankly, only a provincial ignoramus would even believe in death."

Please allow me to share an anecdote from my former life. This one time, en route to a shooting location in Nuremburg or Nagasaki or Newark, the production company sent exactly the wrong kind of car. In place of an elegant black Lincoln Town Car they sent a customized superstretch Cadillac limousine with all the interior upholstery trimmed in purple chase lights. The carpet's stench of Ozium was in direct ratio to the number of bachelorettes who'd retched up Long Island iced teas and semen in the backseats, and to make matters worse this particular car had a faulty battery or bladder or alternator or whatnot that wouldn't hold a charge. And to skip ahead, my mom and dad and I found ourselves standing on the shoulder of some Third World turnpike while a team of automotive

191

paramedics arrived in some towing company ambulance and attempted to give the limo's heart a shock using two scary-looking nipple clamps. No amount of car defibrillation could restart that odious bus; nor did my parents and I desire to reenter its lumpy interior pungent with expelled bodily fluids.

This is exactly how I feel looking down on the ungainly corpse of poor Harvey Peavey. Once more betrayed by his failed heart, he lies on the not-sanitary carpet of LAX, the bumbling chauffeur whose soul departed in tow with Satan. The paramedics shout, "Clear," and jolt him with another shock, but no way am I reentering that mess.

"Lucky him," says a voice. The blue spirit of Mr. Crescent City steps up beside me, both of us looking down on Peavey's corpse.

I ask, "Where's your body?" I glance around, but there's no overdosed rag doll slumped in any of the plastic airport chairs. A short line of three or four people is forming outside the locked door of a handicapped bathroom. Even now that I'm postalive, the thought of using a public toilet fills me with terror. To Crescent City, I say, "Those private toilets are reserved for crippled persons."

Crescent nods his shaggy head at the corpse and says, "Did you hear what he said? Right before he died he called you a liar."

In truth, I called me a liar. I was only using Peavey's mouth.

"I heard," I say.

Incredulous, Crescent says, "You can bet he's in Heaven by now."

I don't say anything.

Softly, under his breath Crescent City begins to chant, "Fuck . . . fuck . . . fuck . . ." without cessation.

That trip when we got the smelly stretch limo . . . on that same trip to some desolate shooting location in Angola or Algiers or Alaska, the cultural liaison for the flyspecked government lamented to us how shipments of surplus cheese from the United States had been waylaid by guerrilla fighters, and losing this crucial source of high-density multinutrient protein meant every village in the region was hungry. And standing there on the shoulder of that godforsaken highway, my mom got a brainstorm. Without missing a beat she snapped her manicured fingers and made a mouth-open, dazzling-idea face. Her brilliant solution was to whip out her mobile phone and make two million dinner reservations for the refugees at the Ivy or Le Cirque. She smiled at the cultural liaison and asked whether any of the starving hordes had any dietary restrictions.

Problem solved.

That, Gentle Tweeter, is not how I want to be. As this Mr. Crescent lunatic, as his ketamine ghost chants that revolting F-word, I say, "Please stop."

The blue shape of him is already dispersing. He falls silent.

"Go," I tell him. "Go collect your body. Take me to my mother. I have some truth telling to do."

The Abomination Advances

Posted by Hadesbrainiacleonard@aftrlife.hell

among the students of Plato, the mythos of the thing-baby continues. According to logographer Hellanicus of Lesbos, the plastic cups and empty prescription bottles form a motley fleet launched on a cursed mission. Alternately subjected to blazing sun and pounding rains, this garbage armada makes its arduous trek across the equatorial belly of the planet, traversing that widest stretch of the Pacific Ocean, this voyage not unlike the voyages of Darwin and Gulliver and Odysseus. And leading this campaign is the thing-child, steeped in this broth of decaying plastic. For the sun photodegrades these grocery bags and dry-cleaning bags. The action of wind and waves churns them, grinding them into smaller particles. As particles cling, its arms grow hands, and those hands sprout dangling fingers of fluttering plastic. The thing-child, its legs bring forth feet. And those feet are fringed with limp toes. Adrift in the center of the Pacific, the pallid thing-child is lifeless, as loose-limbed as a drowned corpse, but still it grows. Nourished on this soup of plastic particles, strands as fine as hair extend from its head. Two bubbles swell, and those erupt to become the shells of ears. Specks of plastic swarm and attach to become a nose, and still the lax thing-child is not alive.

Note how similar is our thing-baby's pilgrimage to that

of the infant Perseus. He of Greek legend who later slew the Gorgons and harnessed the winged horse Pegasus, as a baby he was locked in a chest and cast adrift. And let's not forget how similar Perseus's ordeal was to that of the Welsh saint Cenydd, who, as an infant, was placed in a willow basket and pushed to sea by no less a hero than King Arthur. And how this story is, itself, echoed by the fate of the Welsh bard Taliesin, who as a babe was tucked within a bladder of inflated skin and floated away. And the story of the warrior king Karna, of Hindu mythology, whose mother cradled him in a basket and put him at the mercy of the Ganges. All of this history and cross-cultural theology sails along with the thing-baby and its plastic armada.

And in so many voyages are all religions made one.

And now the juggernaut is thronging past the Hawaiian Islands. The decomposing beach balls and toothbrushes are agitated by the seas, and they break down to undifferentiated flakes and specks and shreds. To coumarone-indene and diallyl phthalate. The photons of infrared radiation and ultraviolet light, these cleave the bonds which hold together atoms. Hydrolysis causes the scission of polymer chains. And these, these disposable cigarette lighters and flea collars, they're reduced to their constituent monomers.

And so suspended in this rich bath, the Neoplatonists believe, the thing-child waxes plump. It evolves lips, and those lips part to reveal a mouth, but the thing-child is still not alive. And within the mouth grow teeth of polyarylate.

Above Wake Island, the flood of thermoplastic polyester compounds and polyphenylene oxide veers north, lingering near Yokohama along the coastline of Japan. There, a discarded wristwatch wraps itself around a growing wrist.

195

The thing-child face floats above the water's surface like a tiny atoll. The broken wristwatch begins to tick. The graven idol opens its eyes, dull eyes that stare up at the ocean skies. And on clear equatorial nights those polystyrene eyes marvel at the stars.

The new lips do tremble and utter the words, "Ye gods!"

Yet, still, the thing-child is not alive.

A Match Made in Heaven

Posted by Madisonspencer@aftrlife.hell

entle Tweeter,

Years before, once I'd been retrieved from my nana's tedious upstate funeral and returned to my natural habitat of Lincoln Town Cars and leased jets, I resumed my campaign of inventing salacious diary entries.

"Dear Diary," I wrote, "what I once felt for musky moose pee-pees I find was merely a fascination. What initially drew me to a leopard's velvety hoo-hoo was not love. . . ."

Here, my parents would be forced to turn a page, pulse-poundingly anxious for my next self-revelation. Their every breath bated, they'd read on, desperate for assurance that I'd abandoned my ardor for lemming wing-wangs.

"Dear Diary," I wrote, "living upstate, among simple, weathered folk, I've discovered a single lover who has eclipsed all my previous animal paramours. . . ." Here I altered my handwriting, making it crabbed and jagged to heighten the tension of reading my thoughts. My pen shook as if I were overwhelmed with strong emotion.

My busybody mom and dad would squint. They'd debate every illegible word.

"Dear Diary," I continued, "I've formed an alliance more

fulfilling than anything I'd ever dreamed possible. There, in that rudely constructed upstate house of worship . . ."

My parents had been at my Nana Minnie's funeral. Both my parents had seen me comforted by the towheaded David Copperfield with his face like fresh-baked bread and his hair like butter, that countrified swain who'd pressed a Bible book into my hands and bade me find strength therein. Now, as they read my diary, most likely they imagined that I was enacting some tantric upstate Kama Sutra with that earnest blond prefarmer.

"Dear Diary," I wrote, stringing my parents along, "never have I imagined this level of satisfaction. . . ."

I wrote, "Until now my eleven-year-old heart has never truly loved another. . . ."

My mother would be reading aloud by now. In the same elegant voice with which she did voice-overs for Bain de Soleil television commercials, she'd say, "I have at last found happiness."

Both my parents would leer at the pages as if they were a sacred text. As if this, my humble fake diary, were the Tibetan Book of the Dead or *The Celestine Prophecy*: something lofty and profound from their own lives. My mother, in her stage-trained, Xanax-relaxed voice, would read aloud, " '. . . from this day forward I commit my eternal love to . . .' " and her voice would falter. To them, what followed was worse than the image of me suckling at any panther woo-woo or grizzly bear nipple. Here was a horror more confronting than the idea of their precious daughter wedding a staunch Republican.

Seeing my words, she and my dad could only stare in disbelief.

" 'I commit my eternal love,' " my dad would continue,
" 'to my supreme lord and master . . .' "

"Lord and master," my mom repeats.

" 'Jesus,' " reads my dad.

My mom says, "Jesus Christ."

My Flirtation with the Divine
Posted by Madisonspencer@aftrlife.hell

entle Tweeter,

Jesus Christ made the best fake boyfriend ever. Wherever my family traveled, at our homes in Trinidad or Toronto or Tunisia, the doorbell would ring, and some aboriginal delivery peon would be at our front step bearing a vast bouquet of roses from Him. Dining at Cipriani or Centrale, my dad would order me the *lapin à la sauce moutarde,* and I'd wait for it to arrive at the table before regarding my plate in pretend disdain. Recoiling, I'd signal the waiter, saying, "Rabbit? I can't eat rabbit! If you knew anything about Leviticus Two, you'd know that an edible beast has to chew a cud and *have a hoof.*"

My father would order the *salade Lyonnaise,* and I'd send it away because pigs didn't chew cuds. He'd order the escargot bourguignon, which I'd reject because the Bible book specifically forbids eating snails. "They're unclean," I'd insist. "They're creeping things."

My mother would put on a serene Xanaxed mask. The buzzwords of her life were *tolerance* and *respect,* and she was trapped between them as if crushed in an ideological vise. Keeping her voice calm, she'd ask, "Well, dear, what *can* you eat—"

But I'd cut her off with a "Wait!" I'd fish a PDA from the pocket of my skort and pretend to find a new message.

"It's Jesus," I'd interrupt, making my parents wince. "He's texting me!" Their own dinners cooling, I'd make them bide their time. If either of them said a word of protest I'd shush them as I pretended to read and respond. Without looking up, I'd squeal, loud enough for the assembled diners to overhear, "Christ loves me!" I'd frown at my little PDA screen and say, "Jesus disapproves of the dress you're wearing, Mom. He says it's too young for you, and it makes you look slutty. . . ."

My parents? I'd become their worst nightmare. Instead of hoisting the ideological banner they'd so proudly bestowed upon me, instead of accepting the torch of their atheist humanism, I was scrolling through the messages on my phone, telling them, "Jesus says that tofu is evil, and all soy is of the Devil."

My parents . . . in the past my parents had put their complete faith in quartz crystals and hyperbaric chambers and the I Ching, so they didn't have a credible leg left to stand on. Throughout this dinner stalemate the waiter had remained steadfast, standing beside our table, and I now turned to him and asked, "Do you, by any chance, serve locusts and wild honey?" I asked, "Or manna?"

As the waiter opened his mouth to respond, I'd turn back to the PDA in my lap and say, "Hold on! Jesus is Tweeting."

My father caught the waiter's eye and said, "Perry?" To his credit, my dad knows the name of every waiter in every five-star restaurant in the world. "Perry, would you give us a moment alone?" As the waiter stepped away, my dad shot my mom a look. Almost imperceptibly his eyebrows arched and his shoulders shrugged. They were trapped. As former Scientologists and former Bahá'is and former EST-holes, they could hardly question me as I merrily keyboarded my devotions to my own choice of belief system.

Resigned, my father lifted his fork and waited for my mother to follow suit.

As they each put a first bite of food into their respective mouths, I announced, "Jesus says I should publicly support the next GOP candidate for president!"

Hearing that, both my parents gasped, inhaling food and choking. Swilling wine, they were still coughing, everyone in the dining room watching them wheeze, as my dad's phone rang. Breathless, he answered it. "A product survey?" he asked, incredulous. "About what? About the *toothpicks I buy*?" Almost shouting, he demanded, "Who is this?" Sputtering, he demanded, "How did you get this number?"

And for that, MohawkArcher666, I thank you whole-heartedly.

A Tiny Golden Overdose
Posted by Madisonspencer@aftrlife.hell

entle Tweeter,
This, this is how the precious little kitten, Tigerstripe, came into my life.

Post-upstate, post-Nana, my parents and I were staying at the ever-lovely Beverly Wilshire hotel. We were eating breakfast in our suite, meaning: I was watching my parents eat. Meaning: My dad was playing his deprogramming games, withholding apricot Danishes and cheese strudels to make me renounce my torrid hookups with Jesus. In retaliation I kept my phone cradled to one ear, billing and cooing and otherwise ignoring my parents' withering glances as I giggled. "Stop it, Jesus! Stop being such a tease!" I allowed my girlish eyes to flit across the white tablecloth, bypassing the flowers and the orange juice, and rest on my mother's glaring expression. Pointedly, I examined her, scrutinizing her lips and neck before resting my attention on her bustline as I said, "No, they're not! No, Jesus, she didn't!"

My mom shifted uncomfortably in her chair. She lifted the napkin from her lap and daubed at the corners of her mouth. With elaborate Ctrl+Alt+Casualness, she looked at my father and asked, "Antonio, my love, would you pass me the sugar?"

Speaking to my fake Jesus boyfriend, just as I'd spoken to my entire fake circle of girlfriends, I laughed and said,

"She's not!" I said, "I'm sitting right here, and she's *not that bad!*"

My father passed my mother the sugar and said, "Maddy, dear, you need to not talk on the phone at the breakfast table."

My mother began, with the utmost Ctrl+Alt+Sadism, to spoon copious amounts of sugar into her coffee.

The phone still pasted to my head, I bulged my eyes at my dad and mouthed the words *I can't hang up.* Silently I screamed, *It's Jesus!*

How to rebel against parents who celebrated rebellion? If I did drugs and pulled a train of outlaw bikers and venereal-warted gangbangers, nothing could make my parents happier.

Acting as if breakfast were sacrosanct family time, my dad was such a hypocrite. Open on the table beside his place was the usual stack of orphan dossiers, among them a photo of two flinty eyes that stared out from a glossy head shot. These stone-colored eyes, they seemed to despise every silly luxury they could see in this sumptuous hotel setting. For the length of a gasp, the trill of my schoolgirl giggling fell silent as my own eyes were held spellbound by the craggy features and churlish expression of that particular Slavic foundling. Entranced was I by that coarse thuggish sneer.

At last my mom broke the silence by saying, "Hang up, young lady."

Turning on her, I attacked with, "Jesus says you're the one who's fat."

"Hang up now," said my dad.

And I told them, "Hey, don't shoot the messenger." Into

the phone, I said, "JC? I need to call you back later." I said, "My imperious, all-powerful dad is being a big booger; you know how that goes." As my coup de grâce, I told the phone, "And you're right about my mom's belly." With exquisite Ctrl+Alt+Deliberateness, I switched off my phone and placed it next to my empty breakfast plate. For the record, Gentle Tweeter, at that repast I'd been served nothing more than a halved grapefruit, a sliver of dry toast, and a meager poached egg. A quail egg, mind you. Such death-camp rations had hardly gilded my mood. Affecting my best Elinor Glyn attitude, I thrust my face at my father and announced, "As you seem so determined to make me suffer . . ." Here I closed my eyes in the style of a true heroine. ". . . I'd rather you just lashed out and struck me!" As other preteens might long for a large allowance or shiny hair or friends, I wanted my parents to strike me. A punch with a closed fist or a slap with an open hand, I dreamed of it. Whether the blow came from my mom or dad, those pacifist, idealist, nonviolent do-gooders, it didn't matter. Across my cheek or into my stomach, I yearned for the impact because I knew that nothing else would shift the parent/child balance of power as effectively. If I could goad them into slugging me just once, forever afterward I could cite that incident and use the memory to win any argument.

Ah, to be Helen Burns, Jane Eyre's childhood cohort who was stood before the students of Lowood School and roundly pulverized by Mr. Brocklehurst. Or to be Heathcliff and have a large stone bounced against my tender head by young master Hindley. Such public abuse was my fondest desire.

Eyes closed, face serenely presented, I eagerly awaited the painful blow. I heard my mother stir her coffee, the tiny song of the spoon ringing within her china cup. I heard the rasp of my father scraping butter on his toast. Finally, my mom said, "Antonio, don't let's prolong this. . . . Go ahead; smack your daughter."

"Camille," my father's voice said, "do *not* encourage her."

I continued to lean forward, eyes closed, offering my face as a target.

"Your mother's right, Maddy," said my dad. "But we're not going to start beating the crap out of you until you're at least eighteen."

In my mind, dear CanuckAIDSemily, I wore a blindfold and dangled a smoking Gauloise from between my lips. I prayed to be pummeled like a girlish punching bag.

My mom said, "We wanted to help you process the grief you must feel about your grandparents."

"We have a present for you, dear," my dad's voice said.

I opened my eyes, and there was Mr. Wiggles. A fluttering, jolly golden fish hovered in my water glass. His protuberant eyes swiveled to ogle me. His gulping little hatch of a mouth gaped open and shut, gulped open and shut. My hard-bitten facade crumbled at the sight of the paddling, gasping little sun-colored sprite suspended in the unconsumed water of my meal. In a word, I was delighted. The name Mr. Wiggles came instantly to mind, and in that moment I was joyous, a hand-clapping, happy child wreathed by my smiling family. Then, tragically, I was not.

In the next moment, Mr. Wiggles foundered. He keeled over and floated belly-up in the glass. My parents and I stared in shocked Ctrl+Alt+Disbelief.

"Camille?" my dad asked. "By any chance did you get the waters mixed up?" He reached across the breakfast table and lifted the glass with dead Mr. Wiggles. Putting the rim to his lips, he carefully sipped around the expired fish. "It's just as I thought."

My mom asked, "Did Maddy get your GHB?"

"No," he said. "I'm afraid her new goldfish did."

My former-pothead, former-junkie, former–speed freak parents, they'd accidentally overdosed my fish by presenting him to me in a glass full of GHB. Meaning: liquid Ecstasy. Meaning: gamma-hydroxybutyric acid. Unfazed, my dad kept drinking even as my pet's tiny golden corpse bumped and bobbed against his lips. He pinched it out with two fingers and passed the tiny victim to the Somali maid. "To the commode," he intoned solemnly, "and henceforth to return to the great circle of life."

Even as I reached for my phone to speed-dial Jesus and relate the details of this latest atrocity, my mom pushed the basket of pastries within my reach and sighed. "So much for Mr. Fish . . . What say we go out today, Maddy, and adopt you a pretty little baby kitten?"

My True Love Rescued from the Jaws of Death

Posted by Madisonspencer@aftrlife.hell

entle Tweeter,

My parents never adopted anything without issuing a minimum of ten million press releases. Tigerstripe was no exception. A documentary film crew shadowed us to a no-kill cat shelter in East Los Angeles, where my father and I weighed the merits of the various abandoned strays. My mother led the phalanx of cameras to a wizened tabby, alone in its wire-mesh cell. Examining the index card on which was printed the animal's curriculum vitae, she said, "Ooooh, Madison, this one has leukemia! Its prognosis is death within four months. That sounds perfect!"

Topmost among the criteria my parents sought in any dependent relationship was impermanence. They wanted homes, employees, businesses, and adopted Third World orphans of which they could divest themselves at a moment's notice. Nothing offers better public relations fodder than something you can rescue and love intensively for a month and then be filmed burying at a lavish funeral.

When I declined the dying tabby, my dad steered me toward an aged calico tom. The shelter staff estimated it had approximately six weeks left to live. "Diabetes," my dad said, nodding solemnly. "Let that be a lesson to you, young lady, for the next time you want another sugary snack."

The documentary cameras followed us from one doomed

kitty to the next. From cats with infectious peritonitis to those with hypertrophic cardiomyopathy. Some struggled with the effort to lift their dying heads as I scratched behind their feverish ears. This seemed less like a cat shelter than a feline hospice. Confronted by kitties suffering from intestinal tumors and terminal pyometra, I felt awful. It's true, they all wanted love and a home, but I didn't want any of them. I wanted something that would live to love me back.

A Siamese lay on disposable paper training pads, too weak to control its bladder. A Persian cried plaintively and blinked gummy, cataract-clouded eyes at me. When my dad saw the long list of medications it required day in and day out, his face brightened into a smile. "This guy can't last for long, Maddy!" With one hand, he coaxed me toward the cat's smelly cage, and he said, "You can name him 'Cat Stevens' and give him the biggest memorial service any cat ever had!"

My mom mugged for the cameras and added, "Children absolutely adore holding little funerals for their pets . . . creating a little cemetery and filling every grave! It teaches them awareness for subsoil bacterial life-forms!"

If my mother possessed respect for any life-forms, her own mother wasn't among them. When my nana died of a stroke on Halloween night, from an errant blood clot generated by her cancer, my mom flew in from Cannes the next day carrying the infamous aquamarine evening gown encrusted with sequins and seed pearls. "Haute couture," she'd said, entering the office of the backwoods mortuary, the dress sealed in a clear plastic garment bag and draped across her arm. The upstate undertaker was dazzled: Sitting on the opposite side of his desk were Antonio and Camille

Spencer. Fawning, he acknowledged that the dress was gorgeous, but then he explained patiently that it was a size four and Nana Minnie's cancer-riddled corpse was a size ten. Without missing a beat, my dad slipped a checkbook out of his inside jacket pocket and asked, "How much?"

"I don't understand," said the undertaker.

"To make the dress fit," prompted my mom.

The poor naive mortician, he asked, "It's so lovely. Are you certain you want me to split the seams?"

My mother gasped. My father shook his head in bitter disbelief, saying, "That dress is a work of art, buster. You touch one stitch of it, and we'll sue you into bankruptcy."

"What we want," my mom explained, "is for you to perform a little trimming . . . a touch of lipo here and there . . . so that my mother looks her best."

"The camera," my dad said, "adds ten pounds." By this point he was penning a steep six-digit number.

"Cameras?" asked the undertaker.

"Maybe you can also take a little tuck behind her ears . . . ," said my mom as she demonstrated by pinching the skin at her own temples until her cheeks stretched smooth and taut. "And a little breast augmentation, a lift, maybe some implants so the bodice will hang right."

"And hair extensions," my dad added. "We want to see lots of hair on the old gal."

"Maybe," my mom suggested, "you could just snip out her kidneys and move them up here a little." She cupped her hands over her own flawless breasts.

My father signed the check with a flourish. "And we've contracted with a tattoo artist." He tore the draft from his checkbook and waved it beside his face, smirking. "That is, unless you have any objections to Minnie's getting inked . . ."

"Oh," my mom said, snapping her fingers. "And no underthings, not a thong, nothing. I do not want the world watching this funeral live by satellite and seeing panty lines on my beloved, dear, dead mother."

I thought my mom might cry at this point of the funeral planning, sitting there in the mortician's office. Instead she turned to me and asked, "Maddy, honey, what's wrong with your eyes? How did they get so red and swollen?" She took a vial of Xanax out of her bag and offered me one. "Let's get you some cucumber slices for that puffiness."

I had, Gentle Tweeter, been weeping nonstop since Halloween. Not that my mother ever noticed.

When I recall my nana's kiss, I taste cigarette smoke. By comparison my mother's kisses were flavored with anti-anxiety medications.

In the no-kill cat shelter, she was once more foisting Xanax on me in an effort to make me accept a large Manx with a thick coat of black fur. It didn't seem to matter to her that the cat had died moments before. My dad lifted its still-warm body out of its littered cage and tried to settle the stiffening corpse into my pudgy arms. "Just take it, Maddy," he whispered. "On-camera it will read as only being asleep. We don't have all day. . . ."

As he gently heaved the drooping, dead Manx in my direction and I recoiled a step, I saw something else. In the same cage, hidden by the recently expired black cat, there sat a tiny orange kitten. This was my last chance. In another moment I'd be driven back to the Beverly Wilshire with a rigid feline corpse in my girlish lap. On-camera, with the shelter's staff as my witnesses, I pointed a chubby index finger at this new orange puff of fur and said, "That one, Daddy!" Making my voice gamine, I piped, "There's my kitty!" The orange object of my desperate affection opened two green eyes and returned my gaze.

My mother sneaked a quick peek at the index card tacked next to the cage. In a dozen words, it told the tiny kitten's brief backstory. That afternoon in the no-kill animal shelter, my mom leaned close to my dad and whispered, "Let her have the orange one." She whispered, "Put back the dead one, and let Maddy have the kitten."

Still holding the drooping dead Manx, my dad gritted his capped teeth and said, "Camille, it's still a kitten." Through a tight smile, he hissed, "That damned thing will live for frigging forever." He gave the furry corpse a shake, smirking, and said, "With this one, maybe she could call her boyfriend to perform a Lazarus number."

"If that's the kitty that our little Maddy has her heart set on . . . ," my mom said, and she reached into the wire cage and collected the shivering orange puffball, ". . . then that's the kitten she should have." Standing so as to allow the cameras full access to the gesture, turned toward them in a slight cheat, she settled the warm handful into my care. At the same time, in a whispered aside to my dad, she said, "Don't worry, Antonio." She motioned for him to lean down and read the index card.

And at that, a photographer representing *Cat Fancy* magazine stepped forward, said, "Smile!" and we were, all of us, blinded by the flash.

Mother of the Year
Posted by Madisonspencer@aftrlife.hell

entle Tweeter,
I never imagined it would be too awfully difficult to be a good mother. That's why my own mother seemed like such a disappointment. Really, what onerous efforts did successful motherhood require? One had only to accumulate a sufficient deposit of fresh spermatozoa within one's womb, and then await the release of a viable egg. From what I could suss out, the whole process seemed more or less automated. The actual birthing involved staffing a sterile, tiled room with an entire documentary film crew, all the grips and gaffers and sound engineers, the cameramen and assistant directors and makeup artists. I've seen the result: My mother blissed out on an intravenous Demerol drip, spread-eagled on a kind of vinyl dais with special leg rests. A stylist is powdering down the shine on her meticulously waxed pubis, and—voilà—the ooze-colored bulb of my newborn noggin pops out. Chapter one: I am born. This miraculous celluloid moment is absolutely revolting. My lovely mother winces a single grimace, but otherwise her dazzling smile remains intact as my slime-slickened miniature self comes corkscrewing out of her steaming innards. Swiftly am I followed into the world by an equally not-attractive afterbirth. Even then, no doubt I was hoping the attendant physician would give me a good wallop. A

real public thrashing. Only a child raised in such complete love and privilege could crave a savage beating as fervently as I did.

Usually my mother played a copy of the video whenever people gathered for my birthday. "We got it in a single take," she'd always say. "Madison was a lot skinnier back then—thank God!" And she'd always get a rollicking laugh at my expense. Such flank attacks are why I so longed for my parents to honestly sock me in the kisser. My blackened eye would trumpet what small torments I daily endured.

You, Gentle Tweeter, you no doubt saw the stills from the birthing film that *People* magazine published. My heartless Swiss school chums certainly saw them, and until the day I died I was to regularly find these photographs—a me the size of regurgitated food, the red of a ripe tomato smeared with cheesy pap and squirming at the end of a ropy umbilical cord—these were stealthily affixed to the back of my sweater with adhesive tape, or they were published in place of my annual portrait in the school yearbook.

Once I was born, I could see for myself that motherhood required no special skills. My general impression was that various glands come to the fore, and you're rendered essentially a puppet or a slave to the timing of bodily secretions—colostrum, piddle, doo-doo. You're always consuming or voiding some vital gunk.

It's this full comprehension of motherhood that prompted me to give my kitten, Tigerstripe, a better upbringing than I had endured. I vowed to show my own mother how this job should properly be done. "Put some clothes on, you people!" I'd admonish my naked parents on the beaches of Nice or Nancy or Newark. "Do you want my kitty to grow up to be a pervert?" I'd locate their pungent stash of hashish and flush it down the toilet, saying, "You might not care about the safety of your child, but I do care about mine!"

Granted, as a distraction from religion, the cat worked perfectly. I no longer returned Jesus' calls during dinner. Instead, I carried Tigerstripe everywhere in the crook of my elbow, lecturing in a stage whisper, always within earshot of my folks, "My mommy and daddy might be drug-hungry sex zombies, but I'll never allow them to hurt you." For their part, my parents were simply glad that Jesus and I had broken up. Thus, they acquiesced as I carried my Tigerstripe with me at all times, in Taipei and Turin and Topeka. He slept curled beside me in my various beds in Kabul and Cairo and Cape Town. At the breakfast table in Banff or Bern, I said, "*We* don't like nonfat, fair-trade tofu sausage, and *we* request that you no longer serve it to *us.*" In Copenhagen, I announced, "*We* would like another chocolate éclair, or *we* refuse to attend the opening of *La Bohème* tonight." Needless to say, Tigerstripe proved himself an excellent companion at the opera, largely sleeping, yet by his mere presence egging my allergic parents to barely suppressed fits of outrage. At La Scala and the Met and the Royal Albert Hall, a trail of shed cat hair and leaping fleas followed us everywhere.

The more I distanced myself in the exclusive company of my new kitten, the more my dad perused the photographs and the files of destitute orphans available for adoption. The more that I isolated myself, the more my mom surfed real estate listings on her notebook computer. Neither of them mentioned it, but despite their soy-based machinations, my stewardship of Tigerstripe resulted in a very fat little kitten. Feeding him appeared to make him happy, and making Tiger happy made me happy, and after only a couple of weeks of overfeeding, to carry him was like lugging around a Louis Vuitton anvil.

It wasn't in Basel or Budapest or Boise, but one afternoon I came upon the doorway to a darkened screening room. It was in our house in Barcelona, and I was passing in the hallway when I saw the door was slightly ajar. From the darkness within, I heard a combination of caterwauls, an inharmonious duet like alley cats expressing their ardor. Holding my eye to the narrow opening where the door had not fully met its frame, I could see a writhing, paste-covered blob on the movie screen within. The squalling was that gelatinous creature, my infant self, clearly not happy to be delivered unto this harsh glare of lights, documentary filmmakers, and burning sage. And seated alone in the center of the otherwise empty seats was my mother.

She pressed a telephone to the side of her face as she watched that, the tiresome video of my new life beginning. Her shoulders shuddered. Her chest heaved. Inconsolably she sobbed, "Please listen to me, Leonard." Her cheeks shining, she swiped at her tears with her free hand. "I know it's her fate to die on her birthday, but please, don't let my baby girl suffer."

My Beloved Is Felled by a Mysterious Condition
Posted by Madisonspencer@aftrlife.hell

entle Tweeter,

Within days of my adopting him, Tiger-stripe swelled as large as a popcorn ball, then swelled to the size of a brioche, feeling as spongy soft as homemade fudge. He had days before ceased going wee in his cat box. Likewise, his plaintive mewing stopped, so now I was compelled to cry in the manner of a ventriloquist, holding my lips fixed in a frozen rictus of a smile as I forged merry kitten sounds for my parents' benefit.

In the comfort of Mexico City or Mumbai or Montreal, over a breakfast of raw tuna sashimi and shrimp ceviche and duck liver pâté, my puss-puss wouldn't eat a bite. My mother and father surreptitiously watched my failing efforts to feed him, sneaking glances from behind their respective notebook computers while I placed my hideously swollen kitty on the breakfast table beside my plate and tempted him with succulent tidbits. To me, Tigerstripe represented my opportunity to shame them both. My care of him would demonstrate proper nonpagan, nonvegan, non-Reagan parenting skills. All of those past lives my mom and dad had brought to my upbringing, I'd eschew them. My strategy would be simply to lavish adoration on my kitty and raise him to a well-adjusted, non-body-image-dysmorphic cat-hood.

217

Here did I fake a tiny *meow* for my fellow breakfasters.

Do you see what I'd done, Gentle Tweeter? Do you see how I'd trapped myself in a corner? In Bangalore and Hyderabad and Houston, my catkin was obviously sick, but I couldn't admit that fact by going to my folks to beg their advice. Over the breakfast table in Hanoi, my father eyed the bloated fuzz ball breathing heavily as it lay on its side beside my plate. Feigning Ctrl+Alt+Indifference, he asked, "How's little Tigger?"

"His name is Tigerstripe," I protested. Reaching to scoop him up and lift him into my lap, I said, "And he's fine." Between motionless lips, I said *meow*. Subtly using my fingertips, I moved the inert kitten's mouth to match. *Meow.*

My father exchanged a raised eyebrow with my mom, and he asked, "Tiger's not sick?"

"He's fine!"

My mom laid her Ctrl+Alt+Serene gaze on the comatose blob now shivering atop my napkin-covered thighs, and she asked, "He doesn't need to see a veterinarian, maybe?"

"He's fine!" said I. "He's sleeping." I couldn't let them see my fear. The quivering fur ball I petted, he felt hot—too hot. Gummy gunk rimmed his closed eyelids and sputtered at his teeny black nostrils. Even worse, stroking his sides I could feel the skin stretched tight, his belly distended. Through his soft fur, his faint kitten heartbeat felt a million-billion miles away. One possibility was that I'd fed him something wrong. Or I'd fed him too much. He was panting now, his kitty-pink tongue protruding slightly, each breath a death rattle. In too many ways, poor Tigerstripe was reproducing my nana's slow, painful passing. Without thinking, my fingertips sought out the spot behind his front leg where the heartbeat felt strongest, and within the thinking bowels of my brain I began counting, *One-alligator* . . . *two-alligator* . . . *three-alligator* . . . between the slow, irregular beats. I noticed that neither of my parents was eating. The sickroom reek of afflicted kitten eclipsed everyone's appetite.

My dad proposed, "How about you and Tiger go together to see a grief counselor?" He swallowed, betraying his Ctrl+Alt+Anxiety, and said, "You could talk about your grandpa and grandma dying."

"I'm not grieving!" Under my breath I was counting . . . *Five-alligator* . . . *six-alligator* . . . between the fading heartbeats.

My mother's worried eyes swept the table until they settled on the pastry basket. Lifting it, she heaved the tasty goodies toward me. "Would you like a muffin?"

"No!" I counted, *Eight-alligator* . . . *nine-alligator* . . .

"But you love blueberry muffins." Her eyes tested me, measuring my response.

"I'm not hungry!" I snapped, counting . . . *Eleven-alligator* . . . *twelve-alligator* . . . My kitty's raspy, rattling breath had stopped. With frantic fumbling fingers I sought to massage his failed feline heart back to life. To hide this effort from my parents I wrapped my linen napkin around Tigerstripe's swollen body. Thus thickly swaddled, his heartbeat became impossible to locate. To mask my panic, I said, "I'm not hungry! Tigerstripe is healthy and happy! I'm not hungry, and I didn't rip off anyone's man banana!"

Hearing that, my mother's face looked Ctrl+Alt+ Slapped. Her hands reached across the table in what must've been some instinctive maternal gesture, some attempted mammalian embrace inherited from our primate ancestors, and she said, "We only want to help you, Maddy, Raindrop."

Recoiling, cradling my still, silent kitten, I countered, my words pure acid, "Maybe we could just desert Tigerstripe on some remote farm outpost upstate? How about that?" My voice rising to hysteria, I said, "Or perhaps we could ship my kitty off to some expensive school in Switzerland, where she could live, socially isolated, among hateful rich pussycats!"

Under my breath I was counting, *Eighteen-alligator . . . nineteen-alligator . . . twenty-alligator . . .* but I knew it was already too late. In Seoul or São Paulo or Seattle, I was half falling, half sprinting as I abandoned my place at the breakfast table and fled back to my bedroom bearing my baby kitten wrapped in his napkin shroud.

In Denial

Posted by Madisonspencer@aftrlife.hell

entle Tweeter,

The long-ago predead, eleven-year-old me carried my bundled feline corpse through Antwerp and Aspen and Ann Arbor. Like the blanket-wrapped cadaver of some expired Granny Joad, another bookish reference, I smuggled poor Tigerstripe through various immigration and customs checkpoints. I wore him strapped to my skin, hidden beneath my clothing, the way my mom and dad had so often played mule for their contraband narcotics. Needless to say, his sour odor did not abate; neither did the faithful entourage of winged parasites, primarily houseflies, but also their adolescent grubs and maggots that appeared on the scene as if conjured by some foul magic.

Whether international security was alarmingly lax, or my parents had placed big-money bribes to the right officers, my sad burden was never discovered. Occasionally, I'd mew quietly, defeated, but I kept my secret always wrapped in that original breakfast napkin. Don't imagine that I was deranged, Gentle Tweeter; I knew my kitty was dead. No one in contact with his deflating fur coat could ignore its constant drip-drip-dripping of cold fluids. Under my sweater, lumped against my belly like a pregnancy, like a miscarriage, I felt the jumble of his collapsing bones.

In the hours since he'd passed, his furry tum-tum had

begun to balloon. And, yes, I might've been temporarily insane with grief, but I knew that my kitten was filling with gas, the excretal product of renegade intestinal bacteria. And, yes, I might've been secretly terrified that I'd fed him something that had caused his demise, but I knew the word *excretal*, and I knew that my beloved was about to burst and that such an explosion would reduce my heart's treasure to a bug-infested carcass. The linen felt sticky against my fingers. To my caressing hands Tigerstripe wasn't dead, but I was careful not to pet him too vigorously.

At present, we shared a stretch limo, my parents sitting side by side with their backs to the driver, withdrawing themselves as far as possible from my not-happy circumstances. My parents' flattened emotional aspect, their somber voices implied that they sensed the truth. Nevertheless in that car between the airport and our home in Jakarta or Johannesburg or Jackson Hole, my mother asked, "How's the little patient?" Her eyes bloodshot. Her voice forcing a Ctrl+Alt+Lilt. "Feeling any better?"

In the limo's plush interior, the perennial flies and rank smell proved difficult to ignore, and one of her yoga-sculpted arms flailed out, seeking the controls for the air-conditioning. Her manicured fingers increased the air flow to a full arctic blast, and she plucked a prescription bottle of Xanax from her bag and upended a few pills into her mouth. She handed the bottle to my father behind his newspaper.

Cradled in my lap, still swaddled in breakfast linen, I carried my heart, and my heart was stiff and cold. My heart was a dead time bomb drooling decayed corruption. In response to her inquiry, I could but meow flatly. Behind the murk of the tinted windows, the outskirts of Lisbon or La Jolla or Lexington fell behind us and vanished. As we motored along, I felt the putrefying juices of my soul mate migrating downward to soil my skort. Smoothed flat, the napkin in my lap would chart jagged islands and filigreed coastlines. Flecked and blotched with the stains of decomposition, the linen would trace a rambling journey in which everything you love falls apart.

This, it was the opposite of a treasure map.

My father? He hardly took notice. In that plush setting, my father was busy behind his newspaper, the salmon-toned pages of the *Financial Times*. Of his person, all I could see were his legs from the knees down, those creased and cuffed trouser legs. I could see only those and his knuckles holding the paper spread in front of him. There, his gold wedding band. While my mom wrestled with her sedated empathy, and I sank deeper into despair, my dad snapped his newsprint pages. He turned them with rustling flourishes. If you'll notice, Gentle Tweeter, a businessman with a newspaper is worse than any Jane Austen heroine flouncing through life in a taffeta ball gown.

"Maddy?" asked my mom. Her words shrill with false good cheer, she said, "How would Tigerstripe like a new brother?"

Meaning: She was pregnant? Meaning: She was insane?

From within his paper fortress, my father said, "Sweetheart, we're adopting." From behind the scrim of wars and stock prices and sports scores, "The kid's from someplace awful."

Meaning: I wasn't paying them enough attention. Meaning: They wanted to feel more appreciated.

"The paperwork took months," my mom said. "It's not as easy as adopting a . . ." And she nodded toward the sodden napkin wadded in my lap.

In response, I offered an almost inaudible tear-choked *meow*.

My father shook his papers angrily. My mother rattled her bottle of Xanax as she tipped back another pill. My hands forgot to be careful, and my fingernails itched at my kitty's soft tum-tum. And at that juncture, Gentle Tweeter, in the spacious seats and enclosed interior of the limo, poor Tigerstripe's distended abdomen burst.

At Last, a Violent Comeuppance
Posted by Madisonspencer@aftrlife.hell

 entle Tweeter,

The earthly remains of my beloved Tigerstripe were to be interred in a toilet of the Beverly Wilshire hotel in an elegant, low-key ceremony patterned after that of my goldfish, Mr. Wiggles. While our personal staff of Somali maids flung open windows and put flame to scented candles, I carried the death-fragrant, napkin-wrapped remains into the suite's master bathroom. The mourners included my parents, who stood near the whirlpool soaking tub. My dad impatiently tapped his foot, the toe of his handmade shoe tick-tocking loudly against the tile floor. The funeral cortege consisted of a trailing black cloud of houseflies. We were, the mourners, literally veiled in buzzing black houseflies.

"Flush it down," my father commanded.

My mom breathed through a perfumed handkerchief and said, "Amen, already."

I stood over the yawning commode, my spirit shattered, unable to relinquish something I'd loved so deeply. So bereft was I that I prayed Jesus would phone, forgetting that I'd only made him up. Jesus didn't really exist, and Dr. Angelou wasn't going to touch this stinky bundle of bones and rotting fur and bring it back to life.

I beseeched, "Shouldn't we say a prayer?"

"What for?" said my dad. "Maddy, sweetness, prayers are for superstitious idiots and Baptists."

"For Tigerstripe's eternal soul!" I pleaded.

"A prayer?" asked my mom.

I pleaded for them to call on Sir Bono or Sir Sting for divine intervention.

"There is no such thing as a *soul*," said my dad. Exasperated, he huffed out a short breath scented with Binaca and Klonopin. "Baby girl, we've discussed this. Nothing has a soul, and when you die you rot away to create healthy organic compost for subsoil life-forms to reproduce in."

"Wait," my mom said. Closing her eyes she began to recite from memory: "Go placidly amid the noise and haste. . . ."

A growing cadre of Somali maids had begun to gather in the space immediately outside the bathroom door.

"Exercise caution in your business affairs," continued my mom, her Botox-infused brow semifurrowed in concentration. "For the world is full of trickery. . . ."

"There is no God. There is no soul. Nothing survives beyond death," lectured my father. Shouting now, he asked, "Didn't those nuns teach you *anything* at that expensive Catholic school?"

My mother droned on, "Speak your truth quietly and clearly. . . ."

"Flush it, Maddy," said my dad, Ctrl+Alt+Snapping his fingers between each short imperative sentence. "Flush it. Flush it. *Flush it!* We have reservations for dinner at eight at Patina!" He shot back his shirt cuff and checked his watch. He waved away the annoying vermin. Meaning: the flies, not the Somali maids who hovered, watching these curious funeral rites.

226

When my voice came it sounded faint. "Forgive me, my kitty." I gave the squishy bundle a big hug against my flabby tummy. "I'm sorry I killed you." My sobs began in earnest. "I'm sorry I murdered you with maternal neglect." I'd proved to be a worse parent than my own parents. With this terrible admission I was rocking forward and back, racked with hoarse sobs, squeezing the not-fresh final graveyard juices from my beloved charge. Yet still I couldn't consign my Tigerstripe to a final watery resting place.

At my father's whispered urging, my mother stepped to my side and cooed, "Maddy, baby girl . . ." She murmured, "You didn't kill the cat. Nobody killed him." She gave me a little pat on the back, leaving her hand to linger on my shoulder, and said, "Mr. Tiger had a genetic condition called feline polycystic kidney disease. It means his kidneys developed cysts, honey. It's no one's fault. He filled with cysts until he died."

I looked up at her, my eyeglasses fogged and streaming with tears, my nose livid and flowing. "But a cat doctor . . ."

My mother shook her head no. Her mournful eyes, the expressive eyes of every death-row public defender and deathbed nurse she's ever played. "Baby girl, there is no cure. The kitty was born sick."

I asked, "But how can you know?" Instantly, I felt ashamed of my infantile, bleating tone, my pathetic words gargled through mucus and misery.

"It was printed on the index card," my mother explained. "Maddy, do you remember the index card taped to his cage at the animal rescue place?" Arrayed on the bathroom's marble vanity were an orange-colored prescription bottle of Xanax, a bud vase containing a trembling spray of purple orchids, an assortment of Hermès soaps heaped in a basket. "According to that index card, Mr. Tiger couldn't live longer than six more weeks." She reached to pluck the Xanax bottle, twisting off the cap. "Why don't you and I take a nice pill?" She said, "Your new brother is coming this afternoon. Isn't that exciting?"

"Drop the cat," my dad ordered. He lifted his hands above his head and clapped them together, shouting, "Ditch the cat, and let's move forward, people!"

Turning to face both of them, dropping my voice to a dragging growl, I said, "You knew?" My tears instantly boiled away. The corpse in my tender hands was teeming with maggots. My voice like a distant Swiss avalanche bearing down upon them with a billion-billion tons of ice and rock, I said, "All along, you knew you'd gotten me a dying kitty?"

A muted bell began to toll. It was the suite's front doorbell. It rang again. The gaggle of Somali maids lingered, watching us from the bathroom doorway. The security cameras were watching.

"You knew my kitten was a goner, and you just let me suffer?"

His face flushed almost purple, his jaw clenched, my father shot a dark look at my mother.

My voice a siren, I wailed, "You should've told me that my baby was going to die!" Cradling my pain, I demanded, "Don't you understand? How could you let me love something that was going to die?"

My mom filled a glass with water and brought it to me. Cupped in her other hand, she offered the pills. "Gumdrop," she said, "we just wanted to see you happy before you turned thirteen." So distraught was she that she actually expected me to drink tap water. *Los Angeles tap water.*

Not looking at me, instead gazing upon my cowering mother, my father squared his shoulders and stretched himself to his full height. "Trust me, young lady," he said. His voice cold, subdued, and resigned, he said, "No one wants to know when their child is doomed to die." For the first time, I could smell fifty-year-old Chivas on his breath. My father was loaded.

I snarled, "Maybe we ought to get Tigerstripe some liposuction and tattoos, and dress him to look like a Whorey von Whoreski version of Peggy Guggenheim!"

Even before the reality of their conspiracy had fully registered, my father strode across the bathroom and snatched the fragile remains from my grasp. He pitched them into the yawning toilet bowl and summarily pressed the flush lever. And, no, Gentle Tweeter, I am not oblivious to how many of my recent dramas had occurred in bathrooms, be they the noxious men's rooms of upstate or the gilded ones of the Beverly Wilshire. And with that, my precious Tigerstripe was gone. Water swirled and splashed, and his tiny corpse was washed away. Lost.

And, whispering in my ear, my mom's voice said, "With all its sham, drudgery, and broken dreams, it is still a beautiful world."

I stared at both of them in mute outrage.

But *was* Tigerstripe truly gone? As my anger built, as the bile swelled within me, fueled by this shocking cystic revelation, the troubled waters also rose within the commode. My loving, former-supportive, former-caring, former-adoring parents had set me up. They'd gifted me a pet they knew would soon perish. The swirling toilet water rose as the acrid emotions climbed in my throat. Tiger-stripe was gone, but his corpse had stuck somewhere in the craw of the hotel's luxurious plumbing, and now not-fresh toilet water spiraled upward to crest the lip of the ceramic tomb and gush forth, splashing across the stone-tiled floor.

The doorbell rang once more, and, as my father turned to answer it, I stepped into his path. Standing between my dad and the bathroom doorway, I swung . . . as I'd once swung the *Beagle* book to decimate a lurid dog dinger . . . I now swung my open hand, jumping, leaping as needed to land a blow across my father's close-shaved cheek.

His expression was Ctrl+Alt+Shocked. The toilet disgorged water. Choked with the dead body of my tiny kitty, it vomited, erupting beside us. No longer a mere commode, it became a cauldron boiling over with decayed cat parts and evil magic.

Not unnoticed by me, even in my churlish state, a strange boy had stepped into the bathroom doorway, a surly urchin whose thorny brow suggested Romanesque ruins and gothic goings-on. Wolves. Stooped Gypsy hags. At the sight of this brooding waif . . . and at the toilet's fury . . . and in response to my violent lashing out, my mother shrieked, and as fast as an echo from my original blow, my father slapped me back.

A Kitten's Tragic Denouement

Posted by Madisonspencer@aftrlife.hell

entle Tweeter,

Yes, my father slapped me.

And yes, I might be an uppity preteen romantic with aspirations to become a long-suffering Helen Burns, but I do know that getting walloped across my sassy, too-fresh-for-my-own-good mouth was a lot less fun than I'd always imagined it would be.

In the well-appointed bathroom of the Beverly Wilshire, as the chilled waters of that kitten-choked commode overflowed beside us, my father's blow fell, scarcely hard enough to turn my head, but the sharp sound of it reverberated hugely in the tiled space. My meaty child's hand hurt more from swatting his rugged face than my cheek hurt from his counterswat. The ready expanses of mirror showed us both: my tiny handprint reddening his face, my own rage darkening my visage. My mom stood nearby accompanied by maids and PAs and assorted hangers-on, her tapered fingers having flown up to mask her eyes from the brutal scene. Bits of orange fur rode the cresting tide, and we were—all of us—swamped. Only the unlikely adopted stranger stood apart from this domestic tragedy. The surly blackguard youth, he was a harbinger of disaster from some distant, strife-torn, blood-besotted fiefdom. This, the glowering countenance of a man-child no doubt suckled by rapacious wolves, this was Goran. This was the taut moment of our first encounter.

In the days and weeks to come, in Nairobi and Nagasaki and Naples, my father would not-subtly transfer his affections from me to this surly refugee waif. As I had so recently channeled my unhappiness through my kitten, my father would come to make indirect statements such as "Goran? Would you tell your sister that she isn't getting anything for Christmas—except perhaps a seat belt extender." Not that we celebrated Christmas. Not that my father even acknowledged me; no, I was Goran's sister or my mom's daughter, but I'd become invisible to him. For my part, as he could no longer see me, I could not speak to him. Thus we ceased to exist for one another.

In Reykjavik and Rio and Rome, I'd already become a ghost to him.

After that came the unhappy episode of Goran slashing the pony's throat at EPCOT Center. After that came Goran stealing my mom's People's Choice awards and hawking them over the Internet. By then my father had begun to soften, but it was too late, because it was soon after that, very soon, that I would be dead for real.

The Abomination Arrives

Posted by Hadesbrainiacleonard@aftrlife.hell

riting in the third century, the Neoplatonist Zoticus predicted that one day a single mighty nation would rule all others. This nation will occupy an island in the center of a great ocean. It will rapidly collect all the wealth of the whole world, and all the kings of the world shall come to reside here. Writing in the fifth century, the Neoplatonist Proclus described this future nation as a beautiful mirage. According to the Egyptian hieroglyphs, it will float on the horizon.

And here will the thing-child wash ashore. It will stride the cloud-colored beaches with no more awareness of its nudity than had the original humans.

There all plastic comes to a final rest. There the center holds, becalmed, in that Sargasso of plastics. The North Pacific Gyre, as that graveyard is known.

And arriving on this scene will stroll a human mother, wandering along that same beach, deep in her own grief. And the woman is essentially alone, accompanied by only one stylist, a publicist, four armed bodyguards, a yoga instructor, two lifestyle gurus, and a dietitian. This woman glimpses the thing-child: a slender sylphlike figure with skin as perfect as only plastic can be perfect. A face as smooth as only a photograph can be smooth. Its hair, a great bale of floss combed to rich fullness by infinite ocean waves. And from all outward appearances is the thing-child a she-child.

And the she-child is of impossible beauty.

And from a distance, upon first catching sight of the she-child, Plato claims that the lonely woman will call out. Stopped, paralyzed by the sight, she'll gasp. The woman shall stumble forward a few steps, her arms raised involuntarily to embrace this vision, and she'll cry out, "Madison?"

For here, to the eyes of a bereft mother, this gift from the sea appears to be a resurrection. And this woman strolling along the beach will be the nominal queen of this wealthy kingdom.

And here is a long-lost child seemingly reunited with its mourning parent. A miracle witnessed by all the attendant entourage.

Tears leap to the woman's eyes. For this stranger, who stands nude on that gleaming beach . . . this stranger is slender and enigmatically calm—not pudgy and grouchy, not willful and sullen—but, still, the resemblance is otherwise perfect. This is the murdered child, glorified. Before she might call out a second time, Plato writes that the woman is choked with emotion.

And thus will evil plant his she-child in the nest of an unknowing bird.

Thus will goodness be cuckolded, according to the papyri of Sais. And evil seeks to fit goodness with a pair of horns.

For this otherworldly beauty, this she-child begotten of plastic and fostered by the sea, it opens its winsome arms to

the human woman. With its sweet voice it says, "Mother."
The she-child advances to embrace the woman, and it says,
"Camille Spencer, I am returned to you." Embracing the
bereaved woman, it says, "I return to you as proof of life
everlasting. I bring you tidings of paradise."

Fata Morgana

Posted by Madisonspencer@aftrlife.hell

entle Tweeter,
Ultimately this is a tale about three islands. As was Lemuel Gulliver's tale. Our first island was Manhattan. The second was a traffic island upstate. The third, we're about to discover.

After our humiliating debacle at LAX, I accompanied my psychic shepherd to a customized CH-53D Sea Stallion, the *Gaia Wind*, for a lengthy low-altitude commute across open ocean. Considering the afternoon sun on the Pacific, the crystalline December air, it's all quite thrilling.

As we fly westward, what I notice initially is a faint glow on the horizon. Even in broad daylight, in the wrong direction, a freakish, premature dawn seems to be rising. A shimmering, blue glow. Little more than three hours after lifting off from LAX, the *Gaia Wind* comes within sight of a new shore. As Gulliver and Darwin before me, I'm glimpsing a new foreign landmass. Carried along as we are by the *whop-whop-whop* of the helicopter's broad propeller, we hover ever closer to this strange, impossible territory of luminous, jagged alps. The sun glints off vast plains. The shadows of passing clouds mottle the land's surface, and pinnacles of breathtaking height thrust themselves up, into the mist. This, this fantasy landscape resembles not terra firma so much as peaks and whorls of whipped cream, all of it enlarged to a massive scale and colored the sparkling crystallite white of table salt. Not that, as former hippies and former macrobiotic dieters, my parents had ever exposed me to salt.

My inebriated consort, Mr. Crescent City, leans forward, his amply veined eyes fixed on this growing vision. His mouth hangs slack, exaggerating his already not-alert facial expression as he says but a single, rapt word. "Madlantis!"

Ye gods.

Contrary to the old adage "Buy land . . . they're not making it anymore," immediately before us is proof that people are, indeed, making land. At least, Camille and Antonio are.

My parents had often mentioned a scheme. It was their stated ambition to resolve many of the globe's most-dire problems with a single dramatic fix. Foremost in their minds was the swirling Sargasso of discarded postconsumer plastic known as the Pacific debris field. Second was global climate change. Third was the dwindling habitat available for wild bears of the polar variety, and fourth was the onerous burden of income taxes they were compelled to pay.

In truth, Gentle Tweeter, their income taxes occupied the lion's share of my parents' attention, but bear with me for the time being.

As a solution to all of these annoyances, Antonio and Camille Spencer had proposed a radical public works project. Even prior to my demise, they'd been busily lobbying world leaders. Like the master puppeteers they were, my mom and dad were shaping popular opinion toward their dream: to create a new continent—a vast floating raft of aerated polystyrene and bonded polymers, with a surface area double that of Texas. In this approximately mid-Pacific location, constantly shifting, perpetually growing, had been the aforementioned Pacific debris field, that far-reaching soup of plastic shopping bags and plastic water bottles and LEGO blocks, and every other bobbing, floating form of plastic refuse that's been caught in the circling currents of the Pacific Gyre.

In the name of ecological restoration, my parents have spearheaded an international fund to meld together the ever-growing mass of plastic, and by churning this stew of Styrofoam, this morass of shredded cellophane . . . simply by partially melting it with injections of superheated air and introducing chemical bonding agents, they've reinvented this sodden ecological horror as a white confection. This synthetic wonderland covers millions of acres, heaped into gleaming mountains and spread in rolling hills where rainwater pools to form freshwater lakes and inland seas. This whipped-foam landscape floats, impervious to earthquakes, and rides high atop the worst tsunami. Its most striking quality is its pristine whiteness, a pearlized . . . an iridescent, immaculate whiteness, with the faintest suggestion of silver.

From a distance, it's a heavenly paradise. Here are the baroque turrets and domes you imagine among cumulus clouds as you lie on your back in a Tanzanian meadow during Easter recess. Not that we celebrated Easter. Yes, I hunted for the requisite dyed eggs, but my parents told me these had been hidden by Barney Frank, who also furnished me an annual oversize basket of carob treats. Not that my mom ever allowed fatty, pig-pig me to actually eat that carob. Not that *anyone* really likes carob.

In my folks' puffed-plastic dreamscape, looming tall are

white spires cresting above bowers of white roses, arches and buttresses, courtyards and gateways bright as spun sugar. It's the white your tongue sees when you lick vanilla ice cream. Approaching the coastline of Madlantis you can discern white ravines and peaks. Before us are reconstituted plastics, seared by high-temperature blasts of air until they look polished. Glazed to glassy smoothness, these pinnacles and slopes aren't subject to geological physics. In a dreamscape, a Maxfield Parrish arcadia: They rise impossibly steep, sheer faces of shining ivory that jut straight up from white beaches as slick as a mirror. Bright as klieg lights.

And yes, I might be a carob-gobbling, sucrose-addicted tubby, chubby dead girl, but I know the word *Arcadian*. I also know a louche tax dodge when I see one.

In the reverse of previous continents, Madlantis existed as maps before it existed as peaks and valleys. This puffed-and-blanched, polygarbage terrain, every slope and crag was planned and modeled by artists, diagrammed on blueprints prior to its creation. Preconceived. Predestined. Every square inch predetermined.

The opposite of tabula rasa.

As they'd believed in the harmonic convergence of the planets and in pyramid power, so did Camille and Antonio promote this virgin continent as a New Atlantis.

Madlantis.

It's doubtful you can fly high enough to notice, but the overall shape of the continent is no mere accident of nature. The stretches of coastline and occasional bays aren't shaped by river systems. No, from outer space you can see how the new landmass is shaped like a human head in profile. The severed neck is oriented toward the south, the crown of the head toward the north. This milk-white, alabaster-white profile forms an enormous cameo surrounded by the cerulean blue of the Pacific Ocean. This Brobdingnagian silhouette, its saggy double chin dwarfs the nearby islands of Japan. The nape of its fatty neck crowds northern California, while its chipmunk cheeks threaten to block the shipping lanes above Hawaii. Needless to say, the newly minted continent of Madlantis was sculpted to look exactly like me.

Seen from outer space, the Earth now resembles nothing so much as a giant coin struck with my likeness. This is the satellite image I'd seen on television monitors and magazine covers at LAX. Here is the white plastic Heaven on Earth named in my honor.

A roundish, landlocked sea serves as my eye. On the opposite shoreline, rambling plastic glaciers suggest the strands of my unruly hair. And despite the fact that the whole is not particularly flattering, it is accurate. It's me but on a gigantic scale. If you asked my mother, she'd tell you that it's only *slightly* larger than life-size. My grieving parents would tell you that they'd conceived of this unheralded experiment in plastic reclamation as a staggering tribute to my memory. To finance their endeavor with public money corralled from every government in the world, my dad promised that it would serve to contain all the petrol-product debris of humanity. Its whiteness would reflect solar heat away from the planet and counteract climate change. Because it floated, the continent could even be towed north to serve as subsidized housing for displaced polar bears. Politicians flocked to support the endeavor.

In actuality, now that it's complete, Mr. Ketamine

informs me that the land's handful of physical residents is already in international court suing for their independence as a sovereign nation. It's no coincidence that these patriotic zealots—known as "Madlantians," and seeking freedom from colonialist oppressors—they are also the wealthiest people in the world, and that under the freshly inked constitution of Madlantis none of them will be subject to taxes upon their lofty incomes. Neither will inheritances be taxed. In addition, this small cadre of residents will all be named ambassadors of their plastic nation and therefore be granted the freedom of diplomatic immunity in all their international treks. That, Gentle Tweeter, is my parents' noble dream: infinite money and infinite freedom. Every major corporation in the world is scrambling to relocate its headquarters there.

By now we've crossed into Madlantian airspace. We're skimming above white plastic mountaintops. We're careening through white plastic valleys. Ahead lies a speck of not-whiteness. Located at the approximate center of my vast global, fat-girl profile is a ship. Mired there, in a whorled pit that suggests the opening of my auditory canal—my ear hole, according to Orthodox Christians, the orifice through which the Holy Spirit impregnated the Virgin—locked in this wasteland as effectively as any explorer's vessel crushed by advancing ice—or as Satan trapped in Dante's icy lake—there is my parents' megayacht, the *Pangaea Crusader*.

entle Tweeter,
Don't imagine for a moment that solar panels and wave energy power any portion of this thunderous helicopter, and approximately a million gallons of dinosaur juice later we set down atop the *Pangaea Crusader*. Ah, the imperial seagoing *palais* that is the *Crusader* . . . Despite the fact that the vessel is virtually an oceangoing space station, painted a gleaming, arctic white and only slightly smaller than Long Island, the *Crusader*'s central salon has been decorated to simulate the interior of a typical shantytown hovel found among the favelas of most Third World megalopolises. Were it not for the fact that we're rocking gently, rolling smoothly atop salty Pacific swells, the yacht's interior could be located in the primitive outskirts of Soweto or Rio de Janeiro.

Through the magic of fiberglass and trompe l'oeil painting, one bulkhead of the salon appears to be a wall of crumbling, asbestos-infused cinder block. To this, the world's leading graffiti artists have hand-applied layer upon layer of gang tags using faux-lead-based spray paint. The overall impression is one of menace, a sympathetic political oneness with the world's violent masses, not unlike the sordid interior of a men's comfort station situated along a densely traveled highway in tedious upstate.

In answer to HadesBrainiacLeonard, yes, this does feel

like an awful lot of scene setting, but please bear with me. We're approaching a poignant episode, a prodigal child returning to the seminurturing bosom of her mother. Thus I focus on the set dressing only because I'm not prepared for the depth of emotion I'm about to suffer.

Eventually, he of the flailing, not-clean pigtail, Mr. Crescent City presents himself before my mom in the yacht's spacious main salon. Unseen, I accompany him for this audience.

Even as I'm posting this, my mom's clutching a tall glass of cherry-flavored cough syrup mixed with an equal part of dark rum, garnished with a dagger of fresh organic pineapple and three maraschino cherries skewered on the balsawood stem of a living-wage paper parasol fashioned by dusky hands enabled through first-world microfinancing.

For someone who protests environmental degradation, it's ironic that my mother is always so polluted herself. It doesn't help that I'm sitting next to her. My ghost self is close enough to share a photo caption with her in *People* magazine, but she's still completely not seeing me.

Seated directly in my mom's eye line, I pop my ghost knuckles. I fidget and pick my ghost nose and bite my ghost fingernails, always hoping she's only pretending not to see me; she's just ignoring me and her attention will snap in my direction at any moment, and she'll shout, "Madison Desert Flower Rosa Parks Coyote Trickster Spencer—*KNOCK IT OFF!*"

However, drunk or sober, there she is: Camille Spencer sprawled on her divan, a drink in her hand, a tabloid magazine nested in her lap. In the wonderfully stagey voice she normally uses only for Somali maids and the Dalai Lama, she demands of her psychic bounty hunter, "Mr. City, can you honestly say you've found Madison's spirit?"

Her voice, it sounds like a trap. Like a cobra ready to strike.

From Mr. K, from under the bushy filth of his lip-colored mustache come the words, "Ma'am, I have found your daughter."

In my mom's eyes is the burning pain your tongue sees when you bite down on a too-vigorously microwaved slice of pizza *quattro stagioni*. "Your proof, Mr. City?" she asks.

"A long time ago," says Mr. K, "you ate some cat shit, and your mama pulled a worm as long as spaghetti out of your ass."

My mom chokes on her drink. Coughing red grenadine blood against the back of her hand, coughing like her own mom, my nana, coughed, she manages to croak, "Did my dead mother tell you that?"

No, Crescent shakes his head. "Your kid told me; I swear."

"And my murdered father?" she asks, stifling her cough with another sip. "I expect you've found him, also?"

Crescent nods.

"You've spoken with him?"

Ye gods. My drug-demented escort is about to expose me as a panicked public toilet pee-pee mangler.

Again, Crescent City nods. As he leans forward, the room's candles uplight his haggard face, like footlights on a stage, the glow gilding his wrinkles and the stubble on his chin. "Your pa, Mr. Benjamin, he told me he wasn't murdered."

"Then you, Mr. City," snaps my mom, "you are a charlatan!"

244

Wasn't murdered?

"You, Mr. City!" shouts my mom. With a wide sweep of her arm she thrusts a pointing finger, and this broad, theatrical gesture evicts the tabloid magazine from her lap. "You are a fraud!" The magazine flutters the short distance to the floor, where it lies faceup. "Because my child is *not* dead! My father was butchered by a psychopath! And my child is *alive!*"

She's gone crazy. I am neither alive nor a psychopath.

On the floor at our feet, the tabloid headline reads, "Maddy Spencer Resurrected." Printed in an only slightly smaller typeface, a subhead trumpets, "And She's Lost 60 Pounds!"

"You don't have to believe anything," says Mr. K, and he tunnels one hand into the rank denim abscess of a pants pocket. He produces a vial of familiar white powder and says, "I can *show* you." He reaches the vial toward her and says, "Go ahead, Holy Mother Camille. Talk to Madison yourself."

Camille Becomes a Tourist in the Afterlife
Posted by Madisonspencer@aftrlife.hell

entle Tweeter,

In the ship's salon, my mom accepts the vial of ketamine offered by Mr. Crescent City, and she scoops a polished fingernail deep into the white powder. She repeats this one-two-three times, inhaling each snootful with a snort so violent that her coiffed head whiplashes backward on her swanlike neck. Only when her fingernail can no longer find its way to the vial does Camille Spencer slump sideways on her divan, and the rise and fall of her world-renowned bosom becomes too faint as to be discernible.

Lest it slip from her chemically slackened grasp, Mr. City quickly reclaims the vial with its precious remaining contents. He asks, "Supreme Holy Mother Spencer?"

The familiar spectacle begins with a spot of blue light glowing in the center of her chest. The blue waxes brighter, shining upward before it grows like a tendril, spiraling, twining almost to the ceiling. At its apex, the blue vine swells into a bud. This bud takes the shape of a body, vague and streamlined. The color, it's the blue your skin sees when you slide between starched-and-ironed sixteen-hundred-thread-count Pratesi sheets. It's the blue your tongue sees when you eat peppermint.

Lastly the features of the blue face appear, my mother's wide cheekbones tapering to her delicate chin. Her eyes come to rest on me, on the vision of my ghost seated beside her, and her mouth blooms, her voice like a perfume. It's this, this elegant spirit, which says, "Madison Desert Flower Rosa Parks Coyote Trickster Spencer—stop biting your fingernails!"

Oh, Gentle Tweeter, success at last. I irritate; therefore I am.

After securing his cache of Special K, Mr. City gently lays two fingers against the side of my mother's slack neck, checking for a pulse. He places a hand on her brow and raises one eyelid, smudging his thumb with coppery eye shadow while making certain that her pupil slowly dilates.

Looking down upon him, my mom's blue spirit observes wistfully, "Maddy never understood why I took so many drugs."

No longer biting my fingernails, I say, "It's me. I'm here."

"You're just a sad projection of my intoxicated mind," she insists.

"I'm Madison."

The hovering, shimmering blue haunt shakes its head. "No," she says. "I've tripped on enough LSD to recognize a hallucination." She smiles as slowly and beautifully as any tropical sunrise. "You're nothing but a dream." Her ghost voice dismissive: "You're merely a projection of my guilty conscience."

I am, she claims, a figment of her imagination.

My mom's spirit sighs. "You're exactly the way Leonard told me you'd look."

You can appreciate my frustration, Gentle Tweeter. The Devil claims me as his invention. So does God. If Babette's to be believed, I'm part of some grand conspiracy launched by my so-called friends in Hell. Now my mother dismisses me as nothing but her own drug-induced vision. At what point do I become my own creation?

Floating, swanning around the ceiling, she explains that since she had been a small girl, pulling weeds and beating rugs on that upstate farm, a telemarketer had phoned to tell her about the future. Early on, she thought he was crazy. His voice was nasal and reedy, like a teenage boy's. Worse, he readily claimed to be over two thousand years old, and that he'd been a priest in the ancient Egyptian city of Sais. He was young and silly, she surmised, or he was clearly a lunatic.

Smiling at the memory, she says, "The very first time he called, Leonard was conducting a marketing research study about cable television viewing habits. . . . You know your grandmother. She'd never let us have cable, but I lied and said we did. You *know* how lonely that farm can get. Leonard asked if he could call me again the next day."

This telephone stranger, he'd known details about my mom that no one could know. And early on, he told her to buy a lottery ticket. He told her what numbers to choose, and when she won he told her where to go to have some photographs taken, and he told her exactly where to send those pictures: to what movie producer. This boy Leonard, he made her famous. He told her how she'd meet her future husband. Every day he'd telephone with more good news about my mom's future. The lottery ticket won. The producer cast her in a film before she'd turned seventeen, and when my papadaddy refused to let her work, Leonard called and told her how to file to become a legally emancipated minor.

This guardian angel, he'd told her to gather flowers and press them between the pages of a book. To honor her father, Leonard said, just in case she never saw him again.

"Your nana seemed to understand," my ghost mom explains. "She bought the lottery ticket for me. She told me that a similar telephone pollster had been calling her since she was a little girl." Patterson, he said his name was. This had been decades before. "Eventually Patterson had told her the exact date she'd bear a girl baby, and he'd asked her to name it Camille."

My mom left that upstate farm and never looked back.

In summary, it would seem that telemarketers have been steering the destiny of my family for at least three generations.

Under the unlikely tutelage of this faceless stranger, my mother's movie career had skyrocketed. As dictated by Leonard, she'd met and married my father, and with Leonard's advice their investments had snowballed. Wherever their far-flung projects took them, in Bilbao and Berlin and Brisbane, Leonard had always known where to call. He'd telephoned every day with new marching orders, and they'd come to trust him implicitly. Before they turned twenty-five, they were the wealthiest, loveliest, most celebrated couple in the world.

After years of coaching my parents to riches and fame, one day Leonard called my mother in Stockholm or Santiago or San Diego, to predict the date and time I'd be born.

"He whispered in my ear," swears my drifting ghost mom. "He whispered merely the *idea* of you."

And in doing so I was conceived.

The beauty of her countenance beaming down on me,

her ghost eyes brimming with soulful tears, she says, "He asked me to name you Madison. We were ecstatic. He told us that you'd be a great warrior. You'd defeat evil in a terrible battle. But then Leonard went too far. . . ."

Moment by moment, she tells me, my life had occurred exactly the way Leonard foretold it would.

"Then he told us exactly when and how you would die."

On some level, she muses, all mothers know their children will suffer and die; that's the horrible unspeakable curse of giving birth. But to know the exact place and time of your child's death is too much to bear. "I knew I was destined to be the mother of a murdered child. All of my film roles had been a rehearsal for that night. . . ."

Camille Spencer. Camille Spencer. Turn on cable television at any hour of any day, and there she is: The long-suffering nun who coaxes deathbed remorse from serial killers. She's the stoic single-mother waitress whose teen son is shot to death in drive-by gangsta violence. The Great Wise Survivor Woman. The Veteran Radical with All the Answers.

Unaware of her ghost, Mr. Crescent City addresses the whole salon, asking, "Do you see the angel Madison? Do you see I'm not a liar?"

It was knowing how I'd die that tempered their love for me. My mom closes her ghost eyes and says, "We knew the agonies you'd suffer, so we kept you at arm's length. I couldn't bear to witness the pain you'd be forced to endure, so we used criticism to prevent ourselves from loving you too much. By fixating on your flaws we tried to save ourselves from the full brunt of your eventual murder."

And by drinking and pill popping. "Why do you think

your father and I took so many drugs? How else could anyone live with the certainty of their child's impending death?"

Smiling wistfully, she whispers, "You remember how awful it was when your little cat died?" Her breath catches, and she closes her ghost eyes for a moment. She steadies her composure. "That's why we couldn't tell you that your Tigerstripe was doomed."

Leonard had told them that I'd invent salacious diary entries inspired by my stuffed toys. They sent me to boarding school . . . to ecology camp . . . to upstate, because it was too agonizing to see me every day, knowing what they knew.

"I even lied about your age," says my mom. "I told the world you were eight years old because Leonard had always foretold you would die on the evening of your thirteenth birthday."

A telemarketer had given her complete foreknowledge of my entire truncated life.

The night my mother had stood onstage at the Academy Awards and wished me a happy birthday, she knew I was breathing my last. As her televised image towered above me on the high-definition screen in a Beverly Hills hotel suite, saying, "Your daddy and I love you very, very much . . . ," she was fully aware that I was being garroted. As she bade me, ". . . good night, and sleep well, my precious love . . . ," my mother already knew I was dying.

Camille Disembodied

Posted by Madisonspencer@aftrlife.hell

entle Tweeter,

You've watched my mother play this scene so many times: a dramatic heroine delivering the expository monologue that provides backstory for some current plot crisis. You've witnessed her in this role so often that it's difficult to separate fiction from this new reality, but never has the scene played with such surrealism. The glimmering blue wraith of her hovers in the salon of the *Pangaea Crusader*. Her words . . . in this new role, my mother's voice is not that of a character. It's measured and frank, the subdued voice of a narrator in a documentary film.

Her blueness kiting about the ceiling, she says, "All preexisting religious doctrines must be made to seem ridiculous, outdated, oppressive, or hateful. That was the mission Leonard decreed."

To make room for a new world religion, Leonard had stated that all religions had to be discredited. Everything held to be sacred and holy had to be reduced to a joke. No one could be allowed to discuss good or evil without sounding like a fool, and the mention of God or the Devil must be met with universal eye rolling. Most important, Leonard had insisted, intelligent people must be made to feel ashamed of their need for a higher power. They must be starved for a spiritual life until they would greedily accept any that would be offered to them.

Since my mother's upstate childhood, all of Leonard's promises had come true. The only reason she'd let me be killed is because he'd promised I would return to my family in even greater happiness. Leonard had long pledged that I would telephone from beyond life and dictate the rules for a new world religion. He commanded my parents to gather the garbage of the seas and to build a heaven on earth. There, on its highest peak, they were to construct a temple. They were to espouse the doctrines decreed by their dead child, and only when they'd done so and the world was swept by this new faith, only then would their daughter return from her grave to lead all people to the actual kingdom of paradise.

"We completed what Nietzsche had begun," says my floating mother. "God would have to be thoroughly killed before we could resurrect him."

Leonard preached that mankind would always long for an organized system of religious beliefs, but, like a scared insecure child, people would hide their need behind a mask of sarcasm and ironic detachment. Each person, he'd claimed, would grow tired of acting as his or her own deity. They would want to belong to something larger, to a sort of family who accepted them despite their worst behavior. This family would be the Boorites.

Boorism, as Leonard had planned, would be a brotherhood that accepted and celebrated the worst aspects of its adherents. Even the details which they themselves despised—their secret prejudices, their bodily odors, their piggish rudeness.

Captivating is my mother, the consummate storyteller. "Through Boorism," she explains, "Leonard teaches us that salvation relies on making your life an ongoing act of forgiveness."

No matter what others say or do, you must never take offense. According to Boorist doctrines, the greatest sin is reproaching others, and humans are given life on earth so that we might test one another with small and large slights. Anyone may spit or swear or break wind, but no one may accept that act as a personal affront.

Every unkind remark or crude gesture by others is a blessing, an opportunity to exercise our own capacity to forgive.

"In theory it sounds vile," says my mom, "but it's really quite simple and lovely in practice."

From even his earliest telephone conversations, Leonard had described Camille's child as a modern Persephone.

As my mother's spirit flits about the room, describing her outlandish scenario—all human destiny covertly string-pulled by dead telemarketers—Mr. City tips his vial of ketamine. He taps a small pile of white onto his thumbnail and snorts it in a single breath. He snorts another.

To touch the hearts of everyone in the world, the child who would die horribly and be returned to life, she would have to be famous. Like a modern Abraham called to sacrifice his son Isaac, the child's parents would need to capture the eyes and ears of the world media. For that lofty purpose, Leonard had made Camille and Antonio Spencer such global role models. All of humanity would know their child and mourn her untimely death. The world would embrace my parents' disdain for organized religions, and the world would subsequently convert en masse when my parents made public their proof of an afterlife.

As they had flocked to soy and hemp, so would people ultimately flock to Boorism.

That's why, Gentle Tweeters, the ultrasound snapshot of my fetus had been published in newspapers and magazines worldwide, months before I was born. The video of my delivery had played on prime-time television and won an Emmy. That squalling, slimy newborn me was known to billions of viewers. As was my kitten, Tigerstripe, show-cased on myriad magazine covers. Birthday by birthday, the entire planet had watched me grow from an infant to a tod-dler to my fleshy girlhood.

The entire planet watched my funeral. Kings and presi-dents carried my biodegradable casket.

For obvious reasons the person who'd slay me would have to be a reviled Judas. My parents had searched long. They'd adopted the basest of blackguards and young cut-throats in the hope that one would be my executioner. It was only when they'd tested Goran, scurrilous Goran, that they knew they'd found their villain. No, what happened at EPCOT was no accident, but rather a carefully choreo-graphed experiment. When they'd given Goran a knife and paraded an innocent, endearing pony before him . . . it was when he'd slashed its throat without hesitation that my mom and dad knew they'd found the player who would eventually end my life.

What Makes a Family

Posted by Madisonspencer@aftrlife.hell

entle Tweeter,

In Athens or Aspen or Adelaide, my parents and I had always created a family. Anytime we were together, our love was intact. We weren't like normal families who live tied to one plot of moldy compost, growing potatoes and carding wool. We had so many houses, in Dublin and Durban and Dubai, that none of them felt like our home. We weren't like those genetically isolated finches Mr. Darwin had found in the Galápagos. No, we were more like those lost tribes wandering around in the pages of the Bible book. In Vancouver or Las Vegas or Van Nuys, all we had that was stable and consistent was each other.

For years, my faults were the glue that kept my parents united. My fat, my quiet bookwormish, misanthropic misbehavior, these were the flaws they sought to correct. And when I seemed to throw myself at Jesus Christ, well, nothing could've cemented their marital bond more effectively. Please forgive me my boast, but for years I was a genius at keeping my mom and dad hitched while the parents of my boarding school peers were constantly wedding and divorcing new partners. In Miami and Milan and Missoula, while our surroundings constantly changed, we had one another.

That is, until now. Which is why God has erected such a firewall between the living and the dead: because the predead always *distort* whatever the postalive tell them. Jesus or Mohammad or Siddhartha, whenever any dead person has come back to offer some banal bit of advice, the living recipient misinterprets every word of it. Wars ensue. Witch burnings. For example, when Bernadette Soubirous stepped into the water at Lourdes in the year 1858, the Virgin Mary materialized only to say, "Hey, don't play here, kid. It's a filthy-dirty medical-waste dump." Even worse, in 1917 when she appeared to impoverished Portuguese shepherd children at Fatima, Mary was only trying to sneak them the number for a winning lottery ticket. Talk about good intentions! Here a helpful dead lady was merely trying to lend them a hand, and those predead urchins Ctrl+Alt+Overreacted.

In summation, the predead get everything wrong. But at this point in history, you can hardly blame them for being so spiritually famished that they'd gobble down anything. Yes, Gentle Tweeter, we may have polio vaccines and microwave popcorn, but secular humanism really only covers the good times. Nobody in a foxhole ever said a prayer to Ted Kennedy. Nobody on a deathbed clasps his hands in weeping despair and petitions for the aid of Hillary Clinton. My parents were in a position to proselytize. I gave them some misguided advice, and now, the headlines: "Camille Files for Divorce!"

I've failed in my eternal mission to keep them together.

Camille in Denial

Posted by Madisonspencer@aftrlife.hell

entle Tweeter,

"Who's Persef . . . ?" I ask my mother.

"Persephone," says she. If Leonard's to be believed, Persephone was a girl so extraordinary that a brute named Hades had only to glance at her to fall madly in love. She lived with her loving parents on Earth, but Hades seduced her and eloped with her to his kingdom in the underworld. In her absence the world cooled. Without her grace present the trees shed their leaves and the flowers withered. Snow fell. Water turned to ice, and the days waned shorter while the nights waxed longer.

With her new husband, Persephone was happy for a period. In her new underworld home she made friends and learned the customs. She became a favorite among her peers just as she had been on Earth. Hades loved her as much as her parents had, but eventually she pined to visit them. After half a year Hades relented. Such was his love that there was little he could deny his wife. Only when she had sworn to return to him in the underworld did Hades allow her to leave.

Upon her return to Earth the snow blanketing her old home melted. Trees flowered and bore fruit, and the days stretched so long that the nights between them were almost gone. Persephone's parents were overjoyed to see her, and for half a year the three lived together as they had before her marriage.

According to Leonard, when six months had passed Persephone bade her parents farewell and returned to her husband, Hades. The Earth slept in her absence. When half a year had again passed, she returned to bring summer.

"That's it?" I ask. "She never goes to college or gets a job or anything? She just shuttles back and forth between her folks' house and her husband?"

With a sad smile, so wan that I suspect the effects of Botox extend into the afterlife, my mom says, "My daughter is Persephone. . . ."

My own response to her speech is complicated. I couldn't accept such a proposal from Satan, but coming from my mother it is more palatable. It's not overly flattering: the concept that I've been born and bred and fattened like a calf for some ritual slaughter. My parents stood apart from me because they knew my life would end so tragically. They even selected my assassin and abandoned me to his deadly manhandling.

Perhaps that explains my carnal preoccupation with the ruddy Goran. Aren't we all entranced by the means of our own future demise?

It's not without appeal, the possibility that I was born already doomed and that everyone I loved knew more about me than I did about myself. If that's the case I'm absolved from doing any wrong. I'm helpless and ignorant, but I am innocent.

What chafes me is the image of Leonard the puppet master, some slide-rule misfit telephoning my mother and jerking her chain. Leonard, seated at his telemarketing console, wearing his headset in Hell, dictating his philosophy to my impressionable eleven-year-old mom . . . the image prompts me to say, "I know him. I know Leonard."

I say, "He's book-smart, but he doesn't know everything."

My mom's spirit looks Ctrl+Alt+Stunned.

I say, "He tricked you. Leonard bought your trust with winning lottery numbers and insider stock market tips just so you'd let me be murdered." The words pour out, unstoppable. "Leonard's a liar, Mom! Boorism is a big mistake!"

I advance to comfort her. My arms spread wide for a nurturing hug, I say, "It's going to be okay. You were just an idiotic eleven-year-old girl. I *know* the feeling. . . ."

The blow lands across my ghost cheek. Yes, CanuckAIDSemily, a ghost can slap another ghost. And apparently a ghost mother can smack her own chubby baby girl ghost. What's more—it hurts.

Granted, my mother's ghost is already fading. Her body sprawled on the divan, the chest stirs. Color rises in her cheeks. The ghost hand that slapped me has almost vanished. Perhaps it's only the idea of the slap that stings.

"You're the liar!" shouts my vanishing blue mom. "You're a hallucination!"

It's not the most sensitive reaction, but I say, "Don't be stupid." I say, "You're leading the entire world to Hell."

What remains of her ghost is invisible. Only her words hang in the air of the salon, almost inaudible as she says, "Whatever you are, you're not my daughter. You're an evil, overweight *nightmare*. My real child is beautiful and perfect, and on this very day she has returned to bring eternal sunshine to all of mankind."

Another Loved One in Jeopardy!

Posted by Madisonspencer@aftrlife.hell

entle Tweeter,

"So why Jesus?" asks the luminous blue ghost of Mr. K. "Why did you fall for Jesus?"

My thumbs twitching across the keys of my PDA, I shrug. At the time I was on the cusp of puberty. I was eleven years old with menarche barreling down on me like a speeding bloodmobile. Meaning: my first menstruation. Meaning: *Menarche* is not some Old Testament who's-it. Any morning I expected to wake up with some huge burden of mammary glands attached to my chest. Thickets of hair would be sprouting in all of my secret places, and I'd be rendered a hormonal zombie. Time and time again, I'd seen it happen at my Swiss school. One day girls would be spunky, brainy flat-chested superheroes, and the next day they'd be simpering Miss Sexy Sexpots.

"So why Jesus?" asks Mr. Ketamine's ghost. We're two ghosts sitting in the main salon of the megayacht, keeping watch over my conked-out mom. The blue of Mr. K's spirit matches exactly the blue that my tongue sees when I eat crushed ice. Not that I get to eat anything, not anymore. Not that I'm shedding any pounds, either.

Continuing to keyboard, I explain that my parents are little more than their physical appetites, their recreational drugs and casual sex. They're just hungry carnal stomachs forever consuming. By dating Jesus, I wanted to sidestep all of the blood and spit and sperm that seemed to loom in my immediate future.

To CanuckAIDSemily, thanks for the heads-up. Reading your latest text, I say, "Fie! Gadzooks!"

Mr. K's blue ghost says, "What's wrong?"

"It's my cat," I say. "It's Tigerstripe."

CanuckAIDSemily tells me that Satan is nosing around Hell, asking everyone whether they've seen an orange-striped tabby. He's offered a reward of one hundred full-size Mars bars to whoever can capture Tigerstripe and turn him in, no doubt for Satan to use as a hostage against me.

Yes, Gentle Tweeter, I did once attempt to flush Tiger down a toilet at the Beverly Wilshire, but that was only after he was dead. And that's different, because I loved him.

Mr. City, he looks down on his earthly body, sprawled there on the floor. His scabrous, pocked face. His mangled ears and nose. "I wish I were dead."

"No, you don't," I say.

"Dead and rich," he says. Even his ghost has crooked teeth, leaning together in some places, missing in others, teeth like the ruins of Stonehenge and approximately the same lichen colors.

I text, asking whether anyone has seen Tigerstripe, and whether anyone is hiding him. This might sound like a case of misplaced priorities, but I'm less worried about Satan getting his mitts on my parents than I am about him flaying the lovely fur off my pet pussycat. Just the idea makes me Ctrl+Alt+Frantic.

"I want to be dead and in Heaven," says Mr. K's ghost, "and making love to Sahara. Did I ever tell you about

Sahara?" The ketamine must be wearing off, because Mr. K's already pale blue ghost is fading.

According to CanuckAIDSemily, Satan has released my prisoners from the Swamp of Partial-birth Abortions. Hitler, Idi Amin, Elizabeth Bathory, they're all set free to terrorize the occupants of Hell once more. Caligula, Vlad the Impader, and Rin Tin Tin, they all have special orders to seek out one special little orange kitty.

Overhead, I can hear propeller blades chopping the Pacific air. It's the unmistakable sound of the *Gaia Wind* setting down on the deck above us. Not looking away from my PDA screen, I pause. Without making eye contact with Mr. K's ghost, trying to sound Ctrl+Alt+Nonchalant, I ask, "Did you and my papadaddy talk at all . . . about me?"

Mr. K's flickering blue silhouette, barely there, nods.

Satan Phones to Bait Our Hero
Posted by Madisonspencer@aftrlife.hell

entle Tweeter,

Aboard the *Pangaea Crusader* my borrowed PDA begins to play "Barbie Girl," and on the device's backlit screen the name of the caller appears as "Your Author." I cautiously put the phone to my ghost ear.

" '. . . Madison knew she would not be able to hide her true nature for much longer,' " a voice says. A guttural, robust voice, it says, " 'Soon Maddy would have to embrace the fact that she personified chaos, and that her reason for being was to bring misery and conflict to everyone whose life she touched!' "

It's Satan. Of course it's Satan. Gentle Tweeter, the dark lord claims to have authored the story of my life—to have written me into being, if you will—and he insists that I'm no more real than Jane Eyre or Huckleberry Finn. Periodically he telephones to read me portions of his so-called novel as proof that he's dictated my every continuing thought and action. In the Devil's version of my life every sentence ends with an audible exclamation mark. At least one. I wish I shared Satan's enthusiasm about me.

" '. . . Already,' " he continues reading, " 'Madison had lured multitudes of souls to eternity in the fiery pit!' " The telephone voice says, " 'And Madison knew that if she didn't strive to complete her infernal mission of total damnation, soon the Devil's hellhounds would locate her helpless kitty cat and utilize it for conducting skin patch toxicity tests of a new feminine hygiene spray!' "

On her divan my unconscious mother stirs, moaning softly. Gradually the noise of helicopter blades begins to subside. Footsteps bound across the helipad overhead, thudding the deck that is this salon's ceiling. Every step brings some hideous revelation a moment closer.

" '. . . Madison knew that, even now, her Papadaddy Ben was coming aboard her parents' ostentatious yacht! He would expose her! The world would comprehend the penis-lacerating, man-hating murderess she was!' "

A Portrait in Goo

Posted by Madisonspencer@aftrlife.hell

entle Tweeter,

Science affords little room for personal feelings. As a supernaturalist, it is not my role to judge or censor events as they occur. No, at best mine is the position of a recording witness. The fantastical might transpire, the sad, the shocking even, but I must maintain a level head and set myself the goal of documenting these. Cold as such an edict may seem, I'm grateful for it; otherwise, I could not bear what happens next.

Aboard the *Pangaea Crusader,* my father appears in the doorway to the ship's salon. He stands there for a moment, squinting against the smoky incense and dim light. "Camille?" he says, his voice subdued, freighted with dread. "My love?" He hesitates as if afraid of what he'll find. Finally, his gaze falls upon the figure stretched the length of the sofa: my mother seemingly dead, and he bounds forward, closing the distance in the time it takes to shout, "Camille!" Like some fairy-tale prince, he drops to one knee beside my drowsing mom. Cradled in his hands, he holds a blue pillow. It's a small bundle of blue fabric.

As for my mother, her irregular breathing is too shallow to be readily apparent. And her cough syrup libation has left a crimson stain around her mouth that suggests nothing so much as the purge fluids: the froth of blood and stomach acid that corpses regurgitate in their early hours of death.

266

Trust me, Gentle Tweeter, I may be thirteen years old and cantankerous and a girl, but I have spent several hours hovering over my own dead body in a hotel suite, hoping someone would arrive to resuscitate me. After observing the myriad noxious changes that beset my own fresh cadaver—lividity, rigor mortis, bowel evacuation—I know what purge fluids are.

To the future-dead, I heartily suggest you don't linger.

My father presses his cheek against my mom's, muttering her name like an incantation, "Camille, Camille Spencer, Cammy, my love," breathing this magic utterance into her still ear. I'm embarrassed to watch, but it's too late to escape. Mere moments before, Mr. Ketamine fled the room. As for me, what I observe seems more intimate than sex. Tears spring to my father's eyes and he moans in agony. "My Camille, my Cammy, how could you end your life?" He sobs his words into her bosom, saying, "How could you? Babette means nothing—she means less than nothing—to me." His body shudders as he presses himself upon her, saying, "I never wanted this divorce. I only left you because our Madison commanded it. . . ."

Hearing this, I'm totally Ctrl+Alt+Taken Aback. Here's more Madison-related human suffering. As if every act of stupidity is somehow my fault.

On his knee, rocking against my mom, he continues to hold the small blue bundle he's carried into the room. Cradled between his chest and my mom's, the blue looks vaguely familiar. And as my dad weeps and keens, the body beneath his begins to stir.

Her eyelids flutter. Her fingers caress my father's hair. So overcome is my dad that he's unaware of her resurrection until she says, "Antonio?" Her fingers find the blue bundle clasped between them, and she asks, "What have you brought me?"

My father, his face, his eyes gasp. His mouth gapes as if he beholds paradise. His mouth thrusts forward to meet hers, and they kiss. They kiss the same way I gobble down peanut-butter cheesecake. They suck each other's faces the way my nana smoked her first cigarette in the morning.

And yes, I might be dead, but I'm not so tactless that I ogle their passionate romantic grappling. Instead, I coolly observe how the oceanic reflections of light glimmer through the portholes to ripple against the salon ceiling. Eventually my parents break their clinch.

Breathless, my mom touches the blue bundle of fabric and says, "Show me."

"Behold, my beloved!" says my dad. He stands, unfurling the blue to reveal that it's a garment. Stretched between his hands is a coarse collar of faded blue. Chambray, my guess is. White buttons march down the front. It's a shirt, and he holds it by each cuff, stretching his arms wide to display it all.

Ye gods, Gentle Tweeter, it's my worst fear. It's my soiled blue chambray shirt from upstate!

"Behold," says my father, his face a grinning blissful cross between tears and joy. "Our cherished Madison has sent us another sign! It was for sale in a vintage clothing store in Elmira, exactly where Leonard said it would be!"

My mother, likewise bleary-eyed, peers at the fabric, inspecting it. Her mouth hangs slack with disbelief.

"It's Madison's image," exclaims my father. "It's her face!"

Hanging there, spoiling the blue fabric, are the stains of

Papadaddy's vile spew. The loathsome fluids that erupted from between the pages of the *Beagle* book in that long-ago tedious upstate public toilet, they've set, creating an abstract pattern like the map of Mr. Darwin's expedition to someplace horrible. They've formed piddling islands and dark continents of a world no one would willingly explore.

"Here!" my father proclaims as he thrusts forward a stained patch for my mother's closer inspection. "Here's her eye!" He shifts another corrupt blotch nearer her face, insisting, "And here's her other eye!" He points to this smudge some huge distance from the first, as if my eyes were in different time zones. As presented the two smudges are vastly different sizes, one no larger than a thumbprint. The other is the size of a fist. The two aren't even on the same level. They're two asymmetrical blobs separated by a gross smear he interprets as my nose.

Please know, Gentle Tweeter, this is not me. It's wiener juice spurted out. It's the face of a deformed monster.

"I can see now! That *is* Maddy's pretty nose!" my mom exclaims. "I can *see* it! The face looks exactly like Madison!"

"Look at her mouth!" my dad gushes, almost weeping. "Oh, her sweet mouth!" Using his fingertip, he traces the irregular outline of a revolting stain, a grotesque mess of indelible ejaculate. A crusted horror.

My mom cries out, "It's a perfect likeness!"

Trust me, Gentle Tweeter, it is not. These revolting residual deposits of frightening man-jelly, they look nothing like me!

My father presses his nose to this abundance of stale ooze, and he inhales, deeply, exclaiming, "It even smells like Madison!"

269

It's this disgusting residue of desiccated goo my mother and father now herald as a visitation from their angelic daughter. Depicted in this most sickening medium, they see me, and the shared passion of the moment brings their beaming, beatific countenances to the brink of a second passionate lip-lock. Their mouths tremble toward touching one another. Their faces yearn forward.

But the moment is spoiled. A new voice enters the room, a young woman's voice, calling, "Antony?" Calling, "Antony, where are you?" At this, my parents freeze. Quickly, they abandon their amorous embrace, almost springing apart, as this new figure enters. Her hair is curled and red, her face bone white. It's Miss Torrid von Torridski from the Rhinelander penthouse, my dad's mistress. My former best friend. The infamous Babette; in her hands she carries another not-clean exhibit.

"Look here!" says my dad, calling my mom's attention to this new object. He spreads the odious shirt across my mother's lap, and he rushes to take this new curiosity from his noxious paramour. "Another sign from Madison!" he says. It's a book. Yes, Gentle Tweeter, it's *the book,* the book I hoped no one would ever find.

As Babette allows my dad to reverently lift the book from her spidery white hands, she narrates. She says, "The child virgin has sent her own unexpressed menses! Madison's blood flows forth to eradicate the blasphemous words of the heretic Charles Darwin!" Her voice climbing to shrill heights, Babette says, "A book that bleeds!" As my father bears the profane book on high, carrying it above his head, kneeling once more to present it to my mom, Babette says, "It's a miracle!"

It's a mess is what it is. The pages are matted together with coagulated wiener blood, pressed as solid as a brick by the weight of a mattress and a guilty conscience. It's not sanctified or remarkable. But to them, these deranged former Indigo Children and former alchemists and former shamanists, it's a holy relic. A big leather-bound, Heaven-sent Kotex.

Buried somewhere within it, written in my mother's hand, is the message, *Set yourself a goal so difficult that death will seem like a welcome reprieve.*

How easily this scene could end there, in this tableau: my father holding the book up . . . my mother on her divan, lifting her arms to accept it . . . the adulterous handmaiden looking on . . . but yet another person has entered the room.

Initially, my impression is that my long-dead Mr. Wiggles has returned to me, for this new presence is hardly bigger than a healthy goldfish. It floats in the air, glittering and fluttering the way a fish smoothly oscillates its yellow-pink fins to tread water. The fairy being, it glows, hovering. This enchantment moves closer.

No one turns to address him, this latest entry, but his tiny face is as smooth as fresh-baked bread. His yellow hair lies as bright as butter against his forehead. It's the rustic swain from my papadaddy's funeral. The primitive evangelist, now a dazzling sprite. My homemade angel from Halloween night. No one turns to address this unlikely import from rural upstate, but I'm so shocked that his half-forgotten name erupts, unbidden, from my lips.

The Inevitable Result of Operating Heavy Farm Machinery While Overdosed on Xanax

Posted by Madisonspencer@aftrlife.hell

entle Tweeter,

In the salon of the *Pangaea Crusader*, I cry, "Festus!" and the twee towheaded visitor turns to regard me with his luminous blue eyes. He actually sees and hears me. More to my surprise, my father's Skanky Skankerton mistress also casts her urine-hued eyes in my direction. She follows my gaze to Festus. Impossible as this seems, Babette sees us both, and her rubbery lips curl like store-brand hot dogs sliced lengthwise and fried in lard for a hardy upstate *petit de jeune.* Her eyes narrow to trembling slits and her shoulders arch like those of a wary barnyard cat. Her ample sweater-bound chest heaves with each breath. Even as I watch with the skeptical eye of a supernaturalist, Babette's fingernails grow from the length of a kitten's to that of a panther's.

My upstate consort lifts one boyish arm straight, his miniature hand, held palm out, no larger than a fully blown pink crocus, and he addresses her. His voice sounding deeper than you'd expect, robust and resonant, he says, "Be gone, vile succubus."

My parents, oblivious, huddle together to examine the *Beagle* book defiled with dingus blood they think gushed out of my angelic woo-woo.

And yes, I may be romantically smitten with this blond

tyke in bib overalls, but I do know the word *succubus*. If this charge leveled by my diminutive hillbilly flame is accurate, it would explain Babette's ability to see me. It might also explain the uncanny hold she seems to exert on my normally Camille-addicted father. My gratitude to Hades-BrainiacLeonard, who reminds us that a succubus is a demon who takes the form of a human female in order to seduce and destroy men.

Holding Babette at bay, wee Festus bids me come to his side. "I venture to this earthly place," he tells me, "on behalf of your grandfather."

"My father's father?" I ask in hope.

Festus regards me, his buttery forehead crossed with a single wrinkle to betray his Ctrl+Alt+Puzzlement. "I refer to Benjamin, who resides in perfect happiness for all eternity in the kingdom of Heaven."

My Papadaddy Ben, he means. "So he is in Heaven?" I ask dubiously. We're standing here looking at Papadaddy's skin-banana slime spouted all down the front of my nice shirt, and he's in paradise?

Festus nods. He studies my expression more closely. "Know you, maiden, any valid reason why Ben should not be in the presence of the Almighty?"

Ah, Festus, how I'd missed his stilted Pilgrim-speak. I ask, "How come you can see me?"

"We two can speak," Festus says, "because I am no longer of the material world."

Poor Festus.

I offer my condolences. "Were you killed by French-kissing?"

"Combine accident," he says with a baleful smile.

273

Forgive my gloating, Gentle Tweeter, but I knew it. From the first time we met at my papadaddy's homespun hayride funeral, I guessed that's how Festus's life would be resolved. A dozen years spent pulling weeds and plucking chickens and then, bam, he's chopped to a pulp by farm machinery. Oh, how I envied his dramatic fate!

He goes on to explain, "Forever am I to serve as an angel." Offering me his peewee hand, he says, "And my mission is to find you, my grail." He says, "I am sent here, Miss Madison, because the Lord our God is in dire need of your help."

The Purpose of My Awful Life—Revealed!

Posted by Madisonspencer@aftrlife.hell

entle Tweeter,

There's a Heaven.

There is a God, and not just Warren Beatty.

Paradise exists, Gentle Tweeter, but that fact provides little solace to those of us assigned to spend our eternity elsewhere. My upstate Festus has become a sparkling, itsy-bitsy angel, while pudgy me is enduring fiery, sulfurous lakes of crap and *The English Patient*. I'm happy for him. Tickled pink. Really, I am, but such inequitable social moments weren't covered in my not-slight schooling on etiquette. Fortunately, this difficult exchange is truncated by the insistent ringing of the salon's telephone. Babette answers it with a curt "Yes?"

Eyeing Festus and me, she listens to the caller. After a moment, she snaps, "No, I do not want to take a consumer product survey." She says, "Emily, how did you get this number?"

My mom's telephone rings, and she retrieves it. My father's rings.

My eternal gratitude to you, HadesBrainiacLeonard and PattersonNumber54 and CanuckAIDSemily. Your timing is spot-on.

"Chewing gum preferences?" asks my mom, incredulous. "Leonard, baby, is that you?"

275

My dad says, "No, I never buy the lambskin ones."

In the ensuing telemarketing chaos, young Festus spirits me from the yacht's salon. We escape down passageways and through hatches. In our giggling flight, we dissolve through bulkheads and Somali maids, tasting paint and semi-digested plantain curry, until we arrive in my long-sealed childhood stateroom. There, we find the drapes drawn, the lights out, the air-conditioning chilling my Steiff bears and Judy Blume paperbacks to archival temperatures. Every stray hair and pot of strawberry-scented lip gloss has been preserved as carefully as a diorama in the Smithsonian or the Museum of Natural History. Dead as we both are, my sturdy squire and I, we are, nonetheless, two unattached persons seeking refuge in a locked room with a bed.

Too steeped in romantic possibility is my ghost heart to ignore this turn of events. I recline on the bed's satin coverlet in what I hope is a not-unappealing pose. Into my ghost mind, unbidden, unwelcome, comes the image of my cigarette-smoking, wigless, panty-free nana stretched the length of my identical bed in the Rhinelander penthouse. To vanquish this image, I pat my postalive hand on the bed beside me and say, "So . . . you're an angel; that's cool." If my Festus is unaware of my history of mauling fragile man parts, I'm not eager to educate him. Neither am I certain whether he knows my soul was damned to Hades. Finally I venture, "So, Heaven's great. Don't you think?"

Festus smiles at me with the same condescending sad-eyed expression my mom uses when she addresses the United Nations General Assembly. A flood of pitying tears, barely contained.

Undeterred, I say, "Yeah, Heaven is tons better than I figured it would be. . . ."

Festus silently continues to regard me, his lips trembling with compassion.

Defensive now, provocatively I ask, "Hey, when the combine machinery tore you to shreds, did it hurt? I mean, did it rip off your hands first? How did that work?"

At this, Festus settles his angelic self on the bed beside me. "Do not be ashamed, Miss Madison," he says. "For I know you've been discarded by creation to spend forever in the scalding anus of Hades." His placid face says this without a hint of malice. "I know that you suffer constant starvation with nothing to slake your hunger and thirst save a mighty banquet of fresh urine and excrement. . . ."

Ye gods. Gentle Tweeter, I am speechless. I haven't a clue where Festus gets his information, but Hell is not that bad. I do not eat caca-doodie or drink pee. Don't you believe a word of this.

Charles Darwin I am not!

"I know also," he says, casting a look of ultimate pity upon me, "I know that you're forced to copulate endlessly with leprous demons and subsequently bring forth their filthy progeny in circumstances of utter degradation."

Hey, CanuckAIDSemily, back me up, here. Nobody is forced to get down with demons, right? As a *virgo intacta*, I have solid proof to the contrary, but there's no way to submit such evidence for Festus's inspection. Meaning: If I even try to show him my maidenhead, the gesture is going to look somewhat slutty.

"I know you exist despised by all worthy beings." Festus

blinks his blue cow eyes at me. "That every sentient creature considers you beneath respect. That in your present state you are more vile than—"

"Shut up!" I interrupt, lying rigid on the bed's coverlet. My chest is heaving. My temper seething. I'd rather spend infinity snacking on putrid poo than be talked down to by some self-righteous angel. Possible boyfriend or not, I'm leaving. I stand. I straighten my glasses. I smooth my skort. "If you'll excuse me," I say. "I'm sure I'm supposed to be fornicating with some diseased corrupt gargoyle or something right now."

"Wait," Festus entreats.

I wait. There it is, my greatest weakness: hope.

"God cast you down unto the Pit not because you are vile, but because God knows you are strong," says Festus. "God knows you are brilliant and courageous and that you are not weak and would not be debased by the torments which destroy weaker souls. . . ." Festus rises and hovers, fluttering in the air near my face. "Since the beginning of time God has intended for you to be His emissary into perdition."

God, Festus explains, knows that I'm pure-hearted.

God recognizes that I'm exceptional. He believes me to be sweet and smart and kind. God does not think I'm fat. He wants me to be his supersecret double agent.

Like nothing so much as a celestial version of Darwin's annoying little finches, Festus jets and darts in his golden fairy excitement, finally taking up a perch on my shoulder. Standing parrot-style beside my ear, he says, "God beseeches you to prevent a grave impending catastrophe."

DECEMBER 21, 1:28 P.M. HAST

My Date with an Angel

Posted by Madisonspencer@aftrlife.hell

entle Tweeter,

Even now storm clouds gather in the sky above the *Pangaea Crusader.* Clouds the color of blue lead, the color my mouth sees when I chew on a graphite pencil, these race toward Madlantis from every horizon, a dark canopy so low that the yacht feels sandwiched between this, this oppressive black ceiling and the gleaming, cotton-colored, plumped-polymer dreamscape. And, no, it is not lost on me that my situation is so like the seafaring *Beagle* adventures of Mr. Darwin. The both of us: boldly cast upon the cruel Pacific to seek our destinies. Being Mr. Darwin's supernaturalist successor, I steel myself to bear witness even as Mr. K paces the passageway outside my locked stateroom door. Even while my upstate squire reveals his divine truths unto me.

"Fear not, Miss Madison," says he. In my sealed stateroom full of stuffed animals and shed cat hair and dead fleas, the angel Festus says, "God has decreed your existence and God dictates your every perfect thought and action."

Angel Festus glows with a soft pink light, like a Park Avenue lamp shade lined with cerise silk, and his light flatters everything upon which it shines: the unread copy of *Our Bodies, Ourselves* on my bedside table, obviously a gift, the spine unbroken . . . a dog-eared copy of *The Joy of French Cooking,* my own favorite bedtime reading . . . a

279

silver-framed photograph of my parents grinning naked on an eco-resort beach in Cambodia. Weensy Festus, his angelic features, his fingers as well as his nose and cleft chin, look to have been piped from a pastry bag filled with buttercream frosting.

As he speaks, his open expression suggests the delicious invitation of a pastry cart, a bakery window, a box of chocolates. "God has gifted you with travails—not to test you, but to *prove* to you your own innate strength." His voice is as soft yet as robust as the ocean swells; his words sound as faint as thunder rolling from some great distance.

"God brings all spirits into mortal bodies so they might test themselves and more fully comprehend their own power," explains this pint-size beau, the upstate cow manure still clinging to his booted appendages.

From beyond the locked stateroom door, another voice shouts, "Angel Madison! Where are you?" A sputtering barrage of flatulence follows, the so-called "Hail, Maddy" of a devoted Boorist. That voice, the quavering vibrato of Mr. K, continues, "I'm really needing to talk to you!"

As Festus explains it, the rapid growth of Hell in recent history is beginning to unnerve God. At current earthly levels of rudeness and uncouth behavior, nearly all souls are damned. "Precious souls as young as three or four, raised on the misplaced multicultural priorities of *Sesame Street*," he claims, "are doomed before they even enter the godless morass of the public school system." In comparison, he says, the flow through the Pearly Gates has slowed to a trickle, and God worries that soon Heaven will be rendered irrelevant, nothing more than a quaint ghetto populated by a few squeaky-clean products of homeschooling.

If some global cataclysm were to wipe out humanity at this moment in history, all souls would go to Hell. No one would be left to breed on Earth. Satan would win, and God would be humiliated.

Therefore, God had used me to infiltrate Hell. Meaning: I am God's secret agent, and even I didn't know my own strategic undercover purpose.

In the burdened silence that follows, I ask, "Why doesn't God like *Sesame Street*?"

"Yours, Miss Madison, is a singular perfection like the flame of a candle," insists Festus. "This is the reason God cast you into the inferno. And why God set you in battle against the worst souls in human history, and why in all of these trials were you victorious." So passionately does Festus deliver this speech. So vehemently. His corn-fed frame fairly dances within his Sunday-school clothing.

Simultaneously, heavy seas lift Madlantis and drop us. Stuttering flashes of lightning flash blazing Morse code in the portholes. Ye gods. All is turmoil without.

"God almighty does not labor to create souls simply for Satan to steal them away," says Festus, his eyes bright with reflected lightning.

The angel says it's my purpose to vanquish Satan and to rebuild God's church on Earth. To roll back legal access to safe on-demand abortion and birth control . . . to righteously forbid marriage between sodomites . . . and to end the financial drain of welfare entitlement programs.

"You will be God's flaming sword of punishment!" This sturdy man-boy angel, his fists raised above his blond head, he flares like an arc, a spark, a stubby bolt of divine fire. His hummingbird wings buzz. His shouts ringing loud as cathedral bells, he exclaims, "Join us, Miss Madison! Join us and rejoice!"

Meaning: I'm supposed to thrash Satan *and* cut funding for public television. Meaning: I'm conflicted here.

And no, Gentle Tweeter, I might be somewhat enamored of my angelic suitor and his flattering message, but I am not deaf to the draconian objectives he describes. It's enticing, the idea of myself as a messianic figure, the hand of an omniscient savior, but not if it means I have to be a dick. In reasonable protest, I insist, "I can't! I can't best Satan! He's too powerful!"

"Nay," my barnyard Romeo says, "but you already have!"

"What?" say I.

"You've already once bested the Prince of Darkness!"

I haven't a clue what my postalive, postfarmer boyfriend is talking about.

"Angel Madison," bellows the voice from the hallway. "We're running out of time!"

"The end of the world is scheduled for three o'clock this very afternoon," says Festus.

According to my noncounterfeit Rolex, it's already one thirty.

Dictating a Desperate Edict

Posted by Madisonspencer@aftrlife.hell

entle Tweeter,

From the portholes of my stateroom aboard the *Pangaea Crusader,* the view in all directions is clear rain pelting polished white. Everything is crashes of blue lightning like blinks of crooked color, like towering neon signs that advertise God's wrath. These flashes illuminate the polystyrene hills and plains that stretch toward every horizon. Unbridled winds lash.

The stateroom door is still locked, but a luminous blue figure slowly enters. At first the blue is a pale glow swelling in the center of the door, bleeding through the wood; then it's a blue stomach lined up and down with a vertical row of shirt buttons. Following that, much higher on the door, the tips of a blue chin and a blue nose appear as a familiar blue form emerges. Last to flow through the locked door is a not-appealing pigtail of braided blue filth. With that Mr. Crescent City stands among us.

Having once more taken leave of his overdosed body, he blinks, looking around at my Gund stuffed monkeys and Steiff bears. His rheumy eyes settle on the radiant golden Festus.

According to the angel Festus, God chooses a messenger every few centuries to deliver an updated game plan for righteous living. Moses or Jesus or Mohammad, this per-

283

son disseminates the newest generation of God's Word 2.0. Noah or Buddha or Joan of Arc, the messenger upgrades our moral software, debugs our ethics, upgrading our values to meet modern spiritual needs. If you believe angel Festus, I am nothing more than the latest version of God's earthly mouthpiece.

"After you prevent today's cataclysm," declares the beaming Festus, "you must halt all human forays into the evil field of stem-cell research."

"Beg pardon?" I ask.

Festus rails, "As God's voice, you must curtail the freewheeling civil rights of women."

Flattered as I feel at being so chosen, I'm not thrilled with the news I'm being given to deliver.

Lifting his tiny arms into the air and flailing his hands, preacher-style, my upstate boyfriend rants, "It is God's will that all women abstain from voting and birth control and driving automobiles!"

While my pint-size Aryan poster child rattles off the rest of God's demands—no more blacks marrying whites . . . no men marrying men, ever . . . absolute mandatory circumcision for all members of both genders . . . veils, lots of veils and burqas—I turn to Mr. K and make my introductions. Not even death negates my years of decorous training in Swiss etiquette and protocol. "Mr. Crescent City, this is the angel Festus." With an appropriate cant of my head, I politely say, "Angel Festus, this is Mr. K. He's a 'psychic booty caller.' "

"Angel Madison means 'bounty hunter,' " says Mr. K. He gazes upon Festus, that golden blaze, as if my upstate swain had summer sunshine coursing through his veins. Giving a deep, blue sigh, Mr. K says, "I wish I were an angel."

It's here, Gentle Tweeter, that the idea strikes me like a bolt of blue lightning. To Mr. K, I say, "You really want to be an angel, huh?"

"I just want to die," says Mr. K, "and have everything be happy and painless. Forever."

"Find God," says Festus, "and you'll find peace."

To that I say, "Angel Festus, shut up." I add, not wishing to offend, "Just for now, okay?" Already I can see that Mr. K's blue is fading from cerulean to turquoise, from azure to French blue. Our time is running out as his not-healthy liver is winnowing the ketamine from his bloodstream. As he fades from robin's egg to powder blue, I offer a bargain. "Take my parents a message, and I promise to make you an angel."

"A message?" he asks.

"Tell them to stop with all the cataclysm stuff, okay?" I say.

Mr. K returns my gaze with puzzled stoner eyes. "And I'll be an angel?"

"Tell them," I say, "that they're stupid hypocrites, and that they shouldn't have *not told me* about Tigerstripe having a gruesome kidney disease."

Mr. K begins to nod, his eyes closed, as if deeply comprehending my words. Eyes closed, he smiles.

"And tell them," I say, "that I accidentally killed Papadaddy Ben by semidetaching his wing-ding because I thought it was a malevolent, rapidly inflating dog boo-boo." I ask, "Does that make sense?"

Eyes closed, Mr. K nods sagely. His pigtail bobs in agreement.

"Also tell them," I say, "that I only invented Jesus on my mobile phone, but it turns out that there is an actual Jesus. . . ." Turning to Festus for confirmation, I say, "Right?"

"Correct," Festus affirms.

To Mr. K, I say, "What's most important is that you tell my mom and dad that I really, *really* love them." Leaning closer to my blue confidant, I whisper, "And please tell them that I did *not* suck on any spider monkey ding-dings or do the Hot Thing with any water buffalo, okay?"

The slack look on Mr. K's face suggests I've overloaded my messenger. As his soul vanishes, gradually leaching backward to wherever he's left his physical body, the pale blue of him fades to grey. The gray goes to white.

The walls of the stateroom begin to vibrate, and a not-unpleasant hum suffuses my bed. The megayacht engines of the *Pangaea Crusader* have started. Outside, increasing gales scour the decks and thrum the rigging.

"Above all, please," I entreat my fading go-between, my meaty hands balled together in prayer, "tell them to die with all the full-size candy bars they can carry."

DECEMBER 21, 1:45 P.M. HAST

The Abomination Spurs a Cataclysm

Posted by Hadesbrainiacleonard@aftrlife.hell

f we compare the ancient codices recorded by scholars since Solon, we see almost identical depictions of the end times. The so-called global Doomsday mythos depicts a beautiful thing-child leading a procession of disciples up the slopes of a gleaming mountain. The mountain rises at the center of the Pacific Ocean, and this ceremony takes place in the waning sunlight of the shortest day of the year.

For the first time, Persephone will not return. Dawn will come, but no one will be alive to witness the next sunrise.

In place of plastics, now the she-child is borne along by a retinue of human beings. Instead of dry-cleaning bags and soda bottles, serving as attendants are earthly potentates and rich chieftains, everyone dressed in costly crimson raiment. This vast throng parades upward across the barren architecture of artificial clouds. Their steps follow winding switchback trails. This procession mounts ever higher, swinging censers of sweet incense and bearing lit candles.

Around the horizon in every direction, great plumes of black smoke rise like tornadoes into the afternoon sky. Underfoot, the ground shakes. This mountain they scale is the tallest in the land. Its towering peak is level, a plateau, and waiting at the highest point is a massive shining temple. This bright palace appears as a pastiche of Gothic and baroque and attic shapes, of domes and spires and colon-

287

nades, the caryatids and cartouches rendered from glistening fluoropolymers. This part-cathedral, part-skyscraper crowns the summit.

It's in this glorious sterile sanctuary, overlooking the entire world, where two millennia of scholars vow that human history will end.

DECEMBER 21, 2:05 P.M. HAST
Thwarted by Continental Drift
Posted by Madisonspencer@aftrlife.hell

entle Tweeter,

We're running. My chubby legs scamper. My tubby knees pumping high, I barrel along, sopping with perspiration. My loafer-shod feet stomp, scale, vault up the steps of a staircase molded into the steeply pitched flank of a nothing-colored mountain. A white, cipher-hued precipice. Scarcely without pause do I leap upward in pursuit of the cadaverous Mr. K, who sprints the stairs ahead of me.

Moments before, we'd emerged from my stateroom to find the yacht deserted. A veritable *Marie Celeste*. An unmanned *Flying Dutchman*. The salon was vacant. The decks not occupied. My borrowed PDA emitted its Europop ring tone, and Archer bade me, "Look outside." He said, "Look out a porthole or whatever."

In this landscape it's hard to miss: A procession of people are walking single-file, ascending the slope of a peak in the middle distance. To a person, they all wear hooded red robes. Thus attired, the thin trickle of them resembles a rivulet of blood flowing uphill, following a narrow channel of steps which zigzags from the base of the white mountain to its peak. If my parents are among them, it's impossible to tell, so identical are their scarlet-hued vestments.

The mountain itself rears skyward, tapering to balance an ornate wax-colored temple at its tip. A much-ornamented cupola, ringed with columns and crowned with turrets. Some colossal shrine graces that lofty apex, but from this far away it looks no larger than a many-tiered, much-decorated wedding cake.

Even as I marvel at this view, I spy Mr. K sprinting down the gangplank in pursuit of the scarlet train of pilgrims. His loping, stumbling marionette figure attains the mountainside steps as I swiftly follow suit. His face, pallid. His breathing, labored. Clearly in cardiac distress, he shouts, "The boats have started! They're starting the boats!"

His words lost in exhausted panting, Mr. Ketamine shouts, "You have to understand, little dead girl, they're launching Madlantis." He throws each word to the winds.

Animated, smiling, he chatters, waving his hands above his head. "You're going to see tsunamis, earthquakes, volcanoes." His words are gleeful. Punctuated with breathless laughter. "Since we're all going to Heaven, it's okay. Everybody's going to die horribly . . . isn't that great!"

Around me, as we climb higher, the dream continent spreads in every direction, a glaring wasteland of immaculate white meadows and tooth-hued villas. At the base of this alpine stairway the *Pangaea Crusader* is mired, embedded in the plasticized lowlands. Judging from her copious exhaust smoke, her megayacht engines are running at full throttle, as if her crew were attempting to escape these millions and millions of acres of seamless heat-processed polygarbage. A black plume spews skyward from her smokestack. At the waterline, the puffed, foamed recycled trash squeaks along her trapped steel hull. The streamlined bow rises and falls like that of a polar icebreaker.

Identical plumes of black smoke funnel up from locations along the horizon, each revealing the site of a similarly embedded, heaving ship.

"The plan is," continues Mr. K, almost singing, "they only need to push Madlantis into the prevailing current. In just a couple miles, the currents will catch us."

It pains me to admit this, but great fortunes have been expended toward the exercising of my perennially not-lean body. Like an aspiring Olympian or a dressage gelding, I've been bullied around indoor tracks. A host of fitness trainers have herded me the lengths of lap pools beyond remembering, and still it seems that I have absolutely no aerobic capacity. None whatsoever.

Mr. K stammers, gulping for air, "We use the continent to shift the alignment of the planet. When the giant huge tonnage of Madlantis comes crashing into North America it's going to wreck everything."

Gentle Tweeter, I am not unaware of this irritating metaphor taking shape. In death, as in life, my blubbery self is going to smash itself against the Americas, the Hawaiian Islands, the Galápagos, Japan, Russia, and Alaska. Giant blubbery fatty-fat-fat me is going to wreak havoc like the proverbial bull in a china shop.

To make matters worse, as I climb, the steps are spongy soft, compressing slightly under my weight. Like foam rubber. Like Styrofoam. Slick with rain, they're treacherous, threatening to springboard me backward into some bottomless pearl-tinted abyss.

Despite our late start we're already coming abreast of the slowest among the red-robed pilgrims. Between the dreamscape and the robes and the billowing diesel exhaust all is bold white, red, and black. Of the people in procession some carry lighted tapers. Others swing censers attached to lengths of chain and trailing tendrils of incense smoke. To a person they all chant the repeating refrain, "Fuck . . . shit . . . cocksucker . . ."

The early winter dusk burnishes every crag to an antique gold. This magic-hour light is the gold my tongue sees when I eat fondue au Gruyère.

We're overtaking more pilgrims pushing and dodging past them on the steep stairway. Most have slowed their gait, for now it feels as if the mountain is shifting, moving almost imperceptibly, as the portly, jowly continent is nudged northward. A thousand million horsepower of marine engines strain to dislodge us from the calm center of the Pacific Gyre, and their gradual success sends jellied tremors through the polyfake tectonic plate on which we're buoyed. The surrounding mountains jiggle like sky-high mounds of vanilla aspic. The less sure-footed pilgrims stumble and fall, screaming dramatically. Perhaps due to his wide experience with drug-induced unsteadiness, Mr. Ketamine remains upright. He bounces ever upward, hurtling two, three, four stair steps in a single stride.

"We must hurry," says Festus, fluttering along. "In less time than it took the Almighty to people this lovely world, the Boorists shall destroy it!"

My running steps begin to slow. My stride slackens with the idea of letting Boorism run its course and complete its not-holy war against humanity, these veal-eating, CO_2-emitting, self-replicating vermin. As the child of Gaia-aware, tree-sitting, monkey-wrenching parents, I can't deny the appeal of a people-free planet. Even more enticing is the thought of having the entire Earth to myself, at least until next Halloween. So blissfully isolated, I'll gorge my way through whole books at one sitting. I'll take up the lute.

"Make haste!" urges Festus, winging along at my side. "Lest your eternally damned parents be force-fed hot excrement!"

Nor can I deny the evil, gleeful idea of *that* scenario—not after all the macrobiotic muck they've crammed down my throat.

It's difficult to accept the idea that everyone's about to die, everything's about to be destroyed, because everyone seems so happy. Smiling. Their manic eyes flashing. Blacks and Asians, Jews and gays, Québécoise and Palestinians and Amerindians, white supremacists, prochoice and prolife, they're all holding hands. They're hugging, kissing even. There's no fear of disease. No social pretense or status indicators or power hierarchies separate them. The crowd is singing my name, grateful for the salvation they believe is imminent. They're happy in the way people are happy while burning books or beheading kings; they're *righteous*.

All the while, Mr. Ketamine's mumbling to keep my message fresh in his mind. His sunset-illuminated face, drawn and gaunt, stained the color of flame, fiercely he's repeating, "No stem cells."

The thoughtful gray bowels of my brain are queasy with motion sickness. They're nauseated with the indigestible memory of my father in New York City saying, "Madison was a little coward."

Ahead of us the procession has come to a bottleneck. The berobed penitents await admittance at a great archway, the entrance to the mountaintop temple. Among us, a quartet of giants shoulders the corners of a sedan chair, a boxed-and-curtained affair whose occupants remain concealed within its red velvet draperies. To my mind, Camille and Antonio are its most likely passengers, and I crane my neck to get a better look. Meanwhile the crowd surges into a not-historically-inaccurate reproduction of a courtyard from some Renaissance Venetian palazzo, the flamboyant dadoes and corbels reproduced in copious amounts of sculpted blah-colored hardened-cellulose froth.

Among this throng of hooded figures Mr. K stands on tiptoe and shouts, "Listen! Everybody listen to me!" Someone has given him a lit candle, and he holds this flaming taper overhead like a stuttering, bright star.

Gentle Tweeter, please understand that effective communication is paramount to me. My parents are so rich because people have outsourced the skills with which they once conveyed their emotions. The public has contracted out their own self-expression. All love must be mediated through greeting cards, assembly-line diamond jewelry, or professionally arranged, factory-farmed bouquets of roses. All epiphanies must be modeled by my mother. People feel only those emotions she prompts them to feel. For them, she is Aphrodite. My father, my dad, is the zeitgeist.

All of my greatest concerns, I've entrusted them to this ravaged ketamine hound who now leaps in place, waving his candle and shouting to attract everyone's attention. Imagine my horror when Mr. K shouts, "Stop!" He whistles for silence, then shouts, "Madison says you're all going to Hell unless you listen!" The assembled crowd begins to turn and stare. "The angel Madison," he shouts, "wants you all to stop cussing and burping. . . ."

Here I've entrusted one person to express all the love I could not. I've asked him to bear all my regrets and resolve all my lies. I sense the tide slowly turning.

Their faces framed in the openings of their red hoods, the confused audience regards Mr. K. They wait, restive, blinking with expressions of puzzlement.

"Madison," shouts Mr. K. He pauses for a moment of absolute hushed silence. "Madison Spencer says the only true path to salvation lies in sucking donkey dicks!"

Ye gods.

It's at that moment that I see my parents. They push back their hoods and stare, their faces exploded in looks of stricken horror.

And without taking another breath, Mr. Crescent City, Mr. K, my psychic bounty hunter, he falls down dead.

The Beating I So Richly Deserve

Posted by Madisonspencer@aftrlife.hell

entle Tweeter,

No one gets it. Everyone gets it wrong.

In the sky-high temple of repurposed plastic, the familiar blue ghost bleeds out of Mr. Ketamine's collapsed body. "I'm not going back," says the blue Mr. K–shaped ectoplasm standing next to me, shaking its head. No one can see us. Every hooded figure is staring at his postalive remains in the center of the court-yard. That pockmarked, pigtailed rag doll. Even now, a team of paramedics pushes through the crowd and begins to check for vital signs.

The ghost of Mr. K tells me, "It's my heart, finally. Hallelujah. I'm gone for good this time."

Under our feet, the topography of Madlantis gives a tiny sideways tug.

Revealed, my parents observe while the medics inject Mr. K's corpse with various lifesaving agents. The bearers of the velvet-draped sedan chair have deposited their burden nearby, but its veiled contents remain a mystery.

Their ceremony interrupted for a moment, the assembled celebrants push back their scarlet hoods. Still holding their flickering tapers, they continue to mutter genital and excretory obscenities. When the attending medics strip the not-clean tunic from Mr. K's not-healthy chest and make ready to attach the leads for a cardiac defibrillator, I see my chance.

The ghost Mr. K sees me and says, "Don't do it, angel Madison."

I have to. There's so much to tell my parents. Not the least of which is how much I love and miss them. That, and how stupid they're being.

"If you're going to use my old body," says Mr. K, "just be aware I was in the middle of a gnarly herpes flare-up."

I look at the ghost him. I look at his crumpled corpse.

"Just so you know what you're getting yourself into," he warns.

I'm so Ctrl+Alt+Grossed-out.

The paramedics shout, "Clear!" And I can't do it. I can't make the jump, Gentle Tweeter, not into that disgusting, inflamed, drug-abused cadaver. The medics deliver their jolt of heart-starting amperage, but nothing happens. All life signs stay flat.

My parents will die without knowing I loved them. They'll go to Hell and be diced by demons with razor blades dipped in margarita salt. They'll get paper cuts across their eyeballs and be subjected to high colonics of liquid Drano.

Once more the paramedics shout, "Clear!" And I don't take the opportunity.

All humanity will be wiped off the face of the Earth. Satan will claim all of God's children. Satan will win. All this is because I can't bring myself to comingle my virginal, intelligent soul with the jaundiced, skeletal remains of a creepy, predecomposed loser man.

"I don't blame you," says ghost Mr. K. "I didn't much like being in there myself."

For a third and final effort, the paramedics shout, "Clear!"

My brains growl a warning: Satan will find my cat.

And I make my jump.

Not since I was entombed in the overly sullied environs of an upstate public toilet have I felt so degraded. These leprous hands! These withered, spindly limbs! The helpful medics have stripped away the majority of my soiled garments, and I find myself with barely a malodorous pair of undershorts veiling my vile pendulous *membrum virilis*. My own burdensome *membrum puerile*. Even as the decorous medics caution me to remain prone on the courtyard pavement, I launch my shambling frame to a scarcely standing posture. Placating latex-gloved hands attempt to stop me, but I stagger a step toward my aghast parents.

My mother and father, they stand beside the curtained sedan chair. Their jaws hang slack. As I career my monstrous new body toward them, my arms thrown wide to give them a loving bear hug, they shudder with not-concealed revulsion.

So weak am I that I fall—Gentle Tweeter, I am always falling—sprawled on the plastic cobblestones.

I, who had once fretted over the prospect of pubescent acne, now I crawl before my father, pitted with the stinging craters of the virulent herpes virus. I who sought to wed Jesus Christ in order to forestall my budding girlhood physicality, I squirm on dying knees, soliciting in a quaking moribund voice for my mother to pay me her loving regard. Prone, covered in sores, I approach my makers on my irredeemably pestilent belly. This form modeled from corruption, once I constituted my parents' bright future, the living confirmation that they had made the politically progressive choices. Now I slither on my naked stomach, exposing my ribbed, emaciated back and dragging the burdensome shame of my heavily soiled pigtail. That braid, so like an exposed prereptilian brainstem. Me, Madison Spencer, their emissary into a better, more enlightened future, I'm reduced to this slinking lizard.

In my gravelly voice, borrowed from a dead man, I declare, "Mommy! Daddy!" Dragging my mostly nude, bony, sweat-lubricated new self toward them, I cry out, "I love you!" I pucker my cracked, well-lesioned lips to bestow an adoring kiss, and I beg, "Don't you know me? I'm Madison!" I cry, "I'm your little sugarplum!"

My new breath tastes the way a pet store smells.

My father's handsome face is a grimace of teeth-baring disgust, revolted by this creature he finds himself forced to punch. To smite mightily. My father, oh, my beloved father, to defend himself and my mother, he's dealt the bothersome task of pummeling me with his closed fists. My hot infectious blood sallies forth. Sickened by my hair and bodily fluids on his knuckles, he's still grimly determined to stop my advance.

With broken fingers I beseech. "I tore off Papadaddy's turgid dinger," I confess, "and I abandoned him to die in a puddle of blood." I tell my parents that I've never actually performed analingus on the lofty bottoms of exotic giraffes. I tell them how I only invented my love affair with Jesus Christ. I tell them everything. My strength fading, I paw the air, and my entreaties are met by the hard soles of my father's Prada wingtips. This atrocity of blood and pus I find myself trapped within, I'm taunting them. Challenging them. Daring them to love me. I'm testing to see whether they recognize, in this tormented grotesque, any sign of their own troubled little girl.

Those two shining paragons, I grovel before them. Showing them what a monster I've become, I beg them to accept me.

"Forgive me for assaulting you in the bathroom at the Beverly Wilshire," I beseech my father. To my mother I say, "I promise to lose weight."

Looking on is Babette, chuckling secretly. The wench, the buxom succubus. Looking on are the blue ghost of Mr. K and the hummingbird-fluttering, golden sprite of Festus. I slither around the feet of my horror-struck family. In nightmarish slow motion I'm reaching my thin strange fingertips to stroke my mom's terrified ankle. "Mommy, I'm here to rescue you."

In response to my professed love, my father continues to hammer me with his fists and feet. Pain blooms within my wasted rib cage. My borrowed heart seizes. And the suffering is indescribable as my blood ceases to flow.

The truth is, Gentle Tweeter, I am always testing their love.

A voice calls out, "The candle! Madison, get the candle!" The source of the voice is Mr. K's ghost. His ghost hand directs my gaze to a spot on the plastic paving stones. There, the lit candle he'd held at the moment of his death has landed. Its wick has ignited the styrene-foam faux cobblestones, and a bubbling fire rises and makes ready to spread to the rest of the temple, the mountain, the continent. Even subjected to my cardiac arrest I'm forced to choose between kissing my panicked mom and dad with wormy, diseased lips . . . or advancing in a new direction to extinguish a rapidly spreading conflagration of potentially epic proportions.

Even as I vacillate in indecision, a lissome hand emerges from a slit in the velvet draperies of the sedan chair. A melodious voice says, "Fear not!" The hand, this perfect ideal of a hand, elegant and otherworldly, its fingers sweep aside the red velvet to reveal the chair's occupant: a winsome maiden. A youthful goddess.

Even as the bubbling fire grows to feed on more plastic steps . . . a Styrofoam pedestal . . . the base of a polystyrene obelisk, the perfect maid enthroned at the center of this populous crowd, this slender girl swings her willowy legs and steps forth from the chair. Her hair is lustrous, supporting a gilded wreath of olive leaves. Her limbs smooth. Her face unmarred by eyeglasses. Her sylphlike frame is adorned in a simple yeoman's tunic of familiar blue chambray.

This ideal maiden points a perfect finger at me and demands, "Be gone, noxious abomination! Retreat, you overweight pretender!" She squares her shoulders and proudly announces, "Behold, for I am Madison Desert Flower Rosa Parks Coyote Trickster Spencer—returned from the grave to bring mankind eternal life."

Denounced!

Posted by Madisonspencer@aftrlife.hell

entle Tweeter,

In a leap, the beautiful stranger pounces. Even as I sprawl, dying on the plastic ground, she launches her winsome form from the sedan chair and lands squarely upon my bared, quivering spine.

Beneath her, I scramble. I crawl to escape. For a struggling moment the perfect child is astride me. Her toned buttocks planted in the small of my back, she beats me about the head with her fists. Clutching my ragged hair, she pushes my face toward the growing candle-kindled fire until my skin blisters. The heat swells my lips like an overdose of collagen, stretching the skin so tight that it splits.

So close are the flames that the tasseled end of my oily pigtail smolders. The braided strands begin to burn like a stinking, slow-motion fuse.

My bones, broken . . . my heart, ailing . . . I'm helpless, unable to raise myself. No one comes to my aid. The ghost Mr. K stands off to one side, sobbing. The succubus, Babette, is off to the other side, howling with demonic joviality, while the assembled Boorites weep and gnash their teeth.

It's clear: My parents don't love me. My parents don't even recognize me. They love *this,* this skinny, Barbie-dolled version of me.

Be warned, my predead followers: When you take occupancy of any physical form you must remain in residence until its ultimate demise. You must suffer until life's accumulated insults render the vessel inoperative. That said, my spirit cannot flee. I'm forced to undergo this painful battering.

I writhe beneath her surprising weight. Twisting to face her. As her uniform, the Barbie-Madison wears the infamous, gunk-despoiled chambray shirt, the tails rippling above her bare legs. As her cudgel she bears *The Voyage of the Beagle,* that book so much annotated with dried blood. Wielding the not-lightweight missive, she pounds my borrowed face. My head lolls, coughing spit and mewling incoherent protest. Scalding tears geyser from my borrowed eyes.

Despite these exertions, the impostor Madison seated atop me, she doesn't perspire. Nor is her breathing taxed by her sustained strenuous efforts. In my own meager defense I pummel her torso with my knobby elbows and knees, but I might as well be slugging the great black-rubber tires of an upstate eighteen-wheeler.

The book's leather binding collapses my nose, flattening it sideways, leaving me gasping. My ears boxed and ringing. My vision filled with bright stars.

Desperate, my fingers grasp a handful of her garment. To this I doggedly hold fast, wrestling the blue shirt from her svelte frame, leaving her not clothed, but to no avail. Modesty does not stem her efforts. To all Boorist eyes we must appear as a depraved naked pervert, a poorly complexioned, libidinous skeleton, grappling to molest a nude lass.

Gradually, I offer less resistance. After the first half hundred thuds, one slug in my kisser is pretty much like another. A trauma-induced lethargy sets in. Not even the pain can hold my attention, and my thoughts wander. Elisabeth Kubler-Ross never mentions it, but there's another stage of dying. Besides anger, denial, and bargaining, there's boredom. Yes, boredom. You abandon yourself.

A strange sense of peace settles. Even as the hardcover tome batters me senseless, my struggling is replaced by a resignation more deadening than Rohypnol. If I'm to die . . . so be it. If she's more to their liking, let my mother and father adopt this pristine Maddy doll. From farther and farther away, I can smell hair smoking. Faintly, I can hear fists smacking jellied meat, my body already splashing-wet with blood.

This isn't anywhere I haven't been before. I've given up. In words muffled with exhaustion I whisper a prayer for my heart to stop.

You, the predead, you must hate hearing this. You hate a backslider, but I am. I'm shirking my life. Not living up to my full potential, I quit.

If there is a grand plan, I surrender to it. I give up to my fate.

Subjected to such a violent skirmish, even the *Beagle* book begins to disintegrate. Coming apart, the pages dissemble, sentence by sentence. Fluttering down upon me are scraps of paper. Penciled words. Of these falling shreds, one appears to be on fire. An edge of the torn page in question flickers with bright orange light. It's Festus, wee Festus escorting the scrap of paper. His golden hummingbird wings fluttering wildly, he hovers, holding it within my view.

There, scribbled in childish blue pen, is written, *Set yourself a goal so difficult that death will seem like a welcome reprieve. . . .*

Here, Gentle Tweeter, my failing brain issues a final inspired belch. Perhaps this . . . this violent engagement is the battle against evil for which my family and generations of telemarketers have been grooming me.

Here is the trial which Leonard has so long foretold.

Survival of the fittest versus survival of the nicest.

To stem this hail of blows I lift my twisted hands to grip the volume. My wasted fingers hold fast, and my trembling arms wrestle for possession of Mr. Darwin's cruel travelogue. Please take note. A magic reversal has occurred: Once again a dying cadaver-man is engaged in a dark tug-of-war with a gamine child.

With a great cry of anguish I seize control of the book. The weapon is mine.

Once more swinging the blood-and-sperm-saturated memoirs of C. Darwin, that disillusioned theologian, I invest the last of my dwindling strength in a great swat that connects with the crown of my adversary's comely noggin. This crippling smack-down drives her backward, stunning her for the moment. That same impact dislodges a final shower of desiccated violets and pansies from between the book's sodden pages.

Likewise do more fragments of the paper detach and cling to my attacker. The castle of Mr. Darwin's mind crumbles brick by brick. A dissolving inventory of the natural world. Blasting my foe is this buckshot of memes: bifurcation . . . crustacean . . . flocculent, and Diodon. They papier-mâché her like a piñata. Wollaston . . . wigwag . . . Fuegians and scurvy. These smother my foe. Her perfect not-nearsighted eyes, they're invaded by a stinging grit of facts and details. All of Mr. Darwin's lizards and thistles. My mom and my nana's long-archived flowery specimens.

The beautiful not-Madison screams in frustrated rage, her peepers pasted over. She's blinded.

In the next instant the smoldering wick of my pigtail flogs her much-combustible paper coating. She's set ablaze as the disgorged words and blossoms attack her with their immolating heat. No longer assaulting me, instead she's beating at her own flanks, swatting to subdue her flaming loins. Even as she struggles to quell the fire, she's clawing away great softened handfuls of herself. Tearing herself to pieces.

At the same time, she's screaming. She capers. Her banshee wails distort her features even as the temperature of burning paper melts and buckles her feet, her knees, her annoyingly slender thighs.

Continuing to clutch the yuck-infused chambray shirt and the flaking book, I cower on the nearby ground. Babbling wildly now, as bloodied and nude as the newborn me in the birthing video, I sob, "I'm sorry I was such a self-righteous coward. . . ."

At this humiliating admission, the impossible takes place.

It happens, on rare occasion, that supernatural phenomena occur for which we've no ready explanation. Two hands come forward to cup the sides of my misshapen head.

My mother's soft, perfumed palms and much-bejeweled fingers lift my ravaged face until I'm looking up, into her eyes. Her arms cradle my shattered body, creating a not-unsentimental pietà, and she asks, "Maddy? Dewdrop, is that really you?" My father stoops to embrace the two of us.

I am seen. Finally, I am recognized.

My parents and I, our little family, is, in that moment, reunited.

It's at this juncture that the impossible, inhuman doll of a girl, she raises her melting gaze to the sky. In a gurgling, liquid voice, the not-Madison croaks, "Heed my words. . . ." Even now, sinking to become a bubbling, smoking puddle, she commands, "Honor me, my followers, with a vast, communal 'Hail, Maddy.' "

Detonated!

Posted by Madisonspencer@aftrlife.hell

entle Tweeter,

As you can imagine, a dense crowd of people expelling pent-up intestinal gas in the presence of an open flame, surrounded by ostentatious, highly flammable architecture, this is a not-happy turn of events. In a flash, the mountaintop cathedral is wildly ablaze. Toga-clad, sandal-shod Boorites run pell-mell in every direction with their extremities exuberantly on fire. The heat softens the underlying peak, and ominous bubbling landslides of molten plastic begin to ooze down the flanks of the precipice.

Smoke blots out the setting sun, plunging this once-pristine world into a darkness illuminated by only the raging orange inferno. On the plains far below jagged fissures crack open, and the ocean begins to seep upward. Even as it burns, the entire continent of Madlantis is slowly sinking. It's the fall of Pompeii. It's the destruction of Sodom. The searing updrafts of wind carry gobs of smoldering, spitting ash, depositing them amid distant artificial forests and combustible palaces, until the world appears to be igniting in every direction.

Blinded and terrified, the Boorites stampede over one another. They stumble and topple into pools of boiling slime. Their screams fall silent only when superheated gases sear their lungs.

Mr. K's emaciated corpus is fully dead, fully involved in flame, and I find myself evicted. Again, I'm a me-shaped bubble of blue ectoplasm. The filthy blue chambray shirt and frayed *Beagle* book must not be wholly of the physical world, because I find my ghost hands still holding them.

Observing the Ctrl+Alt+Chaos, angel Festus comes to my side. He grips the edge of my ghost ear in his golden fingers and says sarcastically, "Excellent work."

For my part, Gentle Tweeter, I'm searching the hectic scene, trying to locate my parents. I'm terrified that my folks are going to be killed, and despite the fact that they're nonviolent, peace-loving, Pentagon-levitating progressives, they're going to give me a centuries-long time-out. We'll be estranged forever.

These theoretical punishments choke my ghost mind when a familiar voice says, "Golly, Sponge Cake, ain't this an awful pickle?"

I turn and see . . . my Nana Minnie. Holding a ghost cigarette in her ghost hand, she leans over to light it off the flaming pigtail of Mr. K's burning corpse. As if this fiery Armageddon couldn't get any worse, beside her is, ye gods, my Papadaddy Ben.

A Dark Episode Revisited—At Last

Posted by Madisonspencer@aftrlife.hell

entle Tweeter,

The last time I saw Papadaddy Ben was Halloween night, the night Nana Minnie died. His scarecrow ghost walked up to our porch in tedious upstate. Now, here he stands. He and Nana Minnie. Surely my education in Swiss etiquette would dictate a casual, easygoing way to inquire about the health of his book-squished, semidetached wing-wang, but I'm uncharacteristically without words.

It's strange how the currently conflagrating Styrofoam volcano echoes the not-happy circumstances of our last fatal encounter. The furious release of polycarbon gases suggests the reek of that long-ago upstate comfort station. The heat of this searing plastic cataclysm recalls the scorching temperature of that summer afternoon.

Speechless, I adopt the detached mien that has so oft of late served me, that of the observant supernaturalist. As the child of former-Gestaltist, former-self-actualized, former-Euthonian parents, I recognize that if anyone ought to be feeling awkward in the present situation, it's not me. My papadaddy played the dooky-brandishing predatory degenerate. Suppressing a lifetime of social conditioning, I resolve not to comment about the weather. Instead, I elect to remain silent and simply to observe my subject for signs of discomfort.

My terrible secret is not mine alone. It is also my grandfather's. As I once waited in the "blind" of my toilet cubicle, ready to endure the worst, now let him suffer my probing gaze. In the stealthy manner of Mr. Darwin or Mr. Audubon, I make a cold inventory of the specimen at hand. I picture the stubby boneless finger that had so menaced me. The infinite tiny wrinkles that carpeted the finger's spongy surface, and the several short, curling hairs that clung to it. I revisit the finger's sour, not-healthy odor.

My nana is the first to speak. "We come on the whirligig. What a ride!"

I appraise them coolly.

My nana perseveres. "Ever since the day he died, Sweet Pea, your grandpa has wanted to see you again."

I make no effort to reply. Let them name the horror. Let them apologize.

"That was a terrible day," Nana Minnie says, patting her heart with one heavily tattooed hand. She brings one porcelain fingernail to her brow and scratches under the edge of her blond wig. "The day he died? Let me think. . . ." Her eyes shift from side to side. "We both guessed you was headed for the traffic island out on the highway."

Papadaddy, the toilet lurker, interjects here. "You asked about it at breakfast." He says, "We was afraid you'd try and cross the freeway, so I decided to drive over there and keep a lookout for you."

I remain steadfast. To judge from the angle of my nana's cigarette, she's upbeat, happy even.

"That nasty place," says Nana, and she makes a face. "Your papadaddy was headed out to collect you when he had himself the heart attack."

I amuse myself by idly looking at my wristwatch. I pretend to warm my ghost hands over the sputtering, guttering campfire that consumes the mortal remains of Mr. Ketamine.

"Died right on my own front porch, I did," says Papadaddy.

"Right on them steps," adds Nana. "He grabbed his chest and keeled over." She claps her hands together for emphasis. "He'd stopped breathing for twenty minutes before them paramedics showed up and revived him."

Papadaddy shrugs. "What's left to say? Not to brag, but I went straight to Heaven. I was dead."

"You was not," insists Nana Minnie.

Papadaddy counters, "I most certainly was."

Undeterred, Nana says, "After they shocked Ben's heart, the ambulance folks wanted to ride him to the hospital, but he didn't want no part of going."

Folding his arms, Papadaddy says, "She's embroidering this next part. That's not what went on."

"I was there, you know," says Nana.

"Well," Papadaddy says, "I was there, too."

"We'd been married for forty-four years," says Minnie, "and he'd never before talked to me that way." She says, "Maybe he was in pain, but that ain't no excuse."

"How could I talk?" says Ben. "I was dead."

Nana Minnie continues, "No, he was bound and determined to go find you, pumpkinseed."

Here, Gentle Tweeter, a theory is slowly coalescing in my supernaturalist's thinking belly.

"After that," Nana says, "he was like a different person."

"I was like a dead person."

Just to clarify, I ask, "You're saying the rescue crew used a cardiac defibrillator on Papadaddy?"

Nana says, "He wanted to go find you at that terrible public toilet." She says, "He was pale and limping. Them paramedics figured he'd die again at any minute."

Papadaddy uses the tip of one index finger to draw a cross on his chest. "I swear," he says. "I died in your nana's arms on that porch."

The paramedics, Nana explains, revived him and made him sign a medical release form. He waited for them to leave, but the moment they were gone he'd jumped into his pickup truck.

Nana leans close to me and confides in a stage whisper, "He called me the C-word!"

"We've been over and over this," Papadaddy says, placating. "I did not."

She coughs. "You called me the C-word, and then you went off to find Maddy at that nasty traffic island."

My grandparents, they Ctrl+Atl+Bicker. They sulk. The patient, observant supernaturalist in me is sorely taxed. Finally, seeking some resolution, I ask, "Papadaddy? Listen. Did you, by any chance, go to the byway restroom and get your elderly wiener ripped off?"

He looks at me, aghast. "June Bug! How could you even ask me that?"

"Because it happened!" Minnie shouts. "Some monster ripped up your privates and you bled to death like a pig!"

"That didn't happen."

"I saw your dead body!" Nana says, "Don't they watch the news in Heaven?" Her gnarled hands frame large, imaginary words in the air. "All the headlines blared: 'Movie Star's Pa Killed in Toilet Torture.'"

At this impasse in what is obviously a well-rehearsed stalemate, even as the continent of Madlantis founders in deep seas and flame-bedecked Boorites dash past us like human comets, I realize I've been mistaken. It's obvious: Papadaddy Ben's soul floated away, and another spirit took possession of his former body. Some ghost or demonic force used the shock of the paramedics' paddles, like a juvenile delinquent hot-wiring a car and taking it for a joyride. Like I just now used Mr. Ketamine's corpse. This strange wiener-wielding corpse rustler is who accosted me in the upstate toilet. Not my precious papadaddy.

Thinking fast, I cagily redirect my grandparents' ire by asking, "Nana, do you know what I miss most about being alive?" Not waiting for an answer, I blurt out, "Your delicious peanut-butter cheesecake!" To my papadaddy, I say, "I'm sorry I wasn't there to say good-bye when you died." Pitching my words with an especially childlike sincerity, I say, "Thank you for teaching me how to build a birdhouse."

I throw my chubby ghost arms around them in an awkward embrace as two red-tinted headlights approach. A strange automobile—spattered with blood, fringed with dripping strands of coagulated blood—cruises magically, silently up the steep side of the erupting mountain. At this most sweet moment of our reunion, a gleaming black Lincoln Town Car comes to a stop beside us.

314

Confronting the Devil with the Awful
Truth Concerning His Mangled Dingus

Posted by Madisonspencer@aftrlife.hell

entle Tweeter,

Nodding his head at the Lincoln Town Car, Mr. K's ghost says, "This is my ride, right? I'm going to Heaven, like you promised, right?"

The driver's door swings open, and a uniformed chauffeur steps out. First his polished, hooflike boots emerge, then his gloved hands, glistening and leathery, followed by the brimmed cap that must hide the two bony rinds that poke up through his not-combed hair. As he stands, he adjusts a pair of mirrored sunglasses that hide his eyes. He carries a sheaf of pages bound along one edge like a screenplay. This he lifts and begins to read from, aloud. " 'Madison felt faint with terror and confusion.' "

And I am, Gentle Tweeter, I do. I feel faint with terror.

" 'Her great, meaty knees wobbled, weak with horror,' " he reads, as if dictating my existence.

In fact, my knees are shaking.

The chauffeur reads, " 'Madison had served her maker well. She'd delivered billions of God's children to the Devil's clutches.' " He turns a page of his manuscript and continues. " 'Madison had betrayed even her own parents and condemned them to eternal damnation!' "

And, so it seems, I have.

Even Babette sidles up to savor my humiliation. To smirk at the sight of my defeat, asking, "How's your psoriasis?"

" 'Little Madison,' " the chauffeur reads, " 'would soon render unto Satan every living soul whom the Almighty had labored to create. All that God loved, Madison had ensured that they would be given over for Lucifer to molest until the end of time. . . .' "

The chauffeur pauses in his speechifying. He opens the rear door of the Town Car, and Mr. K readily climbs inside. The driver leaves the door open, and additional blue ghosts make a beeline for the car's rear seat. The rapidly accruing spirits of Boorites burned to death, suffocated on toxic fumes, or drowned in the surrounding seas, these recently departed flock enter the door the driver holds ajar. They stuff themselves within. So many, so quickly that they blur, they pack themselves into this, this vehicle they think will ferry them to the heavenly hereafter.

" 'Madison thought she was so intelligent,' " the chauffeur reads. " 'But she was not. In truth, she was stupid. The silly cow, she'd brought about the downfall of all humanity. . . .' "

Slowly, so as not to draw his focus, I shuck my cardigan sweater. Stealthily, I don the defiled shirt, doing up the buttons gingerly, lest my fingers come into contact with the crusty spooge that so richly patterns the stiffened bodice.

" 'Little Maddy,' " the driver reads, oblivious to my actions, " 'would have no choice but to submit herself for Satan's repeated carnal pleasures. . . .' "

Positioning myself to protect my aged grandparents from the Devil's wrath, I pry open Mr. Darwin's gummy book and display the defaced chapter about Tierra del

Fuego. There, the sonorous travelogue remains unreadable beneath a thickish coating of horrors. Most prominent on those two facing pages is the outline of a squished ding-dong silhouetted in red.

" 'Poor, fat Madison Desert . . . whatever . . . Trickster Spencer,' " reads the Devil, " 'would soon become the dark lord's concubine!' "

And although the satanic driver has yet to notice the open, bloodied book and its vile illustration, many others do take note. Nana and Papadaddy both peer at the dinger outline and commence to giggle. Likewise, the golden angel of Festus takes a gander and his eyes widen in mirthful recognition. Other souls, those burned-alive spirits in transit to the Lincoln Town Car, they also venture a glance at the gory exhibit I present, and they, too, begin to snicker.

Paying them no mind, the chauffeur turns to a new page of his missive. " 'Madison will serve Satan in Hades, and she will bear him many odious children. . . .' "

Gathering my courage, I push the befouled book forward for his inspection. "How?" I shout. "How will mighty Satan consummate such an unholy union?"

His speech interrupted, the Devil looks up from his script. Reflected in both lenses of his sunglasses are the pages of the *Beagle* book.

"Mighty Satan," I ask, "were you not jerked off by Darwin's gore-slickened observations about the Cape of Good Hope?"

The driver slowly lowers his sunglasses, revealing yellow goat eyes, the irises running side to side.

Written down the outside margin in my nana's hand, the words *Atlantis isn't a myth. It's a prediction.*

"Were you not," I persevere, "in fact *castrated* by your only intimate encounter with the diminutive Maddy Spencer?" By now, Gentle Tweeter, despite all my decorous upbringing, in defiance of all my self-censoring social conventionality, I'm screaming. "Satan, oh dark one, does your wiener not ache at this proof that little Madison gelded you? Did she not reject your evil advances in the not-sterile environs of a public upstate potty?"

Stymied by my revelation, the liveried Devil can only stammer.

Gentle Tweeter, I have succeeded in my last-Halloween vow to kick some satanic ass. The damage inflicted at my chubby hands has far surpassed any I dream I'd ever had of my own ability. Here is proof that I exist as someone beyond Beelzebub's sweaty pedophile fantasy. What mere fictive character could so cripple her author?

More telling than any verbal response, the driver's crimson hide flushes even deeper scarlet. His horns elongate, lifting his cap. His claws lengthen, pushing off his gloves.

Heedless of the cataclysm taking place around me, I keep up my harangue. Immolating plastic mountains create a flaming skyline. All creation is this mix of tragedy and farce as a trio of people approach. The succubus, Babette, my former best friend, leads my mom and dad forward, prompting them with the murderous point of a large, ornate knife. It's the same antique blade with which Goran executed the pretty Shetland pony.

The sight of my parents, brought forth in the Devil's presence, clearly to be utilized as hostages, this unnerves me. Regardless, I boldly thrust out the corrupt book, asserting, "Show us, dark master, if anything remains of your butchered wing-wang." Puffing my chest to showcase the gummy chambray shirt, I demand, "Is this *not* your *demon seed*?"

Livid and trembling, Satan dashes his script against the ground. He turns and reaches into the Town Car, extracting something pale. Dangling from his fist is an orange rag. Given a vigorous shake by his outraged arm, it emits a plaintive *meow.*

Ye gods. It's Tigerstripe.

Before I can shush him, angel Festus seconds my challenge. "Yes, Prince of Lies, show us your chopped-off pee-pee."

Nana escalates the chorus, shouting, "Show us! Let me see your twisted little wormwood!"

And in response, wicked Satan calmly turns to the demon holding my parents, and he says, "Kill them. Kill them both now."

entle Tweeter,

You think it's going to be a breeze, watching your mother get murdered, but it's not. I've witnessed my mom get lynched by redneck backwoods sheriffs, and I've watched her bludgeoned by the henchmen of Big Tobacco, and chomped on by the bulldozers of Big Coal, and garroted by the hit men of Agribusiness.

Once my mother was bitten in half by a renegade manatee. Blood poured out of her eyes. Blood gushed from her ears. Her guts pushed up and out of her mouth. That's how I knew she was dead. It took days to film. It took an entire team of special effects wonks just to get the blood right. Easily a hundred people were present on set. Stylists and makeup people, grips, dialogue coaches. Caterers. You name it. All of these people stood around, yawning and eating potato chips, and watched my mom gasp and choke on her own gore.

The happy memories of ordinary kids might include their homemaker mothers phoning Bulgari to have jeweled tiaras sent 'round for approval, or Tasering the Somali maids, but my fond recollections include looking on as my mother was burned at the stake by a cabal of Big Pharma drug companies.

I'd sat in a folding chair and peeked between my chubby

fingers while she was stoned by angry Puritans. I'd perched on my father's lap and held my breath as her lovely face disappeared into a rank pool of quicksand.

And she never flinched, my mom. She never winced.

The director shouted, "Action!"

And my lovely mother died beautifully every time.

She died bravely. She died cleanly. She died thin and noble and calm. When the script dictated, every time, she died perfectly. Her final words were always so eloquent.

She never required a second take.

My father, my dad I've heard expire loudly and wetly through a hundred locked bedroom doors.

Whatever I expected, it's not like that in real life. On the flaming peak of that plastic volcano, as the continent of Madlantis sinks into the Pacific Ocean, Babette lifts the large knife and plunges it into my father's heart. A beat later, at Satan's command, she swings the ornate cake knife in a wide arc to slash my mother's throat.

DECEMBER 21, 2:53 P.M. HAST

The Inevitable Result of Overly Intellectual-
izing and Suppressing What Would Otherwise
Be Appropriate, Natural Expressions of Grief by
a Precocious Albeit Insecure Adolescent, Who,
Frankly, Has Been Through the Trauma Olympics
Lately, What with the Deaths of Her Grandpar-
ents and Her Nice Fish and Her Sweet Kitten, Not
to Mention Her Own Prematurely Cruel Demise,
but Who Keeps Plugging Along with Her Plucky
Chin Held High and Does Not Succumb to Blub-
bing, but Has Striven Gamely to Rise Above Her
Circumstances, Dire as They've Become, and
Who for the Moment Finds Herself Unable to
Embrace Yet Another Unhappy Turn of Events
Posted by Madisonspencer@aftrlife.hell

entle Tweeter,

The Camille-shaped and Antonio-shaped
balloons of blue ectoplasm inflate. Floating
before my eyes are the international tycoon
and the media superstar. Their ghost eyes meet mine.

Just as I feared it would, back there in the PH of the
Rhinelander hotel, my ghost heart balloons like an aneurysm full of hot tears. It bloats like a deceased kitten in
the backseat of a limousine. It's astonishing, but the
heart of me engorges like a rapidly inflating, much-turgid
man-banana in a fetid toilet. And just like all those things,
my heart explodes.

Forgive me, Gentle Tweeter, but what takes place at this juncture is not something one can keyboard. Such are the limitations of emoticons. Upon contact with my parents' ghosts, I suffer all the emotions which failed to manifest themselves in my life. And for the first time since Los Angeles and Lisbon and Leipzig, I'm happy.

entle Tweeter,

My mother looks over the melting, flaming landscape that surrounds us. Baroque ruins stand outlined in smoke against the ember-filled skies. Scalding ocean waves sweep inland as the continent sinks lower. Superheated convection winds carry the poisoned fumes of everything to kill everyone and everything everywhere.

Surveying this scene of total planetary annihilation, my sweet mother, her ghost, gasps and says, "How lovely!" She says, "It's just the way Leonard predicted. . . ."

In ancient Greek times, she explains, a wise teacher named Plato wrote the story of the destruction of an enormous island nation called Atlantis. Plato, she says, was quoting an Athenian statesman who traveled to Egypt and learned the Atlantis disaster story from priests in the temple of Neith. Blah, blah, blah.

Those Egyptians weren't actually historians, adds my freshly slaughtered father. They were oracles. They weren't recording the past; they were predicting the future. And the great land that, according to Plato, was destroyed in "a single day and night of misfortune . . . ," it wasn't called Atlantis.

Explains my mother in a not-altogether not-smug tone, "That great doomed nation would be named Madlantis."

Smirking, my dad says, "It's not as if the Bible got it correct, either. It's not the rebuilding of the Temple of Solomon that signals Armageddon . . . it's the building of the *Temple of Madison!*"

Looking on, moving with a slowness that betrays his supreme hauteur, the Devil stoops to deposit Tigerstripe on the ground so he can once more lift his manuscript and regale me. " 'Terror seized young Maddy,' " he reads. " 'Her own mommy had confirmed the worst. All of her was as calculated and predetermined as the peaks and valleys of Madlantis. Madison Spencer was no more than a story told by people to other people, a rumor, a silly fable. . . .' "

My ghost mother begs, "Forgive us, Maddy, my sweet, for not telling you the whole truth about your little kitten."

My ghost father places his faint blue hand on my shoulder. "We only wanted you to know love. And how could you ever bring yourself to love so deeply if you truly knew how brief a lifetime can be?"

"Leonard," adds my mom, "he preordained that you should cherish your kitty and lose it to death. He said that pain would plant courage in you. . . ."

Satan taps his foot impatiently, holding the car door open. So great is his growing contempt that the manuscript in his hands begins to smolder and combust. "Heaven awaits!" he shouts.

With a gallant sweep of his arm, my dad ushers us toward the waiting Town Car.

My mom looks out over the scorched, churning field of flame. Reaching a blue ghost hand into a pocket of her ghost robe, she extracts a jumbo-size bottle of ghost Xanax and pitches it into the blazing distance. With this sacrifice she shrieks, "So long, gender and racial wage inequality! Good riddance, postcolonial environmental degradation!"

Following her lead, my dad cups his hands around his mouth and shouts, "Sayonara to you, oppressive popular culture simulacra! See you later, phallocratic panoptic subjugation!"

"We're going to Heaven!" cries my mom.

"To Heaven!" seconds my dad.

They both start strolling toward the car, but notice that I'm no longer in their company. Hesitating, they turn and look back to where I'm rooted.

"Come on, Maddy," my father calls joyfully. "Let's go be happy together, forever!"

Oh, fie. Oh, Gentle Tweeter. I can't bring myself to tell them the truth. I am still a coward. In two shakes of a lamb's tail, surly demons will be sponge-bathing them with hydrochloric acid. Curmudgeonly harpies will be ladling lukewarm pee-pee down their throats. What's worse is that every damned Boorite will likewise be there, tortured, and not liking my folks.

Here, the gray entrails of my brain retch forth a last, desperate scheme. One final gesture to prove myself courageous.

Persephone Makes a Bid for Her Freedom

Posted by Madisonspencer@aftrlife.hell

entle Tweeter,

How could you ever bring yourself to love so deeply if you truly knew how brief a lifetime can be?

All the great myths aren't in the past. Glory is not limited to the days of yore, and not all the heroic acts have been performed. As proof I grab my cat. I slap the bitter words from Satan's mouth. Yes, CanuckAIDSemily, an irksome girl ghost can backhand the Prince of Darkness, smack across his Ctrl+Alt+Scalding kisser. I snatch up Tigerstripe, and I sprint away. I don't fancy returning to Hell and being humiliated. Nor do I hanker to enforce God's pronouncements banning birth control and gay marriage.

Henceforth I will prove my own existence. I will prove that I steer my own destiny.

As my former-Wiccan, former–Green Party, former-living, breathing parents once strove to save polar bears and white tigers, I make my bold move. Into this scorching tableau so evocative of my father's ignited draft cards and my mom's inflamed brassieres, I scramble.

Behind me my damned parents shout from the windows of the Town Car. "Leave it, Maddy," says my mother. "The sad old Earth is so *yesterday's news.*"

The blissed-out souls of burned-alive Boorites continue

to pour into the Lincoln, each righteously certain that their destination is a well-deserved celestial reward.

My former-recycling, former-biodiesel, former–Earth First! father shouts, "Let the silly sperm whales and mountain gorillas just burn, honey! Get in the car!"

After all their years of trying to rescue illegal aliens and crude oil–marinated sea otters, this is my opportunity to try to save my parents. Perhaps to save everyone. Attired in my ooze-despoiled shirt, bearing my cat and my *Beagle* book, I frantically bolt down the mountain. Lugging my kitty as I'd once carried that fragile jar of sloshing tea, I take flight into the blazing canyonlands where artisan pinnacles soar overhead. Into this bland, washed-out, cataract-colored landscape I flee, rescuing the only creature I can.

Oh, my soul's beloved, I feel the rhythm of his ghost heartbeat beneath the melody of his purr. Oh, my Tigerstripe, I breathe the ghost sweetness of his fur. Such is the perfume your heart smells when you feel love.

In the distance a spark of blue flashes. It's the shade of electric blue my nose sees when I sniff ozone during a lightning storm. It's the blue my fingers see when I touch the sharp point of a baby pin. It's something not so much identifiable as it is inevitable, and I chart a course to reach it.

The angel Festus flutters, buzzing his tiny wings in my hot pursuit. He's singing God this and God that. His angelic voice sings how the Lord commands me. The power of Christ compels me. "Return to God," he sings, "as the Almighty is your real maker!"

Satan steers his Lincoln behemoth on my heels. He's honking his horn and flashing his lights as obnoxiously as any long-haul trucker barreling down an upstate throughway. "Abandon yourself!" Satan howls in anger. He shouts, "It was no accident when the autodialer of Hell connected you by telephone to your bereaved family. I direct your every move! I am your true father!" Whether he's chasing me or herding me, I'm not certain.

Me, my stout legs are dashing over the white plastic terrain even as it shatters like the Ohio River beneath the escaping feet of Eliza in *Uncle Tom's Cabin*. Baying at my chunky rear end are my mother and father, my nana and papadaddy. Shouting after me is the soul of Mr. K. So, too, is the succubus, Babette, demanding my immediate capture.

Yet, Gentle Tweeter, I am not helpless. I'm an escaped slave in a blazing world.

I'm Persephone reinvented, determined to be more than a daughter or a wife. Nor will I settle for some celestial joint-custody agreement, shuttling back and forth between residences in Heaven and Hell the way I continually jetted between Manila and Milan and Milwaukee. My new goal is the reunion of all opposites. I will strive to reconcile Satan and God. In doing so, by resolving this core conflict, I will resolve all conflict. There will be no separation between perdition and paradise.

As all of creation founders around me, only my purring kitty, gathered snug in my arms, only Tigerstripe trusts that I know where I'm bound.

The End?

ALSO BY CHUCK PALAHNIUK

CHOKE

Victor Mancini, a medical school dropout, is an antihero for our deranged times. To pay for elder care for his mother, Victor has devised an ingenious scam: he pretends to choke on pieces of food while dining in upscale restaurants. He then allows himself to be "saved" by fellow patrons who, feeling responsible for Victor's life, go on to send checks to support him. When he's not pulling this stunt, Victor cruises sexual addiction recovery workshops for action, visits his addled mom, and spends his days working at a colonial theme park.

Fiction

DAMNED

Madison is the thirteen-year-old daughter of a narcissistic film star and a billionaire. Abandoned at her Swiss boarding school over Christmas, she dies over the holiday, presumably of a marijuana overdose. The last thing she remembers is getting into a town car and falling asleep. Then she wakes up in Hell. Literally. Madison soon finds that she shares a cell with a motley crew of young sinners: a cheerleader, a jock, a nerd, and a punk rocker, united by their doomed fate, like an afterschool detention for the damned. Together they form an odd coalition and march across the unspeakable landscape of Hell—full of used diapers, dandruff, WiFi blackout spots, evil historical figures, and one horrific call center—to confront the Devil himself.

Fiction

DIARY

Misty Wilmot has had it. Once a promising young artist, she's drinking too much and is working as a waitress in a hotel. Her husband, a contractor, is in a coma after a suicide attempt, and his clients are threatening Misty with lawsuits over a series of vile messages they've discovered on the walls of houses he remodeled. Suddenly, Misty's artistic talent returns. Inspired but confused by a burst of creativity, she soon finds herself a pawn in a larger conspiracy that threatens to cost hundreds of lives.

Fiction

HAUNTED

Haunted is a novel made up of twenty-three horrifying, hilarious, and stomach-churning stories. They're told by people who have answered an ad for a writers' retreat and unwittingly joined a *Survivor*-like scenario where the host withholds heat, power, and food. As the storytellers grow more desperate, their tales become more extreme and they ruthlessly plot to make themselves the hero of the reality show that will surely be made from their plight. This is one of the most disturbing and outrageous books you'll ever read, one that could only come from the mind of Chuck Palahniuk.

Fiction

LULLABY

Ever heard of a culling song? It's a lullaby sung in Africa to give a painless death to the old or infirm. The lyrics of a culling song kill, whether spoken or even just thought. You can find one on page 27 of *Poems and Rhymes from Around the World*, an anthology on the shelves of libraries across the country. When reporter Carl Streator discovers that unsuspecting readers are reading the poem and accidentally killing their children, he begins a desperate cross-country quest to put the culling song to rest and save the nation from certain disaster.

Fiction

PYGMY

A gang of adolescent terrorists, a spelling bee, and a terrible plan masquerading as a science project: This is Operation Havoc. Pygmy is one of a handful of young adults from a totalitarian state sent to the US disguised as exchange students. Living with American families to blend in, they are planning an unspecified act of massive terrorism that will bring this big dumb country and its fat dumb inhabitants to their knees. Palahniuk depicts Midwestern life through the eyes of this indoctrinated little killer in a cunning double-edged satire of American xenophobia.

Fiction

RANT

Buster "Rant" Casey just may be the most efficient serial killer of our time. A high school rebel, Rant Casey escapes from his small-town home for the big city where he becomes the leader of an urban demolition derby. Rant Casey will die a spectacular highway death, after which his friends gather the testimony needed to build an oral history of his short, violent life.

Fiction

SNUFF

In the crowded greenroom of a porn-movie production, hundreds of men mill around in their boxers, awaiting their turn with the legendary Cassie Wright. An aging adult film star, Cassie Wright intends to cap her career by breaking the world record for serial fornication by having sex with 600 men on camera—one of whom may want to kill her. Told from the perspectives of Mr. 72, Mr. 137, Mr. 600, and Sheila, the talent wrangler who must keep it all under control, *Snuff* is a dark, wild, and lethally funny novel that brings the presence of pornography in contemporary life into the realm of literary fiction.

Fiction

TELL-ALL

For decades Hazie Coogan has tended to the outsized needs of Katherine "Miss Kathie" Kenton, veteran of multiple marriages, career comebacks, and cosmetic surgeries. But danger arrives with gentleman caller Webster Carlton Westward III, who worms his way into Miss Kathie's heart—and boudoir. Soon, Hazie discovers that this bounder has already written a celebrity memoir foretelling Miss Kathie's death in an upcoming musical extravaganza. As the body count mounts, Hazie must execute a plan to save Katherine Kenton for her fans and for posterity.

Fiction

ALSO AVAILABLE
Stranger Than Fiction

ANCHOR BOOKS
Available wherever books are sold.
www.anchorbooks.com